A BENCH BY MEMORY LAKE

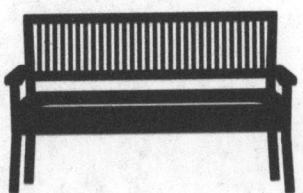

JOHN VANCE

BLACK ROSE writing™

ISBN: 978-1-61296-907-7
PUBLISHED BY BLACK ROSE WRITING
www.blackrosewriting.com

Printed in the United States of America
Suggested Retail Price (SRP) $18.95

A Bench by Memory Lake is printed in Adobe Caslon Pro

To Reagan Rothe and Dave King of Black Rose Writing; to my children
Hope and Jimmy for their love and support;
and to my wife, Susan, for her enthusiasm and keen editorial eye.

A BENCH BY
MEMORY LAKE

As on the smooth expanse of crystal lakes
The sinking stone at first a circle makes;
The trembling surface by the motion stirr'd,
Spreads in a second circle, then a third;
Wide, and more wide, the floating rings advance,
Fill all the watery plain, and to the margin dance.

Alexander Pope

Chapter 1

There was no need to wait until morning to begin her life anew. Early evening would do just fine.

Even though it had been an exhausting day at the wheel, Livy Garner decided to walk down to the lake before unpacking her bags. After sharing a long and much needed embrace with her best friend, Livy took the already prepared frozen margarita and asked to be pointed in the direction of the lake she had heard so much about. Leaving her friend to check on supper, Livy made her way to the single bench that seemed to lord over the sunset tinged water. She wondered if the ripples pushed by the steady late April breeze were welcoming or warning her. Perhaps they were doing both.

Shuttering as the slush of the frozen margarita touched her lips, Livy reacted to the gathering chill of the evening. The temperature must have fallen into the low forties by now, about what she expected for this part of Minnesota. But May was less than a week away, and the summer months awaited. She expected the upper mid-west had its share of miserably hot summer days but not as many as she would have experienced in Washington D.C., where the pleasant spring always gave way to the many insufferable days of incessant heat and humidity—or so she had been told. Although she was charmed by the cherry blossoms earlier in the month, she vowed not to be around to see them next year. After that, she wasn't sure where she'd be.

Livy's husband was almost four months into his first term as a member of the United States House of Representatives, and his wife only agreed to remain with him throughout last year's summer and fall campaign and then through his swearing in during the first week of January. Even though they were about to commence a formal though unpublicized separation, she bowed to his insistence that they remain together in Washington for his first two months in office. Why she gave him another month and a half after that she couldn't quite understand. Did she somehow expect them to reconcile sometime in March? No, she wanted no reconciliation. Perhaps she was merely deferring to her keen sense of fairness—"I tried. I even gave him another month he didn't ask for, but unfortunately we couldn't make it work." Or was it possible she was simply afraid to re-start her life at the time. Perhaps she felt reluctant to begin anew until the divorce was finalized.

Yet, she had done it. After seven years of marriage and nine months of planning her way out of it, she collected her clothes and a small trunk jammed with personal items, parted from her husband without rancor or tears, and headed from their rented house in Alexandria toward 495 and then up to 270 in Maryland. One night on the road and then northwest to her best friend's house some fifteen minutes outside of Minneapolis. Yes, the drive had been exhausting, but also exhilarating—all eleven hundred and fifty miles of it.

"How do you like the view, Livy?" The long-legged, tousle-haired, and effervescent Jennifer Montgomery had made her way down from the house.

"I love the view. But, alas, it's fading fast. What time is it?"

"Almost eight. In a minute or so we can head back to the house and chow down."

"I can't tell you how happy I am to see this day come to a close."

"Well, you drove a lot of miles today, little one."

"643 and eight-tenths to be exact."

"A tasty meal, two or three more of these margaritas, and then a good night's sleep and you'll be ready for the...ah, never mind."

"Ready for what? Why did you stop?"

"I was about to lapse into the cliché—'ready for the first day of the rest of your life.'"

"I don't know. Is it really going to be that or will it merely be the first day of a temporary delay of the rest of my life?"

Jenny laughed boisterously, as she always did when her best friend demonstrated her wit. "Livy, what the hell is that? 'The first *day* of a temporary *delay*.' You'd better clean up your syntax before you return to the classroom, dearest heart. Oh, by the way, did you sign up for classes as Livy Elman or as Olivia Garner?"

"The former."

"Good."

And Livy felt it was right, though perhaps to many not at all proper, that she return to graduate school under the same name she had when she began work on her Master's over eight years earlier. But then Olivia Allison Elman attended classes nineteen hundred miles away at UC Davis, having recently finished a Bachelor's degree up the road at Cal State, Chico. Her best friend from Chico, Jenny Lindstrom, had planned on going to Davis with her, but decided two weeks before classes began to head toward another Davis, accepting a marriage proposal from the man in her life, Davis Montgomery, who was then pitching for the San Francisco Giants.

Perhaps it was envy of her friend's blissful announcement that prompted Livy to respond favorably to the advances of a young California State Assemblyman. She had met him through Jenny's Davis, who was cultivating friends in the political as well as in the sports world. Ten months later, at age twenty-four, Livy married the thirty year old Peter Garner, leaving UC Davis behind for the move to Stockton.

During the first three years of her marriage, Livy saw Jenny regularly, especially when the Giants were on the road. But when Davis signed a lucrative free agent contract with the Minnesota Twins, Livy began experiencing periodic attacks of anxiety. Her general mood deteriorated, and she hated that she saw Jenny only when the Twins traveled to the Bay area to play the Oakland A's. All was coming undone, as far as she was concerned. She already evaluated most of her husband's habits and priorities and found them sorely lacking. At the same time, he was asked to assume the duties of the governor's legislative secretary, who stepped aside for health reasons, therefore forcing Livy to move again—this time to Sacramento.

The unsettling manifestations of Peter Garner's political ambitions became more pronounced as he successfully jockeyed to become the Lt. Governor's chief of staff. But with the governor's two terms coming to an end and the Lt. Governor's retiring from active politics, Garner decided to cash in his chips for a run at a congressional seat in the next election. With his less-than-enthusiastic wife at his side, Garner squeaked by a tough primary field, and won a narrow victory in

November. Now almost six months later, Garner was a thirty-eight year old freshman congressman with a bright political future but no attractive wife to introduce at any forthcoming social events in Washington or back in California.

Looking further out into the darkening water, Livy smiled at how matter-of-fact the summation of her life sounded inside her mind. "That's it in a nutshell," she might have added to anyone from high school or college who wanted to know what she'd been up to these past seven years.

"Livy, you look charmingly contemplative. But you're swaying from side to side. I think you're beginning to weave out of fatigue. Want to sit down while I go up and set the table?" Jenny pointed to the lone bench facing the lake. In the encroaching darkness, the bench was illuminated by a backyard torch lamp Jenny lighted when she joined Livy near the lake's edge. "Come on, my weary world traveler, sit down."

"All right. Just for a minute. But sit here with me."

"Okay, but my margarita's about a quart low—so get your sea legs back soon."

Livy laughed. "I will. Just give me a minute, captain." She always loved when Jenny gave her spirits a much-needed transfusion, especially with her colorful metaphors—mixed or otherwise—and her irreverent wit, whether in person or during their many long-distance conversations on the phone.

The women sprawled on the single bench near the edge of the lake. Livy collapsed one of her legs under the other. "I'm beginning to shake from the cold but I like the feeling of that breeze and the sound of the water coming right at me."

"I know what you mean. There's something utterly intoxicating about the lake and this old bench. Can you believe I've sat out here all bundled up during the winter, until my face went completely numb?"

Livy ran her hand over the arm rest and on the slats underneath her. The wood felt gouged and pitted—somewhat like her sensibilities the past several years.

"This bench looks and feels a little worse for wear, Jenny."

"It was a tough winter. Wind, snow, sleet—the whole nine yards."

"Going to paint it for the summer?"

"Nah. The distressed look is part of its charm. Besides, it would lose its historical value if I painted it."

"So who sat on it? Someone important, I'm guessing?"

"You got that right. Eisenhower sat on it as he planned the D-Day invasion in '44. Later, JFK met Marilyn here for a little hot action. And after that, John, Paul, and George decided right here to put Ringo in the band."

"Come on. Did anyone from Washington actually sit on it?

"Well, the estranged wife of a newly-elected United States congressman is sitting on it now." Jenny stared at her friend, clearly intent on drawing something from her.

"I should drag you into the lake for saying that. But give me a good meal, a few more margaritas, and a good night's sleep and I'll open up, I promise."

"Wait. Didn't I say you needed the same thing a little while ago?"

"My exposure to politics has taught me that it's not important who says anything first, but rather who gets quoted in the *Post* or on cable."

"Wow. Profound, Confucius. Simply profound. No, the closest thing to royalty this bench has seen are the butt cheeks of several over-paid professional athletes."

"The most notable being Davis Montgomery, who just happens to be your over-paid spouse?"

Jenny slapped her friend on the thigh. "Did I say over-paid? I deserve to be pilloried for such blasphemy." She finished her frozen margarita and turned the glass over, holding it up for her friend to see. "It's time to retreat to the bosom of Cuervo Gold."

Livy appreciated that Jenny already pulled out several of her standard gestures and expressions marvelously honed when they were undergrads at Chico.

"Come on, Jenny. Stay another minute. You're a Minnesotan now. You can take the chill." Livy once more gazed at the lake, completely missing her friend's dropped smile. "So, a couple of your husband's baseball teammates have been out to your place and have come down here and sat on this bench, I take it."

Jenny quickly reestablished her impishness. "Lounged more than sat. One of the boys even 'lounged' on it with another player's wife."

Even after all these years, Livy face flushed whenever Jenny indulged her bawdy side. "And who told you that?"

"No one told me that."

"Let me guess. You were the other ballplayer's wife?"

"Right. My husband had a bet with one of his teammates."

"And the teammate lost?" Blushing or not, Livy could get in a good one from time to time.

"Amusing, sweetie-pie—really, really amusing. No, the most famous person on this bench—other than my Davis, of course, has been none other than Nick Lockhart."

"Jenny, you look at me as if I ought to know who that is."

"Take a trip to the sports page every once in a while, will you?"

"Sorry." Livy ran her finger inside her glass for the last trace of frozen margarita. She turned her head and took another glance at the disappearing sun. "So you were about to tell me about Nick Lockhart."

Jenny slid closer to Livy, who enjoyed the warmth of her friend's body touching hers as the temperature continued to fall. Livy was most thankful she decided to come in April and not in December or January as she initially planned. "Well, up in these parts, Nick's *numero uno writer de la sports*. Head sports scribe for the big Minneapolis paper. He also has a bi-weekly column in one of the big sports magazines. You do read those from time to time, don't you?"

"Sorry again." Livy couldn't believe she was actually embarrassed by her wobbly knowledge of sports. She barely knew Jenny's husband was a pitcher, let alone remembered any of his statistics.

"Livy, don't you see a dentist or dermatologist from time to time? They have waiting rooms, remember? Magazines scattered from hither to yon?"

"I bring a book whenever I have my teeth cleaned or a blemish examined."

Jenny brayed another of her patented laughs. "Good one, Livy. Looks like the margarita is doing a nice job of pulling out your dormant sense of humor. Tell you what. You're beginning to quiver from the rugged conditions, so I'll finish the tale of Nick Lockhart in the house. Let's go have some supper."

Livy was indeed shaking noticeably, but she wasn't sure the vibrations were caused only by the chilly night air. As they climbed the wooden steps to the house, she took one more glimpse of the lake, its darkness variegated only slightly by the final slivers of light from the setting sun.

"Does this lake have a name?"

"Sure does. And has had one for several hundred years. According to legend at least, sometime in the late 1600's or early 1700's—somewhere in there—a French trader or trapper—one of the two—by the name of Auguste Memoré— lived around the lake, perhaps right here where you're standing. The locals later called it Memoré's Lake—and later the Anglicized "Memory's Lake." In the early twentieth century it was trimmed a bit, so now and we just call it "Memory Lake.""

Livy's continued to stare at the lake, until she heard the slapping of the water caused by the sudden vigorous breeze. Satisfied, she turned and followed Jenny up to the house.

Chapter 2

Livy no sooner entered through the rear of the house when she was startled by the sound of the kitchen telephone. She stopped, took a step back, and blocked Jenny's attempt to close the door behind them.

"It won't bite, Livy. It's a telephone. We have those in Minnesota now." Jenny noticed her friend wasn't smiling. "Are you all right?" The phone continued to ring. "It's not my husband. He's lounging in the bullpen right now. I just checked. The Twins are up by four in the eighth. I'll just let it ring. It's probably someone sitting in a cubicle in Kuala Lumpur wanting to sell me the one thing I'll need to survive a Minnesota summer."

The machine picked up on the sixth ring. Jenny's recorded voice filled the kitchen. "If you're a friend, leave a message. If you're trying to sell us something, get lost and never call again. Have a nice day—or evening, whichever is applicable."

"Hey, Jenn, it's Peter. I'm calling to see if Livy got there all right. I assume the two of you are out to dinner."

Jenny now understood why Livy remained motionless in the doorway. "I'll talk to him, Livy."

"No, Jenny, don't. I told him I'd call tomorrow."

Garner continued with his message. "Okay, I guess I'll try to call again in an hour or so." Jenny loped to the phone.

"Peter? Peter, this is Jenny. I was just taking the garbage out and got stuck in one of the cans. Livy made it, but she barely stayed awake through dinner. I sent her down to bed half an hour ago. She said she was going to call you tomorrow. Uh, huh. Well, I understand, but she's here—in one piece—and is now out like a bag of nails."

Jenny glanced over at Livy, hoping she would be amused by the fractured simile, but her friend's expression remained troubled and pensive.

"No, I really doubt she'll open her eyes before mid-morning, but if she does I'll tell her to call you, I promise. Thanks for calling. Bye." Jenny hadn't lied for Livy since they were undergraduates at Chico, but she found her skills had not at all atrophied in the years since.

"Thank you, Jenny. I owe you one."

"You're welcome. But you owe me nothing. I forgive all debts."

The women shared a look, each wanting the other to raise the subject of the failed marriage of the former Livy Elman and the current Congressman Peter Garner. Livy heard the distant sound of the Montgomery's grandfather clock ticking incessantly in the living room. She wasn't sure if the sound reflected the sense of time wasting or of time leading her toward an inevitable act to forever change her life. Fortunately, Jenny cracked the silence.

"I'll call him myself tomorrow, if you want. You don't have to talk to him."

"No, I do, Jenny. I have to talk to him. I have to tell him something final, but I don't know when that should be."

"Let me refill your glass with more slushy stuff." Jenny hummed as she pressed the button on the blender, but she knew a cheery attitude wasn't what her friend needed right now. By the time she took her finger off the button and filled both their glasses, she altered her demeanor to that of someone about to commence an intervention. She turned with a serious expression splashed on her face—only to see Livy staring out the kitchen window toward Memory Lake.

"I wish it weren't so chilly out. I would really like to sit on that bench right now."

"I'm afraid you'd have to daub some of this frozen margarita on your pretty face to keep warm." Damn, Jenny thought. She was back to cracking wise.

"Peter isn't ever going to accept that it's over between us."

Jenny leaned back against the center island in her spacious kitchen. Livy remained with her back pressed against the door leading down to the lake. Jenny recalled that whenever her friend wished to raise a serious personal issue, she often preferred her space—literally. During those moments, Livy didn't care for hand holding or being touched in any manner. Peter Garner's habit was to caress his wife whenever she was upset or worried. Livy once told Jenny that Peter would offer his "now, nows" and his "there theres" not to comfort but rather to prevent her from disagreeing with him. He had to have his way, and more often than not Livy dropped the matter and informed him she was fine, if for no other reason than she hated his hovering and being imprisoned in his arms. He had never struck her and she was certain he never would—but she still felt unfairly abused, although she could never articulate to anyone but Jenny why she felt that way.

"Livy, I think your being here for the next year or so will convince him it's over."

"No, you don't understand." She uncharacteristically raised her voice. "He can't *afford* to accept it." Livy opened the back door and took a halting breath of cold air. She shut the door again and turned to her friend. "I'm sorry for raising my voice like that."

"Think nothing of it, *mi amiga*. You've driven a long way and you're hungry. We'll talk about Peter tomorrow—that is, only if you want to."

Livy finally felt free to leave her position against the rear door. She took a seat at the intimate table in the breakfast nook. "Thanks for understanding. I can't tell you what it means to me that I'm here."

"And, again, you'll be here for at least a year. Longer if I have any say about it. I'll just bribe one of your professors to flunk you so you'll have to enroll for another semester to complete your Master's."

Livy couldn't help smiling. "You may not need to offer a bribe. It's been a long time since I've been in the classroom, you know."

"Oh sure, Ms. Mensa. Anyway, I think you'll find the accommodations here acceptable. You have the whole suite in the basement—complete with your own bathroom, shower, tub, flat screen, and refrigerator. And then when Davis is away on road trips you can sneak up the stairs and climb into bed with me. We'll cuddle, eat popcorn, and watch HBO. And if you want a little girl-on-girl action to relax at the end of a busy day, I'll...call a friend of mine who will rock your world. She's Amazonian—six-two and one-eighty-five."

"Have I ever told you that you are utterly shameless and vulgar?"

"Not often enough. So it's a miracle we're still best friends."

Livy tried to affect disapproval but it was impossible in the face of Jenny's puckish expression.

"Okay, let's get back to what we were talking about outside. Your friend the sports writer. No, no, wait. Before you do that, tell me again where your husband is tonight."

Jenny briefly paused. "Davis is in Detroit. First of a two-game set with the Tigers. Then on to Baltimore for another two. He's pitching the first night against the Orioles."

"I know."

"What? Did my 'dumb-as-a-donut-about-sports' best friend actually do a little research?"

"No, Peter told me before I left. He's driving up to see Davis pitch." Livy's face scrunched into an adorable wince.

"Oh. So, let me see. We've got three minutes on the timer before we eat. So let's get back to Nick Lockhart."

"You said he's the most famous celebrity to sit on the bench by Memory Lake."

"Without question. He's won a ton of awards for sports writing, including two Hearsts and two Pulitzer nominations."

"Wow. Even sports-dumb old me knows the names Hearst and Pulitzer definitely merit Nick his title of the most famous to sit on the bench by Memory Lake."

"Tell me about it. He's also been National Sportswriter of the Year a couple of times and he's won a 'SABR' award or two for his writing and even one for his oral presentation at their annual conference. He's blessed with a fabulous speaking voice—to go along with his good looks."

"Excuse me. Saber awards?"

"It's an acronym—S-A-B-R—for The Society for American Baseball Research. Nick won the Seymour Medal for the best book on baseball history for his work on the '61 to '65 Minnesota Twins—who were once the old Washington Senators, and then..."

Jenny stopped momentarily when she saw Livy's pained reaction to yet another reminder of the place from which she had just escaped.

"I'm listening, Jenny. The Senators moved to Minneapolis in 1961. Go on."

"And then they went to the World Series in 1965. Lost to those smug Californians down in the smoggy south—the Dodgers—and wouldn't make it back to the Series until 1987."

"You're quite impressive, Jenny. So what ever happened to my apartment mate, the anti-historian "dates don't mean a thing unless they lead to the best sex you've ever had" friend I used to know? So Nick won an award for his book on the Twins first five years, and..."

"He's also cluttered his trophy case with a bunch of other awards given by Minneapolis and Minnesota groups. He's appeared fairly often the past few years on ESPN—including a number of their "Sports Reporters" show. And David Letterman had him on twice."

"Okay, now you're talking. I can finally relate."

Jenny reached over and pinched her friend's wrist. "You really aren't as dumb about sports as you let on, are you?"

"Dumber. So I guess you should give me a crash course just in case Nick Lockhart comes by to sit on the bench."

"Don't laugh. He's likely to do just that any time now. He's back from some business in Chicago and will soon drop by for a little bench time."

"What do you mean?"

"He comes over fairly regularly just to go down and sit on the bench. He used to live directly across Memory Lake. I'll show you tomorrow, but the large house sitting on the property now wasn't there when Nick was a boy. There were two smaller houses then, and he lived in one of them."

Livy tended to her margarita, and Jenny could tell she was intrigued by the thought of Lockhart having once lived across the lake. Livy dragged the inside of her index finger along the rim of the glass, collecting the salt and then depositing the crystals on her lower lip. "How old is he, Jenny?"

"He's older than twenty-one and younger than sixty-five."

Livy exaggerated her sigh. "Let me guess—to have won all those awards and gained such a reputation he's closer to sixty five than twenty-one."

Jenny offered another Cheshire-Cat grin. "Nope."

"Closer to twenty-one? Really?"

The grin remained. "Nope."

"Jenny, stop."

He's as close to twenty-one as he is sixty-five. Split the difference and you have forty-three—his age."

"Oh."

"What's this? You look disappointed."

"No, I'm not disappointed. I just wondered, that's all." What made her uncomfortable was that Nick Lockhart was the age of someone she would likely date were she presently free to do so. Livy felt the rush of anxiety. Was Jenny planning on some matchmaking?

Jenny frowned. "You look as though you hoped he was closer to sixty-five."

"Don't be ridiculous. What does it matter how old he is?" Jenny said he was handsome and had a great speaking voice. Livy once again deposited salt on her lower lip. She feared her manner gave away the fact that her curiosity was aroused. Had she time to ponder the matter, she might have attributed her reaction to a lifetime habit of carrying through to its ultimate degree her relationship with every boy or man for whom she felt an interest. She'd spend the first fifteen minutes of an initial date imagining the male as a potential lover, husband, and father. Such fantasizing had its benefits, as she was able to save herself time and discomfort by turning down so many requests for second dates, but it also had its undeniable drawbacks. For instance, by judging each date by such ultimate standards, she was unable to enjoy any ephemeral relationships that might provide a woman with assorted delights and titillating memories. But the most harmful effect of her practice was that it led to her marrying Peter Garner, who later made a mockery of her confidence in her own judgment. Yes, Peter. The fact that they were still married made her curiosity about Nick Lockhart even more absurd.

"Livy, I have to say that Nick is a gentleman and very cerebral. He—"

"Do you even know what 'cerebral' means?"

"No, but I know it's good to be that. Seriously, if you're afraid he'd hit on you in your delicate state, I can assure you have nothing to worry about."

"I never even gave that a thought, but...no, sorry."

For all her self-deprecating humor, Jenny was most prescient when it came to her best friend. "Ah. You're afraid I'll try to set the two of you up for romance. That's it, isn't it?" Libby didn't have to answer. "My dear friend, I promise you I will do no such thing—overtly or subtly. I understand the position you're in with Peter. Besides, Nick's...well..."

"He's gay." Livy sighed in relief.

"No."

"Married." She tensed her facial muscles.

"No."

"Here we go again. What is he then?"

"I'm not sure why, but for all his celebrity and attractiveness he seems gun-shy with women."

"He isn't a misogynist, is he?"

"Not in the least. He loves the superior sex. What I mean is he's very comfortable around women, but seems reluctant—yes, that's the word—reluctant to get too serious with anyone."

"Hmm. He's probably been hurt badly and hasn't gotten over it." With the margarita salt on the tip of her nose as well as on her bottom lip, Livy sensed that she was showing too much interest Nick Lockhart. "How much longer till we eat?" On cue, the oven buzzer went off.

"All right, Livy. Let's break for chow. What do you want to drink? Pinot grigio? Or do you want to stick with margaritas?"

"What are we having?"

"Food."

"Funny."

"More specifically, '*La especialidad de la casa hoy.*'"

"What can I say but *Olé?*"

"You can also say what you want to drink."

"If it's not too much trouble, I'd like to stick with margaritas."

"It *is* too much trouble, since I'm the one *stuck* with having to make them. But for you I'll endure the agony."

Livy felt as warm and cozy in a domestic environment as she had in a number of years. Her best friend was in vintage form, delighting her house guest with her humor, teasing, and especially her unqualified support and affection. Livy understood that tomorrow she would have to call Peter and in the days ahead, she'd have to make the most difficult decision she'd ever faced. But for tonight she decided to submerge herself in margaritas and in the laughter Jenny Montgomery would surely provide.

Chapter 3

Upon awakening in a strange bed, Livy was surprised she felt completely at home. Noting the time on the digital bedside clock—8:20 a.m.—she muttered what for her passed as an uncharacteristic profanity at having been in bed for close to ten hours. But after a moment, she smiled knowing that for the first time in several weeks she had given herself completely over to her body's need for sleep. The night before, in a hotel room along the interstate, she was too keyed up to sleep much at all.

Previous to that, she fought a losing battle against her anxieties, which increased the closer she approached the move to Minnesota. Peter had been respectful of her mood—or was it his own pride—to forgo the romantic overtures he wanted to recommence after several years of forgetting them. Livy and Peter had an unspoken agreement that if he wanted sex, he should simply wait until they retired to the bedroom, where he would fondle her breasts gently but briefly and rub his palm on the inside of her thigh before attempting to engage in intercourse. Yet in the last several months, he wearied of the attempt to elicit some kind of passionate response from his wife. Therefore, their "lovemaking" was a silent affair—"business-like,' as Livy thought of it—a habit, a practice, and an obligation from which she now was released. Still, she didn't feel at all free, even though she had awakened in the basement apartment of Jenny and Davis Montgomery's Minnesota residence, over eleven hundred miles away from her and Peter's rented home.

Livy went about her morning routine of stretching and showering. The towel, much plusher than the ones Peter favored, felt good on her skin. It was pleasant to know her husband had never used this towel. She placed her foot on the edge of the tub and dried her beautifully shaped thighs and calves. She was proud of her body, which put on only four pounds since she married, and she believed her muscle tone was even better than it was then. But even this acknowledgment brought a frown to her lovely face. Her husband almost daily reminded her to maintain her impressive figure through diet and exercise. Apparently, the additional twenty-two pounds he added since they wed wasn't a concern in the least. In fact, Peter thought the extra weight served him well whenever he donned one of his eight suits. Realizing her husband was proud to show her off, and when he was working in the California legislature and later in the Lt. Governor's office, she conceded to her vanity and took pleasure in the attention she received whenever she came to the state house or went out with her husband for a political event.

But she felt none of that delight during last year's campaign for national office. From January through the election in November, Peter became even more concerned about his wife's looks. He insisted on approving everything she wore in public, vetoed her decision to lengthen her auburn hair, and refused to allow her to wear sunglasses when she accompanied him. Worse, he began feeding her lines to speak to potential voters and to the press.

Throughout the late summer and fall, she acquiesced to all of his suggestions and demands, because she knew she would be leaving for Minnesota after the election. She wasn't sure whether it was her duty to obey him or the price she had to pay to leave him, but she went along with everything he wanted. As for her hair, she liked it falling just above her shoulders, but again the reason why she nevertheless considered growing it longer had never been clear to her. Did she hope it would change his feelings for her? He once told her that his affections for a college girlfriend evaporated when she decided on an ankle tattoo. Perhaps Livy believed longer hair would alter her image enough to make his acceptance of their parting easier. Or did she want to grow her hair simply to spite him? That is, to anger him enough so that he'd want to let her go?

As Livy brushed her teeth, she avoided looking at herself in the bathroom mirror.

Jenny was wrapped securely under a heavy blanket. Before leaving the house, she checked the thermometer outside her back door—30 degrees Fahrenheit, or -1 Celsius as her Canadian-born friends liked to call it. Normally, she would have waited at least until late morning and for warmer conditions, but at this moment she wished to be alone. She earlier cracked the door leading to the basement and didn't hear Livy moving about. After filling a small thermos of coffee, Jenny headed down with her blanket to the bench by Memory Lake.

The rising sun had already brightened half the lake. Jenny much enjoyed watching the subtle colors of the water emerge as the morning progressed and in feeling the sun caressing her face, knowing that it gave her blonde hair and light features a temporary reddish hue. She preferred to think the color alteration reflected something within her—her deeper and more passionate side. Yet, she felt no melancholy when the lake succumbed to the darkness, because the next morning the cycle would repeat itself. And even during overcast, rainy, and snowy days, Memory Lake remained stirring and eloquent as it embraced and replenished itself with the precipitation in either liquid or frozen form. And the water was no less inspiring when the ice formed along its edges and then further out during the coldest days of a Minnesota winter. Jenny found in the lake's natural permeations—in its "moods," as she termed them—a metaphor for what intrigued her most about her own life. The change that never really changed what was permanent underneath. Simply put, she depended on Memory Lake; it was there for her anytime she needed it to calm her and alleviate her fears. A strong element of sameness and security was what she always desired—and now it was in danger of coming to an end.

Jenny daubed her eyes with the edge of the heavy blanket. She didn't want Livy to see any evidence of her tears, but it was becoming more difficult to pass a day without conceding to her emotions. Unable to shake free of the thought, she was already mourning the loss of this place—this bench next to her lake.

As she sipped coffee from the thermos, Jenny closed her eyes and heard the slight rustling of the water, stimulated by the gentle though persistent breeze. How different her feelings were now from what they were when she first sat down on this bench with her husband four years earlier. She easily recalled what she said to Davis on that day.

"Yes, the view of the lake is very nice, but it isn't exactly Russian Hill."
Jenny had become quite fond of their $900,000 condo in San
Francisco's Russian Hill area. *"Looking out at a lake—no matter how
nice—just doesn't have the same impact as seeing San Francisco Bay, you
know what I mean?"*

Jenny did her best to hide her disappointment over having to leave
the Bay Area, but at times her efforts completely failed her. She was
excited by her husband's generous contract offer from the Twins and
how it had made him feel, even though she had all along expected the
Giants to match it in order to keep Davis Montgomery pitching in
San Francisco. But when the front office mentioned to the press a silly
point about Davis's slightly elevated earned run average the previous
season as reason for holding to their original offer, her husband lost all
desire to remain with the Giants and eagerly signed with the Twins.

Unlike his wife, who was a California girl, Davis hailed from upper
New York State. He therefore thought nothing of facing late falls and
winters in Minnesota. Besides, he assured his wife, they'd get back to
the San Francisco area when the Twins made their one trip to play the
A's in Oakland and as often as she liked in the offseason. Already
having experienced periodic bouts of depression since her early
twenties, exacerbated by several traumatic events in her life, Jenny
nearly panicked at the prospect of moving to Minnesota during the
middle of winter and accordingly spent February and March with
Davis in Fort Myers, Florida, where the Twins held their annual
spring training. She finally had her first look at the house Davis
wanted to buy early one morning in the middle of April, after the
Twins' season already began. She liked the house very much but
couldn't help wishing it was located in California.

But after her husband excused himself to make a call that day,
Jenny found herself alone on the bench by Memory Lake. The early
morning sun had elevated high enough to bring half the lake into
bright display. Jenny was intrigued by the murmuring sound of the
water made by the wind and afterwards liked to think the lake was
whispering just to her. Incredibly, she remembered, her anxieties
disappeared. That night at a Minneapolis hotel restaurant, she
surprised herself by ordering a glass of white wine. For some six years
her reliance on the bourbon her father habitually drank had increased

to the point that immediately before the move to Minnesota she regularly had three or four drinks during the late afternoon and evening when her husband was home and several more than that when he was on the road. She knew she was in big trouble when she required one at ten-thirty in the morning.

Her husband sensed nothing of his wife's growing dependence on alcohol. In fact, he liked to brag that his wife preferred a "real man's drink" to those "frilly" Cosmopolitans and Mimosas. The Montgomery bar was always well stocked, owing to the number of guests they entertained after Giants' games and especially in the off-season. As a result, Davis never checked the level of the bottles to see how much she consumed when he was on a road trip. He always trusted Jenny's judgment on the choices she made and the amount she spent. Besides, she earned her own money from the occasional modeling assignment and the editing projects she did from her computer at home.

Much to her surprise, Jenny weaned herself completely off bourbon within three weeks of moving into the new house. She would take the social cocktail or glass or two of wine without desiring anything stronger. She now felt little need to imbibe unless it was in a social context—alone with her husband, with friends, or at a party or official event. She found making frozen margaritas much to her liking because she could control the amount of tequila she added. She began sleeping better and waking up without the residue of the previous day's intake of hard liquor. And for her new serenity and improved health she thanked Memory Lake. She became convinced the purgative and restorative powers of the water had changed her life. She would sit alone on the bench and recall the events and poor choices she had made previously and come to terms with the causes of her anxiety and depression. She knew it was fanciful, if not absurd, to think so, but she believed Memory Lake spoke to her or at least took an active interest in comforting and assuring her. Logic held that the lake "belonged" equally to the other houses that surrounded it, but to Jenny the body of water was her own—an extension both of her property and her sensibilities.

But here she now sat, battling the return of both her anxiety and her depression. She had to face it. Her husband's career was evidently in decline. He had, for him, a very mediocre season the year before, and this one had gotten off to an unimpressive start. The team had an option to renew his contract after this season, but Davis warned his wife that they wouldn't do so unless he quickly "returned to form." Unfortunately, he was now thirty-eight, and she knew the impressive skills that made him for over a dozen years one of the best starting pitchers in major league baseball weren't likely to be recaptured—ever.

She desperately wanted Davis to assure her he would retire if the Twins didn't pick up his option, because then they could remain in their house and she could look forward to spending many hours sitting on the bench by Memory Lake—her life remaining stable and serene. But her husband, like so many other proud athletes in a similar position, wasn't quite ready to walk away from the game he loved. For several years he boldly pronounced that he wanted to pitch until he was at least forty. Given the reality of his situation with the Twins, Davis had already begun considering other teams he believed would seek his services if he was cut loose. Jenny squeezed her fists under the heavy blanket as she replayed their conversation of three nights ago.

"Jenny, don't be too upset. Wherever we go we can always move back to Minneapolis after I do retire."

"But we will have lost this house, Davis."

"Come on, honey."

"I don't want to leave here. I don't want to go."

She recalled his disappointment over being unable to reassure her with his promise to move back to the area. He didn't push the point, even though he felt he hadn't received any gratitude for so willingly respecting his wife's desire to live in Minnesota. She pulled the blanket over the back of her neck as she retreated from thoughts of what might soon come.

"Jenny? You down there?" Livy stood at the back door.

"Yes, Livy. I'm coming up. I decided to start my morning by freezing my ass off. The coffee's on the counter."

After Livy returned to the kitchen, Jenny daubed her eyes with the blanket one last time. She would present herself as she always did to Livy—in control and in full entertainment mode.

Chapter 4

"It's the best sleep I've had in months. I love it down in my basement suite."

"You know you always wanted to be locked up in a dungeon, Livy."

Livy offered a half smile at the appropriateness of Jenny's flippant metaphor. "It's so much better without the chains, though."

"My, my. It's only the middle of the morning and we're already confessing to S&M fantasies."

Livy laughed freely, as she only did when Jenny was in her company or on the phone during one of their periodic thirty-minute chats. Peter Garner's sense of humor was what Livy labeled "American Gothic"—after the iconic and bland Grant Wood painting. Peter often attempted understated wit, but the effect was as awkward as the polite laugh his wife felt obliged to offer for his poor attempts at "dry" humor. He preferred shopworn jokes—most often reflecting "little town" rather than "big city" amusement, she thought. And Peter rarely engaged in humor with sex as the set up or punch line, and on several occasions he complained to her about Jenny Montgomery's "potty mouth." Yes, he had actually called it that.

Although never admitting it to anyone other than Jenny, Livy relished bawdy jokes and allusions, complete with profanity and references to every sexual act imaginable. That is, from the mouth of someone else—particularly Jenny—for Livy couldn't bring herself to tell such jokes or make the more graphically lewd allusions. She wondered if she was a hypocrite because of this inconsistency, but Jenny once told her that the world is made up of two kinds of people—the entertainers, of which there were but a few, and the broader audience. Livy, she said, was fortunately in a special sub-category of audience members, because she "got it," whereas most of the larger audience never would.

Regardless, Livy delighted in the prospect of being entertained by the humor she most liked without having to apologize to her husband. And now she had immunity from Peter's censure about so many things she preferred and he didn't. The thought seemed almost incomprehensible to her.

"What would you like for breakfast, my fugitive friend? I have everything—eggs, bacon, toast, cereal, fruit, and a pantry full of vitamin supplements."

"I'll just have coffee for now."

"Okay—then we won't have to wake the chef. I thought that this morning we could—"

The phone interrupted her. Livy sighed and began tapping her fingers at the breakfast table. Jenny went to the phone and checked the caller ID. "It's a 202 area code."

"Are the first three numbers 205?"

"That they are."

"Just as I thought, it's Peter." The phone rang for the third and then the fourth time.

"I'll tell him you're still asleep."

Livy rose from the table. "I'll talk to him now."

"Put it on speaker, luv."

Ordinarily, Livy would have deemed Jenny's request a joke, but without hesitation she did as Jenny suggested. "Hello, Peter."

"How'd you know it was me?"

"Area code and the 205 prefix." Livy assumed he was calling from his office in the Rayburn House Building.

"Oh, right, right. Anyway, I expected to hear from you by now. It's ten o'clock. I was getting worried."

Jenny grinned at Livy. Both women realized the congressman had failed to consider the one-hour time difference."

"It's just past nine here, Peter."

"What? Oh, right. Stupid me. Central time. I didn't wake you, did I?"

It was hard for either woman to tell if Peter's question was a reflection of his awkwardness or deliberate sarcasm.

"I've been up."

"Oh. For how long?"

"Peter, I said I would call you, and I would have later this morning. Jenny told you last night that I made it here, didn't she?" Again, it was the same ritual. He would often ask her a series of questions so that in some Socratic way she would come to see that she was wrong or unappreciative of his efforts or his needs.

"So—how are you feeling, baby?"

Baby. She hated that pet name coming from him—at least she had for the past several years. She knew what he wanted her to say. That she was a bit frightened being so far from Washington—or a little unsure of her decision to separate—or somewhat less resolved to return to school—or that she was already missing him. But she experienced none of these feelings. "Thank you for asking. I'm feeling just fine. Peter, I..." Livy hesitated and looked at Jenny, who understood what her friend wanted to say and encouraged her with a nod. "I really think I've done the right thing—for the both of us." Livy grimaced. Why had she added the final phrase? How she wished for once in her life that she could be abrupt and even cruel.

There were several seconds of silence before Peter responded. Livy knew he was struggling to suppress his anger. "Okay. I'm sure that spending a little time with Jenn will be good for you—but not for me, I'm afraid." He laughed without sincerity. "Look, I've got to go. I've been invited to the Majority Leader's office for coffee and a chat. I think he's taken a liking to me, actually. That's the key in politics, as I've often told you. I'm very anxious for you to meet him."

"I already did, Peter—right after you took your oath in January."

"No, I mean, *really* meet him—in a social setting—ideally for dinner. He thinks you're a very beautiful woman. He told me so."

Livy felt the strength leaving her legs. She wanted to hang up and sit back down. "Peter, I'm fine. Get to your meeting, and I'll..." She couldn't finish with "...and I'll talk to you later." Instead she chose "...and I'll say goodbye now." She hung up the phone immediately so that she wouldn't have to hear him announce his intention to call again soon.

"You okay, Livy?"

"I think so. But then I don't really know. Why didn't I just tell him that it would be best if we didn't talk—at least for one stupid week?"

"Look, it's not going to be easy to change the habits of the past seven or eight years."

"The habits of a lifetime, you mean."

"A lifetime? I know spending an hour with Peter is like spending a decade with anyone else, but..."

Now was as good a time as any to start unpacking all of her emotional baggage. "Jenny, I've always been this way. You know, peace at all costs. Always the one to make accommodations and all that."

Jenny grinned. "Whereas I've always been the one to make *reservations*."

"And I've always been the one to have them."

"Wow. Oscar Wilde, eat your heart out. I believe we've just engaged in another exchange of wit. Dearest friend, you deserve a cup of java for being more than my straight man." Jenny poured the brew into one of the mugs the two of them had in their apartment when they were undergrads at Cal State Chico. "Remember this piece of earthen ware?"

Livy looked at the mug and experienced an instant flash of nostalgia. But the feeling was quickly replaced by a less delightful reminder. "It won't come as any surprise to you that I've hated confrontations of any kind—ever since I was a little girl. I was the model child, my parents proudly bragged. I took correction well. I never talked back. I wanted to be just like my mother when I married. She too was the calm that prevented many a tempest. My parents never argued about raising me—about politics or about money. I suppose they had disagreements and that my mother asserted herself from time to time—but if she did, she always did it in private. She and my father felt such mutual respect for each other. It made coming home *always* a pleasure for me." Livy paused, knowing she had crossed a boundary she usually respected in her conversations with Jenny. Her friend's smile was gone. "I'm sorry, Jenny. I shouldn't have rambled on about my parents."

Jenny spooned the sweetener and milk into her friend's coffee. "No, no. I'm here in my professional capacity as confidant. Look, I greatly envy the relationship you had with your parents. That card just wasn't in the deck of fifty-one I was dealt, I'm afraid. But I found the right guy, which has more than made up for what I didn't have as a child and a teenager."

"Looks like each one of us has gotten half of the perfect sandwich, then."

Jenny grabbed Livy's hand. "I'm sorry. I didn't say what I did to make you feel bad. Besides, you're going to move on now and who knows what incredible pleasures await you."

"Yes, I want to move on, but how can I when Peter is either holding on to me and pulling me back—or standing in front of me to block the way?"

Jenny knew what she would do in such a situation. She would call Peter and lay it all out. Or she'd fly back right away and confront him in his office or in the rotunda of the Capitol, if he refused to discuss it on the phone. But she was sophisticated and caring enough to realize her best friend was a different sort. Whereas Jenny fought and scrapped through her formative years, Livy was able to sit back passively and enjoy the many benefits of supportive parents. "Livy, you've just got to prepare yourself for the confrontation I know you're desperately hoping to avoid. Peter isn't the type who takes the hint, you know. Or rather, he isn't the type who will *accept* the hint."

"My point exactly, Jenny. Still, look what's happened so far. I told him we needed to spend time away from each other, and eventually he gave in to my desire to come here and return to school."

Jenny took a long sip of coffee before following up. "I'm curious. Didn't he argue that you could go to graduate school at Georgetown or Maryland or to one of the other dozens of universities much closer to D.C.?"

"Yes, he did, but I insisted that I wanted to live here with you and Davis for a year and that I'd be miserable if I had to stay there."

"And that won the day with him? I find that very hard to believe."

Distracted, Livy opened and closed the refrigerator door before answering. "No. I convinced him that it wouldn't help him politically if others saw me unhappy. That they'd make conclusions about the stability of our marriage—even though their conclusions would have been absolutely right. I even...never mind."

"Wait just a flippin' second. You can't pull that old one on me, Livy. 'Never mind' my *gluteus maximus*. You even did what? Look at you. You're grinning like the Cheshire Cat."

Livy made no attempt to hide her delight. She ran her finger around the rim of her coffee mug. "I'll have to admit I surprised myself by coming up with such a brilliant plan."

"Tell me, you little conniving vixen." Jenny's face seemed to have stretched two inches in all directions, it was so animated.

"I made friends with a reporter for the *Washington Post*, who was writing an article on the new congressional spouses. I told her I was planning on going back and finishing my Master's and that...and this is the good part...that Peter was fully behind my desire to further my education—which wasn't totally a lie—*but...*"

"Oooo, I know this is going to be good." Jenny held her mug of coffee suspended several inches off the table.

"But I sort of suggested that Peter was supportive of my coming to the University of Minnesota—here to live with my best friend, the wife of perennial all-star pitcher Davis Montgomery, where I could fully concentrate on my studies without the distractions of life in the Nation's Capital."

"You are wicked, little one. But Peter must have busted a hemorrhoid when he read that." Jenny's coffee mug remained suspended.

"Oh, he wanted to all right, but the article also singled him out for high praise for being so such an enlightened modern husband. In fact, he just received laudatory mention in two leading publications. And another magazine is preparing a piece on him, along with some comments about my casual style being a welcome addition to the Washington fashion scene or some such nonsense."

"Don't be modest, Livy. I've long admired your fashion sense. But I should brag a little and say that I was voted by one of the naughty men's magazines the 'Wife I'd *Most* Like to be Caught Dead in a Dugout With.' That makes me a 'WIMLCDDW'—which, if you write that down, looks like an ancient Roman calendar misprint. So you're telling me that Peter was checkmated? And that you had him by the budda-bangs, as it were?"

"The what? No, I didn't know all that was going to happen. But it worked out so that he had no choice but to let me come here. He had a nice poll bump in his district back home and one of the woman commentators on CNN suggested his chances for a future Senate seat just improved considerably. Still..."

"What? Don't tell me. You said what else in that *Post* article?"

"When the writer asked me how often I'd be coming back to Washington, I could only answer "Often enough.""

"Well, you didn't lie—that is, if you meant 'none is often enough.'"

"But Peter didn't take it that way. He literally expects me to fly back often. Of course I tried to tell him I didn't think I should, but he simply refused to acknowledge what I said and prefixed everything with 'I know you'll soon feel...' and 'Soon you'll no doubt want to...' I just stopped trying to convince him otherwise. I figured I'd be more able to make my case for a divorce if I were here in Minnesota."

"Yeah. And he knows that all the political capital he's earned through his new and undeserved reputation as Mr. Enlightened Husband will immediately evaporate when word gets out that you both are calling it quits—or at least that you are."

Livy placed her mug forcefully on the table, spilling some of the coffee in the process. "Oh God." Jenny's accurate assessment had unnerved her.

"Whoa, whoa. I didn't mean to upset you. Let's just retire that topic for the rest of the day, okay?"

Livy retrieved a kitchen towel. After she wiped up the spilled coffee, she went to the window.

Jenny finished her coffee. "Livy, tell you what. We'll get dressed and head into Minneapolis. We'll have an early lunch and then take in a matinee. Unless you want to shop, that is. I could easily be convinced to alter the plan if that's the case." Jenny saw Livy looking out toward Memory Lake.

"Jenny, there's a man sitting on your bench."

Chapter 5

Nick Lockhart scanned the most recent correspondence from his attorney and then turned his attention to Memory Lake. He was now at the age when reaching back was becoming more common. To him Memory Lake and the property directly across from the Montgomery house was a visual signifier of his past—his history. Recently, he had sifted through the box of old family photographs he received from his mother before her death. Lockhart examined his face in these photographs for any hint that he knew then what awaited him in life. But studying these snapshots and some of his schoolwork from those years failed to provide him with the same sense of understanding as did the time he spent on the bench by Memory Lake. His only disappointment lay in the fact that his old house was gone—as was the house next door to it, where he had often gone to play with a neighborhood friend. The large and expensive home standing there now had in effect evicted a large part of his past.

Now past forty, Nick concluded that the single most delightful consequence of reaching middle age was rediscovery. Though busier than at any period since arriving at the height of his career as a sports writer, he managed to spend some time re-collecting on disk so much of the music he listened to on vinyl and cassette tape since boyhood and through his teenage years. He also took the time to watch movies from the 1980s especially—those he once saw and those he missed the first time around. He even explored his trunk and thumbed through memorabilia from his junior high and high school years and a pile of sports and music magazines he rescued from his mother, who always took pleasure in ridding the house of "junk." And of course he kept his massive collection of baseball cards, some of them still bearing traces of the bubble gum that came with each pack. Each card conjured a place, a mood, and even, he believed, a smell reflective of what he experienced as a boy. How badly he wanted to tour his old house just one more time. Nevertheless, his memory and imagination permitted him to walk every step of the residence, to touch each piece of furniture, even to touch the walls of his bedroom—his inner sanctuary, where he read his first issues of *Sport* and *Sports Illustrated*. It was while sitting at his small desk and looking out the window at Memory Lake that he made up his mind to devote all his energies to sports writing.

A good athlete in high school, lettering in three sports, Nick believed that he only played so he might write more effectively about baseball, football, and track. He never thought to take up a sport in college, even though he received football scholarship offers from two small schools. His concentration was totally on sports journalism from the moment he graduated from high school, and he decided to work a year as a sports section intern at a paper in Mankato before enrolling at the University of Minnesota. But during the end of his internship, the sudden onset of his paternal grandmother's Alzheimer's resulted in an alteration of his university plans. The money saved for his education had to go toward his grandmother's care, and now it was too late to take advantage of the two scholarship offers he had earlier received. That his parents would have to borrow the money to fund his college tuition was unthinkable to him; therefore, he felt his best option was to join the military for a couple of years and take advantage of the educational benefits of doing so. After talking to a recruiter, who assured him he had a chance to do some journalism while serving, young Nick joined the U.S. Army. And there was another benefit to his decision. Carl Lockhart had served in Vietnam in the late 1960s and came home with a Bronze Star and Purple Heart for his actions in the infamous Battle of Hamburger Hill in May of 1969. Nick knew his father was disappointed, although he never said anything, when his son displayed no interest in serving. Now that he was indeed enlisting, Nick's discomfort over having disappointed his father completely disappeared. Two years later, Nick was able to matriculate at the University of Minnesota as a twenty-one year old freshman. After he returned from the service, he never again lived in the house on Memory Lake. And soon the house was sold and then demolished to make way for the new up-scale residence.

"Is that Nick Lockhart, Jenny?"

"One and the same. He's forty-three now but as you can see, he's tall and broad shouldered—not at all fit for the refuse heap."

"Jenny, I sincerely hope you aren't planning anything that would embarrass me—or him."

"Now would I ever do such a thing?"

"Jenny, I'm really serious. Don't try anything funny. I didn't come here to begin a new social life, you know."

"I realize that. You're just here to study and write your papers and get your Master's. But as they say, all work and no play..."

"I mean it. I'm very serious, Jenny."

The slight intensity in Livy's tone informed her friend that the teasing should stop—at least for now. "No, no, don't worry. I won't try to arrange anything that might place you and Nick in a compromising position—oops, I mean compromising *situation*."

"I'm *still* legally married, remember."

"And that has stopped so many women—I mean those who know their marriage is over even if not legally— from having a romantic fling with another man, hasn't it?" At least Jenny wasn't teasing.

"Quit it. I've removed the word *fling* from my vocabulary. And it will stay removed for as long as I'm here—understand?"

"So you flung *fling* out of your vocab, eh? Oh, all right. From now on, I won't even kid about such a relationship between the two of you. Besides, his two engagements ended in disasters, so you can trust that he wouldn't be interested in a third."

Livy shaped her right hand into a claw. "And how did we go from a fling to a third engagement?"

"You're right. I spoke out of turn. Okay, let me get you some more coffee."

"Thank you." Livy stepped away from the back door window and returned to her place at the kitchen table."

"Here you go." Jenny placed the mug before her best friend. "I'll now move on to another topic—completely unrelated to the one we were just talking about. Now, you know if you and Nick just had dinner together, it wouldn't be classified as an engagement—or even a fling."

.   .   .

Lockhart once more scanned the correspondence from his attorney. He couldn't fathom it. How did he suddenly go from being the darling of his newspaper to someone they were considering dumping? He knew the why, but still the how gnawed at him. How does one who hadn't a significant blemish on his record in the areas of journalist accuracy and fairness—not to mention his exceptional command of English prose—about to become a journalistic *cause célèbre?* Just because he made the decision to sit on a story to protect an athlete's privacy? Yet, Lockhart knew it was more than that—so much more than that.

He read his attorney's suggestion that he appeal to the "court of public opinion" before deciding whether he would file suit.

Nick, to remain above the fray is all well and good, but your best bet is to at least make some noise about bringing suit. You can have the media run everything by me if you like. Say nothing, but give me permission to raise the possibility of filing. What do you think?

Lockhart understood that a legal fight against termination by his paper would evolve into a national story, commanding the attention of all sports media and all strict First Amendment advocates. The case would probably take years to resolve and might well wend its way up the judicial chain, and perhaps even to the Supreme Court. And with each step, the scrutiny on Lockhart would intensify, leading to a full invasion of his privacy, which he could not abide. Yet how could he take his potential termination without fighting back?

"Hey, Nick."

Lockhart folded his attorney's letter and placed it inside his light jacket. He rose and hugged Jenny. "Hope you don't mind my being down here this early in the day."

"Not at all. As both Davis and I told you, you're free to plop your hindquarters down on this bench anytime you want."

Nick turned his head slightly to the right and noticed Livy coming down the steps to the lake. She didn't want to come down with Jenny for fear of making it look as though she was being presented to the sports writer. She smiled and offered a cheery "Hi."

"Nick, this is Livy Garner—excuse me, I mean Livy Elman—whose only claim to fame is being my best friend. We go back to the dark ages at Cal State Chico. Livy, did you know that Nick spoke at our alma mater a couple of years ago?"

"Really?" Livy shook Nick's hand outstretched hand. She liked that he didn't "wimp out," as Jenny liked to say, but applied some pressure to his grip. "Yes. I had a great time, and the students were wonderful. Very nice to meet you, Livy." His smile was sincere and completely non-threatening.

"Livy's staying with me for the next year. She's about to begin classes at Minnesota. Shooting for her Master's."

Livy prayed Jenny would provide no other details about her situation—at least not while they were all standing near the bench. But she had to admit that her friend was right about Nick Lockhart. He was a gentleman and quite a good-looking one at that. She thought his eyes met hers respectfully. Too many men she had known lifted their brows as a way to suggest inappropriate interest. She and Jenny also laughed about the number of men who apparently believed they could mesmerize a woman by staring at her for ten or more seconds at a time—the kind of look she saw too much of in Washington. But Nick's eyes shifted away from hers until he was ready to address her again.

"What will you be studying and writing about in your thesis, Livy?"

Livy's shoulders leaned back slightly. She was frankly unprepared for his interest in her academic work. Her husband never once asked her what she would be working on when she went back to school. He spoke of her plans only in the general sense of her "not needing to get a Master's" or her not realizing that, at her age, she was "going to get sick of the classroom" and the "homework" after a couple of weeks as an "older student."

"I thought of a project when I began the M.A. program at UC Davis that I now want to write while I'm at Minnesota." She stopped as though she was certain Nick was only being polite. She didn't wish to embarrass herself by going on about her academic plans. Too many perfunctory "Oh, and what do you do?" questions at political parties and weary receptions had made her vow never again to expose herself to wandering eyes and rude interruptions.

"I see. But what is your project, exactly?"

She stared into his eyes for a moment for any indication that he was in fact uninterested. "Well, I don't want to bore you." She inwardly cringed at hearing such a banality from her own mouth.

"Livy, he's dying to know. Just look at him. He has but seconds to live."

Leave it to Jenny to add the requisite dose of irreverence. Fortunately, Nick wouldn't let the moment plunge into embarrassment. He laughed and assured Livy he would indeed like to know. "Unless, that is, your topic is too sensational for Jenny's tender ears."

Livy offered a laugh of her own in appreciation of his remark. "No, nothing like that. I decided when I was at UC Davis that I'd write on the fate of Vietnam War veterans after they returned home." She noticed that Lockhart's smile lifted but then dropped. "No, no. Not the devastating effects the war had on them. That's been covered in numerous studies, of course. Instead, I want to write about the Vietnam Vets whose lives turned out successfully. About what they believed their military experience, especially in the war, had to do with what they accomplished. Did it truly contribute something valuable? It all started with a long talk I had with my father, who was a lawyer and who had been in the Army in the 60s. He told me..." She suddenly ceased, fearful that in spite of Lockhart's seemingly genuine interest, she had gone on too long and was now beginning to tax his patience with unwelcome details.

Nick opened his hands. "Well, what did your father say?"

She couldn't believe he was still curious. Jenny was the one beginning to fidget.

"I'll make it quick, I promise. He told me he would never have gone to law school—or college at all—had he not served in the Army. He said he wasn't mature enough for college after high school and that he learned self-discipline in the service. Anyway, he made clear he'd always have a fond spot in his heart for the military because of what he went on to accomplish."

Lockhart's brow furrowed. "So he served in the 60s—do you recall which years?"

"Yes, he served from May 1967 to May 1970—and was a corpsman in Vietnam from October 1967 to October 1968, when he was wounded himself."

Jenny clapped Livy on the shoulder. "And almost fifteen years after he was discharged, his lovely daughter Olivia came into this world."

"Thanks for announcing my age, Jenny."

"I didn't announce it. I just gave anyone with a love of mathematics a chance to figure it out."

Nick smiled warmly. "You're not alone, Livy. Jenny also enjoys embarrassing me about my age whenever she gets a chance."

"Well, sometimes I don't really enjoy it. And when I don't, I remind myself that it's a dirty business but someone has to do it."

Nick seemed hesitant to speak, but Livy's expression encouraged him. "Your father was in Vietnam a short time before my dad went over."

"Really?" Livy guessed that Nick's father had him when he was in twenties, while her father made it to his mid-thirties before she was born. She was slightly taken aback by her calculation. Why did she think of that first? She wanted to ask more about the senior Lockhart's experiences in Vietnam and share those of her father, but her natural caution—if that's what it was—prevented her.

Nick glanced at the water. "Well, I do need to move along and let you both enjoy this splendid and cool morning down here at Memory Lake."

"Say, Nick, how about all of us having a threesome?" Jenny waited until Livy's face began to alter. "Good grief, my dear. I meant the three of us having lunch one day this week. I apologize for her, Nick. She has a mind that should be scrubbed raw with soap. Anyway, how about lunch? I'll treat."

Livy's eyes locked on the ground underneath the bench.

Nick nodded. "Sure. I'd enjoy that—very much. Well, it was so nice meeting you, Livy. Just call me about lunch, Jenny. And give my best to Davis."

"I will. Bye, Nick."

The women watched Lockhart walk up the steps and then out of sight.

"Funny. He usually hugs me goodbye as well as hello. I think you intimidated him, Livy."

"Oh, right."

"You know what?"

"I'm really afraid to ask?"

"You need to interview Nick Lockhart for your thesis."

"Was he in the military?"

"He was, but I was referring more to what he could tell you about his father." Jenny grinned in triumph while Livy began evaluating everything she said since meeting Nick Lockhart.

Chapter 6

"Jenny, I can't believe I'm sitting in the middle of the Mississippi River. Or I should say I can't believe I'm sitting in a gorgeous restaurant situated on an island in the middle of the Mississippi River."

"But you are, my dear." The women just sat down for lunch at the Nicollet Island Inn, one of Jenny's favorite dining spots in Minneapolis.

Livy was embarrassed by her flimsy grasp of geography. "I must admit that whenever I conjure images of the Mighty Mississippi, I never think of Minnesota."

"Few people do. And we up here are very resentful of that fact. Say 'Mississippi River' and one almost invariably nods and goes, 'Ah, yes. Old Man River. The Deep South. Nawlins'. Or way up there in St. Looey.' Just once I'd like to say, 'Where the hell do you think that damn thing starts from?' Minnesota, that's where. It's a Yankee thing too, you know."

"It's Mark Twain's fault, Jenny."

"Damn right it is. I'll tell you one thing, Livy. Had old Huckleberry Finn come up this way, we would have showed him a damn good time. Would have knocked the freckles off his you-know-what, you can bet on that."

The women spent most of their hour at the Nicolette Island Inn reminiscing about their Chico days. Jenny was careful to keep the conversation restricted to all things other than Livy's relationship with Peter. Livy seemed confident her friend wouldn't spring any difficult questions about her marriage or offer sisterly advice on how to handle her separation. Livy of course realized that her friend wanted to do just that, but appreciated that Jenny was apparently allowing her to choose the moment when the topic could be broached.

"Can I ask you something?"

Jenny was a bit startled by Livy's question, mainly because she was about to articulate the same words to Livy. "Depends on whether it would violate my privacy in any way. If it does you have my permission to ask it."

"Thanks. I read about the suicide of that basketball player's wife's last week, and I started thinking more seriously what it would be like to be married to a professional athlete. I mean, you've told me what you've done and the lifestyle you've lived…"

"And have grown devoutly accustomed to."

"Right. But do you see other wives having difficulty coping with being a… how shall I say it?"

"A sports wife?"

"Yes, okay, a sports wife."

"Well first, Livy, there are two kinds of sports wives."

"Okay."

"One kind—comprising the largest number—is represented by the woman who's married to a man who only works at his job or career so he can afford to devote every other conscious hour to watching sports and memorizing statistics."

"Come on, Jenny. My question was a serious one." Livy twirled the small amount of pinot grigio remaining in her glass.

"So is my answer. Want another glass of wine?"

"Not sure. Just go ahead and finish explaining your first category of sports wife."

"Thank you. This woman must, at all times, be razor sharp, so she can answer such thought-provoking questions as 'How many players chewed tobacco on the 1946 Chicago Cubs?' and 'What was the largest number of hot dogs Babe Ruth ate at one sitting?' Seriously, most wives know what it's like to watch old hubby's gut expand along with his alcohol blood level—when the home team isn't performing well. She knows how ridiculous her homely and out-of-shape man looks wearing Tom Brady's authentic NFL jersey. By the way, I once dreamt about having champagne in bed with him, did you know that?"

"The homely, out-of-shape guy or Tom Brady?"

"Cute. Anyway, this sports wife must also deal with the sighs, gasps, howls, and groans whenever she walks in front of the big screen or forgets to buy her husband's favorite beer, chip, dip, or wing sauce. And then she's forced to endure the culinary offerings prepared by her supposed grill master—undercooked brats and blood-tinged chicken and eight-inch high burgers. It's a sad commentary when the height of a meat patty outdistances the full length of his male offering."

"Enough." Livy laughed so hard that she, and not Jenny, was the one drawing attention from the other diners. And Livy could find her friend's account especially effective because, unlike the wives Jenny described, Livy knew very little of their experiences. Peter Garner sought the acquaintance of California and D.C. area athletes—such as Davis Montgomery—but merely for political reasons. Garner had never devoted much thought at all to sports. That would have been understandable if he was a connoisseur of fine food or the fine arts—but he was neither.

"Jenny, I guess I will have another glass of wine." Livy signaled to the server. "So now on to the category of sports wife you belong to."

Jenny uncharacteristically took a few moments to begin. Livy was struck by the serious expression on her friend's face, as she shuffled the salt shaker between her hands. Jenny's tone was similarly reserved. "Livy, it can be the greatest life. That is, when your husband is happy, productive on the field, on the rink, on the court, or on the course. But I know other sports wives whose husbands are marginal players at best. They may not be around for a second year in the big leagues. So their wives—or live-in girlfriends—often resist the urge to celebrate their lifestyle for fear they'll become accustomed to something that will shortly end. They can be way too cautious—even somber and depressed—because of this fear. Did you ever start dating a guy you really, really desired and then acted miserable or distrusting because you were certain his affections couldn't last? Well, the same is true for some of these sports wives."

Livy assumed from Jenny's nearly lifeless explanation that she must know several women going through the same thing. "I guess I never imagined that part of the life."

"Yeah—it's no fun, let me tell you. Then of course there are those wives whose husbands cheat on them—or they suspect they do—so that every away game becomes almost unbearable for the more sensitive players' wives. Not all, for some of these women are pretty damned tough, and some give out as enthusiastically as their husband's take in—if you know what I mean."

Livy did; still, she wasn't used to Jenny speaking this long without attempting to amuse. "Jenny, do these women ever—how shall I say it—commence the cheating before they suspect their husbands of doing so?"

"I've known a few who have, but often the wife's straying is revenge or a response to being hurt or confused."

Livy couldn't bring herself to ask if Jenny and Davis Montgomery fell into this category of high-profile sports marriages. Besides, she would have been horrified if they had. No, there wasn't any way they were unfaithful to each other. Jenny's demeanor had to be prompted by something else. Again, likely the fate of a good friend who found herself in this situation.

The server placed the two glasses of wine before them. Jenny finally offered a smile. "You see the pretty young thing who just brought the wine?"

"Yes." Livy was looking forward to the punch line.

"The last time I was in here, she was utterly gushing."

"Did you come on to her or something?"

"Hey, leave the bawdy stuff to a real pro—namely me. What I mean is that Davis and I were in here the last time, and she recognized him and just about offered herself to him on a bread plate."

"And you did or said what?"

"My darling husband faked it beautifully. He thanked her for her gushing and signed two autographs. One for her and one for 'her younger brother.' He kept one hand below the table—doing what I have no idea..."

"Jenny, stop." Now Jenny was back to her familiar ways.

"So I didn't have to say anything to either of them. Anyway, you can tell what a memorable impression I left on her."

"Right, she's shown no indication she's ever seen you before."

"Another one of the joys of being a sports wife—my kind, I mean."

"Jenny, I swear if they ever name me Queen of the Universe, I'm naming you Head Jester."

"Promise?"

"Cross my heart. Okay, now that your future service to me is assured, let's get back to the sports wives in your category. I'm intrigued by what you said about those wives not wishing to get used to the life out of fear that it will all be taken away from them. Without naming names or teams, are you close to anyone who's in that situation?"

Jenny stared into her glass of Cabernet Sauvignon. She swayed it slightly, so that the wine splashed against the sides of the glass. She wanted desperately to be alone for a few minutes on the bench by Memory Lake.

"Jenny, you okay?"

"Yes. I'm just getting light-headed inhaling the fumes from the wine. Well, turn-about is fair play." Jenny raised the glass to her lips. The sip of wine steadied her. "Your turn. Tell me about being a pol-ee-tician's wife."

Livy's expression made Jenny wish she hadn't asked the question the way she had. Both women were uncomfortable with each other's sudden awkwardness.

"Tell you what, Livy darling—that can wait for later. Now, it's time to go back to our Chico days and discuss which professor or two—or three or four—we most wanted to take up residence in our private spaces. And I'll start. You remember Dr. Hammerstein, don't you?" Livy nodded, the smile returning to her face. "He's the one I would have given first entry to. I called him Thor in my fantasy scenarios. Get it? *Hammer*stein becomes Thor?"

Livy kept a straight face, tinged with insincere boredom. Jenny snapped her fingers. "Check, please."

Chapter 7

Nick replied to the request via email. Once again, he'd been asked to interview Twin's pitcher Davis Montgomery—and once again Nick politely declined. He decided on the day he sought Montgomery's permission to sit down at the bench by Memory Lake that he wouldn't interview or write any kind of in-depth story about the Twins star pitcher, because keeping Davis and Jenny as friends would make difficult maintaining his journalistic integrity. Nick even refused to inform Davis beforehand if a story about him was about to be published in Nick's paper.

Had he not been friends of the Montgomerys, Nick would have written that the Minnesota Twins' four-man starting pitching staff rotation was in need of both a transfusion and a therapist. The two youngest starting pitchers had so far failed to live up to promise. The reliable third member continued his solid, though unspectacular work. But most disappointing was the sudden collapse of their ace, Davis Montgomery.

The previous season had been a nightmare for Montgomery personally and the organization and fan base collectively. Before last season and since being brought over from San Francisco, Montgomery won at least nineteen games a year, highlighted by a season in which he had twenty-six wins and only five losses. The following year, the record slipped a bit—to twenty-one wins— although it was still one of the top three records of any American or National league pitcher for that year. But during a round of golf in Florida before the start of last season, Montgomery hurt his right shoulder after swinging his club and hitting a large tree root near his ball. He wasn't too concerned since the pain subsided after a few days, and when the season began his control and accuracy on the mound was unaffected. But immediately he could tell that his velocity wasn't what it was the previous year. He had lost over five miles an hour on his fast ball, and the speed of his second pitch, the slider, was affected as well—the result being that Montgomery was now unable to blow his fast ball by most hitters as he had always done. His earned run average shot up while his number of recorded wins fell precipitously. Last year's record was an uncharacteristic and unimpressive 14-16, with a high earned run average—but worse, his effectiveness deteriorated as the season wore on, as the pain in his shoulder returned.

Montgomery dismissed the suggestion of off-season shoulder surgery, refusing to believe there was anything serious that needed to be scoped. He insisted he'd just had a bad season—his first ever—and that all would return to normal this year. Finally, he flatly dismissed any notion that his advancing age would make that return most difficult if not impossible. But his publicly expressed optimism was soon shaken, for he now stood with a record of 0-2 with an embarrassingly high ERA. He tried to chalk up the poor start to the time of year—asserting that it now "takes me until May to get loosened up," a remark that only testified to the reality of an athlete's advancing age, even though Montgomery refused to see it as such.

Nick knew that under normal circumstances he would have written sympathetically about Davis's collapse and especially about the pitcher's dismissal of both the seriousness of his golf-related injury and the realities of getting older, but again his personal relationship with Davis and Jenny made that impossible. His paper's sports editor wasn't happy when Lockhart earlier announced that the assignment of covering the Twin's pitching staff would have to go to another reporter, but the editor had little choice but to honor the wishes of his highly acclaimed sports writer. There was always the fear that Lockhart would pick up and move to New York or other large cities where his column periodically appeared.

But his recent decision to honor another principle fractured the usual editorial desire to please Lockhart. In fact, the paper had recently entered into serious discussion about cutting all ties with their star sports writer. Yes, if they did drop him by not renewing his contract, the story would go national. Lockhart was frankly surprised that it hadn't already done so.

.   .   .

Jenny and Livy returned to the Montgomery home after lunch and a cursory tour of Minneapolis. Jenny pointed out so many landmarks and shared so much history of the area that Livy believed she'd be lucky to remember half of it. Still, she wanted to learn more about the entire state of Minnesota as well as the Twin Cities. She felt no similar curiosity when she and Peter arrived in Washington D.C. at the end of December in preparation for the swearing in of the 115th Congress early the following month. Peter wanted to move in mid-December, but Livy told him he'd have to go alone, since she was determined to spend Christmas with her mother in California. She begged off a tour of Washington that Peter arranged for them and another freshman congressional couple soon after they arrived, and it was all she could do to hold herself together on the day of the swearing in, as the photographer lined up the new House representatives with their wives, husbands, and families. Livy felt miserably hypocritical when she and Peter had their photo taken—but she couldn't refuse to pose for the shot, rationalizing that it was, after all, Peter's day and that their ultimate future hadn't yet been fully determined. She was very hard on herself for entertaining the latter thought. She knew what she *wanted* their ultimate fate to be. But before now she hadn't mustered the courage to make such an unalterable decision.

"Drink, Livy?"

"Better not. You made me guzzle that second glass of wine at lunch, so I think I'll wait until tonight."

"Coward. All right, then. As much as it pains me to endure your 'delayed gratification syndrome,' I'll make some coffee and we can sit in here and talk further about your...*our* immediate futures."

Jenny wished to talk about Livy's short- and long-range plans. Still, she accepted that her best friend would have to bring the matter up herself without too much prodding. Another glass of wine on top of the other two just might encourage a looser tongue, but Livy wasn't interested. Later in the day, Jenny would crank up the blender for another date with Señorita Margarita, and then—perhaps—Livy might be in the mood to loosen her tongue. Besides, she'd had a good night's rest, and must now be feeling confident Peter wasn't going to drive to Minnesota and refuse to leave until she accompanied him back to Washington. Even so, Jenny was disappointed Livy turned down the offer of a drink. It scared Jenny for a moment. She understood she had wanted another because it would help keep at bay her growing anxieties about Davis's fate after this season. If the Twins cut her husband loose after this season, she would be leaving this house for another one in another city, where Davis might pitch for another two or three years. Once more, Jenny couldn't bear the thought of moving—of losing her connection with Memory Lake—of the satisfying and necessary mornings and evenings sitting on her bench.

"Jenny, what's wrong?"

"What? No, no. Nothing's wrong." Jenny suddenly realized that if she and Davis did move, it would likely be in the late fall, at least six months before her best friend had completed her Master's at the University of Minnesota. Livy had come from Washington with Jenny's invitation to live here at least until next June.

"Jenny?"

"Okay, I'll admit it. There is something wrong."

Livy took both her hands. "What is it?"

"I forgot to buy that crappy cheese spread for the nachos I was going to serve this afternoon. Now we have to munch on cheap old jumbo shrimp cocktails."

Livy shook her head in amusement. "You really should be tied to a log and set adrift on Memory Lake."

"Great idea! We'll fix our coffees and take them down to the bench for serious caffeine-induced conversation."

"I'm game."

Jenny was relieved her friend characterized her troubled look as a set up for another of her comedy routines. When they finished depositing the artificial sweetener and the one percent low fat milk into their mugs, the women headed out the back door.

Chapter 8

"And he's going on ESPN with this? When? A couple of days? Okay thanks, Hugh. Keep me informed. Bye."

Oddly, Nick felt relieved to learn from his attorney that the proverbial other shoe had finally dropped. Former Vikings back-up quarterback Paul Vanderkellen had agreed to appear on ESPN to discuss his troubled past and to cast part of the blame at Nick Lockhart.

Vanderkellen came out of college two years earlier replete with all the laurels and "can't miss" tags. The first quarterback taken in the second round of that year's NFL draft, Vanderkellen quickly signed his contract with the Vikings, who set about grooming him for the starting role, which they assumed he'd claim by the end of his second or his third year in the league. Vanderkellen was blessed with impressive size and arm strength, and the only question about his play dealt with his decision making on the field. During his senior year in college he'd occasionally have lapses in concentration, although he'd invariably "wake up" and show exactly why he was one of the most highly recruited athletes out of high school and why he was named to several All-Conference and All-America teams. The Vikings, as well as other interested NFL organizations, thought they had the temporary lulls of concentration figured out. Vanderkellen's parents divorced at the end of his junior year in college, and his fiancé broke their engagement half way through his senior season.

Vanderkellen's rookie year was non-eventful, since he wasn't required to play at all. But the following year, the team's starting quarterback suffered a hip injury in the eighth week of the season. The back-up quarterback took the reins, and the coaching staff hurried to bring Vanderkellen up to speed in case he was needed to play. Because of NFL rules, the Vikings were unable to trade for a veteran quarterback since it was past the sixth week of the season. A week later, Vanderkellen came into the game against the Detroit Lions in the second half, after the backup quarterback suffered a broken hand, but played disastrously. Three interceptions and a fumbled snap marked his NFL debut. His decision making was poor, and twice he pulled out from behind center before the ball was snapped.

Fortunately for the Vikings, their original starting quarterback returned the following week, which rescued the season. Ostensibly owing to Vanderkellen's utterly dismal play, the organization bit the bullet and released the young quarterback at the end of the year. But a week before the announcement, sports writer Nick Lockhart received a phone call from a very anxious young woman.

"Mr. Lockhart, my name is Kaitlin Terry. I'm the former fiancé of Paul Vanderkellen. I want to let you know that Paul gambled on college games when he was a senior, and I'm pretty sure he's still doing it with NFL games. I know he owes people a lot of money and I'm afraid for him. He once told me he deliberately threw an interception in his senior year because he had to keep the score down."

She said all of that in what seemed to be one breath, leaving Lockhart no chance to interrupt. When she finished her opening salvo, it took him several moments to process what she revealed.

"And how do you know all of this, Ms. Terry?"

"As I said, I was his fiancé. He told me."

"Might he have been kidding with you?"

"No. And before you ask, he wasn't drunk or on drugs—and neither was I."

Again, Nick paused before proceeding. "You said he deliberately threw an interception to keep the score down?" Sitting at his computer, Lockhart quickly went to the site of Vanderkellen's college team and opened the record for the young man's senior season. "Do you recall which game he was referring to, Ms. Terry?"

"Yes. I was at that game." Her voice softened into sadness. "I was at all his games."

She told Lockhart the specific opponent and that Vanderkellen threw the interception as his team was about to score late in the fourth quarter. Lockhart saw the result on his computer—a 31-21 victory by Vanderkellen's team. He checked the betting line for that afternoon—

Vanderkellen's team was favored by twelve. Kaitlin's story was therefore plausible. Had Vanderkellen's team scored either a touchdown or a field goal, those who took the opponent and the twelve points would have gone from winning their bets to losing them.

"Can I ask why you're telling me all this?"

"Because I think the only way he'll stop gambling is if he gets out of football."

"Is that your real reason?"

Now it was her turn to pause. "No. I think he needs to be scared enough to stop."

"You're still angry at him, aren't you?"

"That's not important."

"I think it is, because it goes to your credibility as a witness or a source."

"Can't one be angry and still tell the complete truth, Mr. Lockhart?"

"Of course, but in the legal or journalistic world it often comes down to what you can prove—not to mention the significance of perception."

"And since I used to be his fiancé, my testimony can be dismissed, is that what you're saying?"

"Especially if he broke it off with you."

"I broke it off with him, Mr. Lockhart—because I couldn't trust him anymore. I saw where his gambling was taking him. The kinds of people he was associating with. And no, I didn't break the engagement because I was seeing another guy I wanted more than Paul."

"I'm sorry, Ms. Terry. Please understand. I have to ask these questions."

She sighed. "I apologize too. I'm mad at him for not being the man I thought he was, but the story's still true and I think he needs public exposure to pull him away from the course he's on. Does that make sense to you?"

"Yes." In truth, Lockhart was still suspicious of her motives. "Can I ask why you didn't—"

She immediately interrupted. "Why I didn't talk to him about what I was feeling?"

"Yes."

"I did. On *four* different occasions. Twice on the phone and twice in person. He didn't want to hear it. He hates me for breaking the engagement. He's so full of himself. Honestly, I tried, Mr. Lockhart, I really tried."

"I'm sure you did, Kaitlin." Calling her by her first name told him that he now believed her. "One last question. Is there anyone else who might corroborate what you've told me about the gambling and about that specific game?"

"Yes."

Nick was frankly surprised she answered affirmatively. "Other players?"

"Yes, two of his teammates. One being the receiver who was supposed to catch the pass that Paul threw right to the defensive back in that game I mentioned."

"Would they speak with me, do you think?"

"The receiver would, I'm sure. I can't say the other one would go on the record, but the three of us have talked about what Paul was up to. Do you want to know who they are?"

Lockhart took down the names, thanked Kaitlin, and said goodbye. That was the easy part. Now he had to decide what to do with the information the young woman had unexpectedly dropped in his lap.

Looking back over the past three months, Lockhart painfully accepted that the decision he finally made was the wrong one for him professionally. But he hadn't yet been convinced he had any other option. In fact, he wondered why he followed up on the matter as far as he did.

•   •   •

"Stay here and enjoy some meteorological intercourse with nature, Livy. Davis is calling me right at 2:00, so I'm going to take the call while lying on my bed, where I have taken many of my husband's calls—of the wild—on many other occasions."

"Jenny, I thought you were more adventurous than that. I have a feeling that you and Davis have 'communed' in every room of your house—and out on your deck, on the lawn, and in the hammock."

"True."

"Just don't tell me the two of you have 'communed' on this bench."

"All right. I won't tell you. You'll just have to wonder. Well, enjoy this hot love bench while I'm away. Ta, ta."

Livy sighed with contentment as Jenny bounded back up the steps leading to the house. Other than her irrepressible wit and personality, Livy admired and envied Jenny's beauty and athleticism, which demonstrated no sign of deteriorating now that she was in her early thirties. Livy long ago conceded that Jenny would easily best her on the tennis court, on the golf course, and on the bowling lanes. But Livy always conquered her friend in all the trivia, card, and board games. Livy loved the skill and strategy one could maintain in a sitting position—and it was impossible for her to entice any of her friends to take her on in chess, for she was that good. Livy recalled the one thing she looked forward to when she first came to Washington was meeting others who knew the game and could challenge her. She assumed these opponents would be congressional spouses but hoped that some would be members of congress, provided the latter would have time enough to sit down with her and play.

In January, she met one of Peter's more senior House colleagues, who enthusiastically volunteered to take her on. He had walked over during the post-swearing in festivities and asked about her background and interests. Having been little more than displayed by her husband on that day, Livy was grateful for a chance to talk with someone without having every word "translated" by Peter—"What Olivia means is that..." and "My wife has this idea that..." being his two favorite interruptions. Peter literally positioned himself between Livy and the other person to make his job of providing context and commentary all the easier. But on this occasion, her husband was drawn away by his party's whip to discuss the first series of votes of the new congressional session, leaving Livy alone with Representative Evan Donnelly.

Livy nestled comfortably into the bench by Memory Lake and replayed her brief relationship with the congressman. After he asked general questions about her family, education, and interests, Donnelly stopped and stared into her face for several seconds.

"I know I shouldn't say this, given the current climate of heightened and, let me add, appropriate sensitivity, but you are a very beautiful and graceful young woman who doesn't seem at all intimidated by your surroundings. Nor do you seem at all wide-eyed and gushingly exuberant by being in the presence of men and women at the highest levels of government. I applaud you for that. It's so refreshing to see someone with such elegance as you possess keeping herself above the madness, so to speak. There is such charm in your aloofness, Olivia."

"You think me aloof, Representative Donnelly?"

"Please, it's Evan. I meant the word in its most positive sense of self-containment, not snobbishness. You are going to be such a refreshing addition to this musty old place." Donnelly noticed Garner approaching. "And here is our new rising star from California. Peter, it was such a pleasure talking to your lovely wife. That she plays chess is not the least of her many enchantments. Perhaps she and I might have a game or two in the immediate future?"

"My wife would be delighted, sir."

Livy offered a muted smile at Connelly to signal her approval of the idea.

After Donnelly stepped away, Garner pulled his wife to the side. "Livy, you know I wouldn't ordinarily want you to play chess with another man."

Livy had looked away, a reaction to the fact that Peter had only played with her once—right after their marriage, when he had patronizingly suggested that she learn the game. He was oblivious to the fact that she had been playing since she was six. Then, Livy flustered her husband as he was beginning his tutorial by cutting him off with "Let's just play."

As she listened to the comforting and subtle sound of Memory Lake breathing contently before her, Livy once more wondered why she chose to play up to her skill level with Peter and not allow him to win, as her good angel encouraged her to do. As the months and then years passed, she would sadly make an art form out of deferring to him on so many occasions, justifying her decision on the grounds that peace of mind required sacrifices and that it wasn't in her nature to be confrontational. But since childhood, she tended to release all her demons whenever she played cards or board games. Friends marveled at how her demeanor altered on those occasions. She frowned throughout the game; she reshaped her facial features into a series of menacing squints; and she periodically, audibly, and sometimes comically let out breaths through her nose.

Peter was easily dispatched the first time he sat across from her, but he immediately insisted on another game, claiming that her quick victory was "a fluke." He lasted no longer in the second game, and the way he glared at her when she almost snarled "checkmate" convinced the both of them they wouldn't be moving pawns and bishops against each other in the future. Garner never mentioned the word "chess" again in her company—that is, until Evan Donnelly parted from them at the Capitol in early January.

"But I want you to play with him if he asks again. He can do a lot for my career. He's in line to be the next chairman of the House Budget Committee, the one I want on the most." Much to his disappointment, Garner's initial committee assignments did not include Budget. "Now listen to me. You have to give him a good game, but you can't win. Do you understand? You'll potentially mess everything up for me if you beat him. Now, promise me, Olivia. Will you promise?" Whenever he got paternally serious, he would use her formal first name.

Snuggled comfortably on the bench, Livy smiled at recalling her reply. "I promise you I'll give him a good game."

It took until early March for Donnelly to extend her an invitation to drop by his office for a game or two of chess. He saw and talked with her on several occasions since the swearing-in, but hadn't mentioned playing. When he finally did, he simply called out to her as she was leaving the Willard Hotel, after her lunch with three of the other congressional wives. He was taking one of his brisk walks up Pennsylvania Avenue from the Capitol.

"Olivia! Great seeing you. Remember, we have to play some chess soon."

"Whenever you're ready, Evan."

"How about this afternoon? Four o'clock in my office in the Rayburn?"

"Fine. See you then."

Livy's three lunch mates cleared their throats and raised their eyebrows in the familiar expression of knowing concern. They extended more plainly their warnings and assessments of Donnelly's "borderline" interactions with the younger congressional wives. None of them had any experience with the congressman to validate their concerns, but they had all been told of Donnelly's questionable behavior.

"I'll be in his office at the Rayburn Building. I should be fairly safe, don't you think?"

"There once was an Oval Office visit by a young lady named Monica," offered one of the other women in rebuttal.

Livy smiled. "Yes, but from what I've heard, the game of choice wasn't chess."

Livy looked up toward the Montgomery house and debated whether to walk back to the kitchen and bring down some hot coffee or tea while Jenny continued her conversation with Davis. The wind had picked up, making the mid-60's temperature feel a full ten degrees cooler. But the lake squirmed just enough to keep her attention. Livy decided to remain where she was until Jenny returned. She curled both legs on the bench and continued her reminiscence.

"Come in, Olivia. Welcome to the inner sanctum." Livy looked around Donnelly's office and appreciated the décor—reflective of a man of middle age, certainly, but of a man with more than average taste in furnishings. She wondered if Donnelly's wife, who rarely accompanied him to social events, had any influence on her husband's choice of framed prints, which included one from each major period of art history—late Medieval, Renaissance, Baroque, Neo-Classical, and Impressionism. The twentieth century was represented by a Picasso.

Donnelly had already set up the chess board and two chairs in the middle of his office. "Can I fix you a drink?"

Livy noticed the bottles of gin, vodka, bourbon, Scotch, pinot noir, and Chardonnay resting on a side table. She wouldn't accept Donnelly's offer, but thought to decline with humor. "Sobriety is the best ally of a chess player, Evan."

"Not where I come from," he laughed. "Then how about a soft drink, or I can get you some tea."

"Tea would be nice, thank you."

Donnelly sent a member of his staff to another office where water was on constant boil. When the staff member returned with the small pot and a cup, the congressman pulled from one of his drawers a bag of Oolong tea. "Sorry this Oolong is bagged. I'm not set up for proper brewing in the office."

"Do you know that Oolong is my favorite kind of tea?"

Donnelly hesitated for a moment before he broke out in a wide grin. "Actually, I do know that. You mentioned it to Tricia Wilcox, I believe."

Livy had to think but remembered she had engaged in a conversation with Wilcox, one of the freshmen representatives, about tea and coffee. How Donnelly learned the information from Wilcox, Livy didn't wish to know. At the moment, it was too flattering to think that the congressman had been interested enough to ask his new House colleague about Olivia Garner's likes and dislikes. For all she knew, Peter had no earthly idea what tea she preferred. He never cared to ask or to observe.

"Then you must know, Evan, that I prefer Oolong because of its antioxidants. It has the polyphenolic qualities necessary for a healthful, hopefully cancer-free living."

"Of course, I did."

"And that it protects against premature wrinkles and helps combat skin disorders."

"As I was just about to say."

"Not to mention that it relieves stress, promotes good bone structure, and lessens the effects of diabetes."

"And we can't forget that it also..."

"Reduces tooth decay."

They broke into laughter at the successful completion of their unrehearsed comedy routine. Livy felt exhilarated by the exchange, grateful she could exercise her wit and particular brand of humor with a man who seemed so much on her wave length. At that moment, she regretted they were going to play chess. She would have much rather have sat and simply talked to this charming man in his late fifties.

Donnelly finally invited her to take a seat at the table, extending her the invitation to play the white pieces, "because, as you must know, the statistical odds favor the white, Olivia."

"So I understand. All right. Here we go."

Livy quickly moved her f2 pawn to f3. Donnelly reared his head back at what he knew was one of the weakest opening moves in the book. The beautiful woman sitting across from him had done nothing to influence the center of the board and left her king vulnerable to a diagonal move. Donnelly quickly moved his queen's pawn to e5.

Livy scrunched her features and scratched the top of her head with her fingers. Donnelly wondered if she realized how comical she looked. Livy smiled and moved her knight's pawn to g4. Donnelly couldn't believe it. She had made the stupidest move in chess. The way was paved for him to bring his queen all the way on the diagonal to h4. He immediately made the move and announced "Checkmate." Livy looked at him with great surprise and then studied the board, lowering her head so that her nose almost touched her king, which was stuck in its place, unable to escape. Donnelly's inarticulate mutterings went from the triumphant to the sympathetic. "Oh, Olivia, I..." He was completely at a loss. The poor woman had no concept of how to play. How else could he explain why she had succumbed to the infamous "Fool's Mate"? Yes, how could she have actually made such a disastrous...? Suddenly, Donnelly had his epiphany. "Olivia, you are so very wicked, do you know that?"

Livy finally raised her head. The smile on her face was almost as wide as the chess board. "Sorry, Evan. I couldn't resist. And you can call me Livy."

"Nevertheless, I'm counting it as a win. All right, Livy. Let's have one more go at it—this time with complete sincerity."

Donnelly stood little chance against his opponent—a fact he suspected but did not fully appreciate until they resumed play. Livy occasionally offered a polite smile, but nothing more that reminded him of the devilish sprite that took a dive in the first game. Still, Donnelly was utterly fascinated by the lovely woman across the table. "Okay, Livy, we're even—one game all. Now, let's play the tie-breaker." He knew he stood little chance of beating her in her a third game, but it was worth another defeat to spend more time in her company.

After Donnelly tipped over his king, Livy stood, shook his hand officially, and reassumed all of her normal personality and charm. They said their goodbyes, with Donnelly clumsily suggesting they meet again for a game of Monopoly, "since I'm sure I'd have no chance against you in any *sophisticated* board game."

Livy ignored the implied invitation to meet again and thanked him for a "stimulating three games." She had without qualification enjoyed Donnelly's company. She knew he was taken with her—which, given his polite behavior, provided her with a necessary supplement of vanity. He had a wit that stimulated hers, and he was patient enough to listen to what she said. Yes, she was then aware others would warn that his demeanor and attentions were all a familiar prelude to something else he desired from her, but when she left his office at the Rayburn Building, she dismissed such possibilities and allowed their time together to buoy her sinking spirits. Now as she rubbed her chilled hands on the bench by Memory Lake, she remembered also how it struck her that she had obeyed her husband's instructions. She had lost at chess to Evan Donnelly. True, she felt free enough to indulge her naughty promptings, but she wondered if the decision to throw the first game was actually another concession to Peter's wishes. Still, she also remained true to herself and won the other two games. At the time she considered it possible that her handling of the chess games was an indication of her slow but deliberate breaking away from her husband and his cloying influence on her life.

Chapter 9

"Whatcha thinkin' about?" Jenny placed her hands on Livy's shoulders, which sent her friend's torso jerking upward. "Whoa, whoa. Didn't mean to scare you, sweet face."

Livy required two deep breaths before regaining her equilibrium. "You shouldn't sneak up on me like that."

"I didn't. I came down the same way I always do. I even said, 'I'm baaaaack.' You didn't hear me?"

"I'm afraid not."

"You didn't look asleep, so you must have been in deep thought."

Livy was embarrassed that Jenny had it so correct. "I think I was just so mesmerized by Memory Lake."

"It'll do it to you, that's for sure."

"So, how is Davis? Is he ready to pitch tonight?"

"Rarin' to hurl."

"He's sick?" Livy was quite sincere in her concern. Accordingly, she was totally unprepared for Jenny's bellowing guffaw.

"No, dearest Livy. 'To hurl' means to pitch a baseball. A 'hurler' is therefore a..."

"A pitcher—I see." Now Livy had a second reason to be embarrassed.

"You're probably thinking back to our Chico days and that night we went out after finals—when I introduced you to the little concoction known as a Mary Pickford, and you barfed all over the rest-room floor." Now Livy had reason number three.

"Jenny, do you realize I've never seen you get sick—even though you drank twice as much as I did."

Jenny's smile dropped as she snapped her head in the direction of Memory Lake. "Just had a stronger constitution, Livy."

"Sorry. Did I hit a nerve?"

"What? No, no, no." Jenny grabbed Livy's hands and brought them to her mouth for a kiss. "The only nerve you hit on me is the one that stimulates all things wonderful. You know I adore you and am so, so, so very happy you're here."

Livy smiled, reassured her best friend was fine. Jenny lifted her head and let the cool wind run flush over her face. Her blonde hair blew back, making her look like a Norse goddess, Livy thought.

"Well, you've now been an official citizen of Minnesota for going on twenty hours. So how do you like your new homeland?"

"Believe it or not, but I feel it really *is* my new homeland."

"Well, it is. But you need to purge all traces of your California Valley Girl accent and start talking like a real Minnesotan."

"You mean like they did in the movie *Fargo*?

Jenny stood over her friend, transforming herself as best she could into a Lutheran schoolmistress. "Oh, yah. You betcha. Welcome to Minnesooooota, Oooolivia."

Livy howled. "That's it. You really have it down. I'd swear you were actually from Fargo, Minnesota."

Jenny altered her demeanor and affected a stately British Anglican aristocrat Oscar Wilde might have created. "My dearest Olivia, there is no Fargo, Minnesota."

"But the movie..."

"The movie's first scene is set in Fargo, *North Dakota*, my dear simple soul with the dark hair nature left untouched by anything approximating a grooming instrument. But to give you complete credit for something about which you are completely unaware, the Fargo 'metropolitan area'—if I may use such a vulgar epithet—comprises Fargo, North Dakota and Moorhead, Minnesota, two cities that touch each other—inappropriately, I might add—in the unspeakable wilds some two hundred and forty miles northwest of where you are presently sitting."

Livy had to brace her forearms against her stomach—the result of unadulterated laughter at her friend's performance. "Stop, stop. I can't breathe."

Jenny decided to be merciful. She sat down and continued in her "normal" manner. "Seriously, many up here wished that little movie had never been made. Besides that, everyone in North Dakota is mad at us for stealing their city." Jenny erased her grin and gazed out at Memory Lake.

"What's wrong, Jenny?"

"Hmm? No, no. Nothing. Just doing something I'm not used to. Thinking."

"About?" Jenny's silence prompted a repeat of the question. "About."

"Davis."

"Is he all right?"

"Not exactly."

Livy moved closer to her friend, whose face had taken on an uncharacteristic frown. "Please talk to me, okay?"

Grateful for Livy's encouragement, Jenny needed no further prompting. She informed Livy about the injury Davis sustained while playing golf, the physical erosion of his skills the past two seasons, and his fear that he wouldn't recover enough to be the pitcher he was. But she didn't share all she and her husband talked about on the phone, even though his words were as fresh in her mind as if he were presently whispering them in her ear.

"And what the hell am I going to do if I can't get the speed of my fastball back up to where it was?"

"Davis, didn't you say that a whole bunch of guys have saved their careers by learning how to throw a cut fastball?"

"Yeah, but I can't get enough speed on it whenever I've tried it. It can't limp up to the plate. The movement has to have some motor on it to be a successful pitch. I've just been waiting for my fastball to come back. I can't figure out why it hasn't."

"It must be your shoulder—the injury, I mean."

"I don't want to hear it. It's fine—or good enough to throw the way I always have."

"But that and the fact that you're now getting—"

"What? Getting old, you mean?"

"Just older in professional athlete years. You're not even forty, and you look great. You're a young man still."

"Thanks for the compliment, honey. But given my profession that doesn't mean a whole lot. But worse than all that, I've now completely lost my confidence. You know, I was so sure this winter I was ready to make up for last season, but even down in Florida I couldn't get enough zip on my pitches. And now I'm the worst starter on the staff."

"It's only April, baby."

"The end of April, you mean."

"It will turn around, at least enough to...I'm sorry. I don't know what I'm saying."

"You meant to say 'at least enough to make me competent or decent enough,' right?"

"Please Davis, let's just—"

"No Jenny, I'm not mad at you. You're right. You're absolutely right. 'Competent' is the best I'm going to be from now on. I know it. And I hate it. I just hate the hell out of it. Damn it, I hate getting old. I hate hearing the press question my ability. I hate having my teammates look at me with pity, the way they did last season and are beginning to do again this season. No one ever looked at me with pity before last year."

"Davis, I understand. Please don't treat me like the enemy, okay?"

"Oh baby, I'm so sorry. I'm sorry I dropped all this on you today. I know Livy's with you, and you guys are having a great time together. But I sure as hell wish you were here."

"If you want me to come down to Baltimore, I will, you know that. Livy will understand."

"No, it's only a two-game set. Then we'll be in Cleveland for three and then back home. You stay with Livy and have a great time. At worst, if I don't pitch well against the Orioles tomorrow night, I might ask you to come to Cleveland so I can cry on your shoulder. Bring Livy with you and you can both visit the Rock and Roll Hall of Fame."

"Just say the word, and we'll or I'll be there. Just promise me that you won't talk about Livy if Peter gets your ear in Baltimore. Livy told me he's coming to see you pitch."

"No chance I'll be spending any time with him, so don't worry."

"Also remember that I love you no matter what happens career-wise."

"I will. Okay, Jenny, I have to go. Love you, and thanks for listening to me whine. Talk to you soon. Bye."

It wasn't the fact that her husband was so frustrated and embarrassed over the way he performed of late that had Jenny so concerned at this moment. Nor was it the swelling fear that he'd be forced to sign with another team and move them from their home on Memory Lake. Rather, it was his belief that he was now "old" in a general sense, regardless of how such a though was belied by his appearance and chronological age.

Livy tapped her friend lightly on the forearm. "Jenny, is there more you want to tell me? Want me to go up and get you a glass of wine? I'll even join you in one if you want."

"No thank you, Livy. I want you to stay on the bench with me.

Livy attempted humor to shake her friend from her sudden onset of gloom. "I won't run off with the bottle, I promise."

"I know you won't." Jenny's reply was flat, as if she had no ability to process anything that was facetious. "Okay, Livy, you're right. There is more. I'll tell you if you want." Jenny continued to look out at Memory Lake, but specifically at the edge of the water closest to her property. Livy had never before seen her like this—not even when she had her heart broken when they were sophomores at Chico, nor at any time since.

"Jenny?"

She finally turned toward her friend. "I'm sorry, Livy. It's just hard to talk about."

"I understand. I'm in the same boat, you know."

"We may be in the same boat, but you're in the bow and I'm in the stern." Jenny managed a weak smile.

"That's my Jenny."

"Really, it's like that. You're looking ahead and can see what's coming that scares you. Me, I'm looking at where I am now and see all that I dearly love shrinking inevitably the farther I go forward. And that really frightens me."

Livy tensed. "You and Davis aren't in trouble, are you?"

"We're not having marital difficulties, if that's what you mean. No terminal illnesses or financial ruin to report either. I'm not having an affair, and neither is he." She took one more look out at Memory Lake. "Yet."

Livy pulled Jenny's chin toward her. "Yet? You expect him to—is that what you're saying?"

"I'm *afraid* he will is what I'm saying."

"Someone you know?"

"Not likely but possibly. But it's probably going to be someone he doesn't even know. Yet."

"Another 'yet'?"

"Davis told me he's feeling old." Livy attempted to protest. "I know what you're going to argue. I told him that he's only in his late thirties and still handsome and sexy as hell. But it doesn't matter what I say. I'm afraid he's going to have to hear it from someone else. From some female else—likely seven to eleven years younger than I am."

Livy now understood Jenny's point. "I see, but before you go any further, I don't want you thinking that you're not a stunningly gorgeous sexual creature still."

"Isn't it the truth, though?" The woman took a break from the sobriety of the moment by laughing at Jenny's remark. But with the brief respite over, their demeanors and thoughts returned to the serious.

"Okay, so you feel the problems he's having with his arm and the shaky state of his career will make him vulnerable to another woman's advances?"

"In a nutshell, yeah."

"Have you seen any indication of such a possibility occurring?"

"Do wives always see the indications, Livy? It's like being afraid of getting hit in the head by a fastball. The only indication is that a pitcher pitches fastballs. You think about it and fear getting hit, but you usually escape. But when it does happen it's because you just couldn't get out of the way." Jenny paused. "That made very little sense to you, I bet."

"Not complete sense, but more than a mere little, I'd say."

"A man thinks, acts, and reacts like he's programmed to do. Most often he has control of his actions and decisions—like a pitcher, you see? But sometimes like a pitcher, a man loses control, misses the mark, poorly calibrates his aim—whatever—and damage results. The batter—or in this case the wife—takes one right against the skull."

"I'll admit that being with a category-two sports wife is teaching me new metaphors to explain life, Jenny."

"You'll have to forgive me. It's an occupational hazard. But what really has me scared is the fact that Davis is approaching that age when men usually go through a psychological losing streak."

"By which you mean a mid-life crisis."

"Right. And losing streaks come in all lengths—both short and excruciatingly long. Sometimes they have no effect on the season at hand, but in some cases they can just ruin a team. If Davis's has the big one at the same time he's going through his career difficulties, it could get very messy—for the both of us."

Livy knew that Jenny's metaphor failed to express adequately the depth of her concern. "Again, I understand, Jenny."

Jenny stood and walked toward the lake. Livy followed her, though remaining two steps behind. "Livy, don't take this the wrong way—I so dearly appreciate your support and your wisdom—but can you really understand? You're not in love with Peter."

Livy knew her friend was right. She never found distressing the thought that Peter might find another woman desirable or worthy of an extra-marital relationship. In fact, she frequently wished he would find someone else, for it would make their break so much easier, regardless of the potential political fall-out. But then she knew it was more her own feelings she wished to save. A new woman in Peter's life would assuage her guilt—the constant presence which so gnawed at her sensibilities.

"Damn, I'm sorry, Livy. I didn't mean anything insulting by what I said." Jenny reached down and picked up a small rock, which she hurled into the lake. Livy was surprised by the distance the rock traveled.

"Wow."

"Just feeding the beast that is Memory Lake."

"No, really. I'm impressed by how far you threw that rock. Did you ever think of trying out for the Twins?"

"Don't laugh. I've shagged with them."

"Shagged? Jenny, you are not going to make me believe that..."

"Calm down, Miss Prim. You're thinking 'shag' in the British and Austin Powers sense. Shagging means to catch and retrieve fly balls hit by the players or the coaches. Boy, you've got so much to learn before I dare bring you to a Twins game."

"Maybe I won't be ready until next season." Livy's face told Jenny that she immediately regretted her cute response, but with the pressure of her worries having been lessened by their conversation, Jenny smiled and embraced her dearest friend.

"Okay, now that I've nearly soured up this lovely afternoon, how about we get in the car, do a little shopping, eat a little bite, have a little drink or three, and then take in a little 7:00 p.m. movie?"

"Can I do a little clothes changing before we head out?"

"I will be happy to grant your little request. Come on, let's put on some little new duds."

As the women made their way to the house, Jenny put her hand to her lips and blew a kiss to Memory Lake.

Chapter 10

Checking the time--7:25 p.m.--Nick was grateful Jenny and Livy weren't yet home, because he sought a good half hour alone on the bench by Memory Lake to ponder the Paul Vanderkellen matter. If he remained alone for another hour or so, he'd have time to return to the kind of retrospection he'd been engaged in more frequently the past several months. He wondered whether he was expected to reconcile completely with his past by the time he turned forty-five or fifty. Regardless, he was trying to do just that. But these contemplations had been knocked off schedule by Paul Vanderkellen's shocking decision to voice his grievances against Nick Lockhart in an on-air confession scheduled for broadcast in about forty-eight hours.

Nick was like so many men and women who placed ingratitude among their top three pet peeves, but his experience with ingrates most often warranted a shake of the head rather than any genuine disappointment, anger, or bitterness. But this was different. He had kept Vanderkellen's dirty secret private, even though his investigation following Kaitlin Terry's phone call in January led to the inescapable conclusion that while in college the young quarterback had indeed deliberately thrown an interception to keep the score down. It wasn't merely the observations made to him by Vanderkellen's former fiancé and an examination of the game film, but it was also the confession of wide receiver Rodney Sims.

"I swear to you, Mr. Lockhart, that right before Paul threw that interception, I asked him to repeat the play sent in from the bench, and I clearly heard him say his receiver was to break to the middle of the field and not out toward the sidelines, where the pass was ultimately thrown. In fact, he repeated what he said right before we broke the huddle. So when we returned to the sidelines after the interception, I was plenty pissed. I got in Paul's face about his throwing it right to the defensive back, and all he could say was, 'Had to do it, man. Had to do it.' Mr. Lockhart, I knew at that moment Paul was in trouble–probably with gamblers. He looked so relieved he'd thrown that interception. While we were showering after the game, I confronted him again and asked if he was in any financial trouble and he slammed me against the shower wall and told me to keep my fucking mouth shut. I mean, it wasn't as if I said I knew what he deliberately did on the field. He just assumed that's what I meant. Even though I was mad as hell for what he did, I was still concerned for him. But he looked at me like I was the bad guy—you know, like someone who'd betray him."

Nick learned from Sims the phone number of the other player Kaitlin Terry mentioned as being certain of Vanderkellen's actions, but when he called, this teammate refused to talk about specifics, although he made clear what his beliefs were. "Mr. Lockhart, I can't let you use my name or mention what position I play—anything that would identify me—because I'm scared what might happen. You know those gambling guys play pretty rough, and I'm married now with an eight-month old kid. Just know that whatever you're thinking about Vanderkellen is the truth of what happened. But I won't go on the record and say that, okay?"

Nick followed this conversation with another call—this time to a source he never once solicited in the fourteen years he had known him. He punched in the 702 area code and then the number of Tom "the Booker" D'Angelo, one of the crowned princes of sports wagering in Las Vegas. D'Angelo had an exceptional ear for gambling gossip and was, as the Booker himself liked to note, "in tune with a host of contacts spanning the entire globe." Lockhart and D'Angelo hit it off when the gambling maven failed in his attempt to buy the sports writer a drink at the Bellagio during a sports writer's gathering, which occurred at the same time the hotel was hosting a poker tournament. With his usual charm, Lockhart politely refused the drink, owing to his "selfish and indefensible" desire to keep his job. D'Angelo laughed and lifted his glass. "Here's to the most honest and best sportswriter in the business," to which Nick quickly added, "But please don't mention his name."

A week later, Nick received a brief note from the Booker regarding the gambling habits of a former NBA player, then a big story covered by the media. Nick believed the information was genuine and perfectly legitimate to use, given the national coverage of the controversy—so he passed it on to another writer, who was covering professional basketball. Over the next fourteen years, D'Angelo five times sent Nick similar information—again well within the ethical parameters of Lockhart's profession. At the end of each letter and email, D'Angelo closed with "Still want to buy you a drink." Never had Nick made the first contact. Never did he fish for information regarding the gaming habits of professional athletes. Seeking details about athletes' personal shortcomings was never Lockhart's way. Often he was forced to tolerate the jokes about his journalistic failure to keep up with the times.

But now he wanted to learn if Paul Vanderkellen was known in the larger gambling circles and, if so, whether the young man was indeed in trouble with anyone who might do him harm.

D'Angelo didn't answer the call, so Nick left the message, "Booker, this is Nick Lockhart. Call me on my cell when you get a chance." He left his number and hung up, glad that D'Angelo provided him his private number with the Christmas card he sent Lockhart ever year. "Never know when you might need to call me, Nick."

D'Angelo called back less than a minute after Nick hung up. After the Booker's playful "I knew you'd eventually need my services," Nick explained why he wanted to talk. D'Angelo required no additional time for research. Everything he needed was in his head. "The kid's deeply into it, Nick. To the tune of seven hundred grand, which he's been paying back at a rate unsatisfactory to those to whom he owes the cash. Seems his career with the Vikings is headed for the rocks and no other team seems interested in signing him, so the final chapter isn't going to make for pleasant reading."

"I see. And what about the college game I mentioned?"

"That I'll have to check on for the accurate figures, but I know that a killing was made when the kid threw that interception and kept the score where it was—or rather, where it needed to be."

"Thanks, Booker. I appreciate your getting back to me so soon."

"After fourteen years of waiting for you to call, I wasn't going to keep you in the outer room, buddy-boy. Call anytime you need something—whatever that might be."

"Be careful, Booker."

"No, I know you're Mr. Saintly Two-Shoes. I wouldn't even try to tempt you. I just hope that once you retire, I can buy you that drink."

"You got it. Thanks again."

"Hey wait, Nick. Are you going to do a story on Vanderkellen? Could be a good one—that is, as long as you keep my name out of it."

"Have no fear. I never even heard of you."

"Well, let's not get carried away, Nick. I just want discretion, not anonymity. Anyway, write up a good one. Peace, my friend."

When he hung up, Nick thought nothing of writing a story. His thoughts were exclusively on arranging a meeting with Paul Vanderkellen.

•   •   •

"Well, as they say, the best laid schemes." Jenny puffed an exaggerated sigh of disappointment.

"Sorry to have ruined your cinema plans, Jenny, but when I saw the film last week in Washington, I immediately determined that it was hardly good enough to see twice."

"I feared as much, but it sounded trashy enough to be worth two hours of my time. I'll pirate the thing on-line and make a final determination at a later date."

"Pirate the thing on-line? Then a judge may be making the final determination, you mean."

"Well, the evening's going to be a good one nevertheless. How do you like this place?" Jenny and Livy were situated in the stylish Long Room at Brit's, one of the city's most unique and popular establishments.

"Love it. A British Pub in the heart of Minneapolis. But I would have expected you to take me to a German or Swedish place."

"You'll learn that up here we're far more diverse ethnically than the rest of the country imagines. If I'm not mistaken, the top five ethnic groups are German, Norwegian, Irish, Swedish, and English—but we have everyone else from way, way outer Mongolians to pale, pale faced Antarcticans, who moved up here for the heat."

"Well, with you being of Swedish extraction, you have to feel at home at least."

"Don't laugh. Davis believes that's why I love it here so. Minnesota—the state with the most Swedes."

"So is Minneapolis called 'Little Stockholm' or is that St. Paul?"

"Neither, because there's a township called Stockholm about fifty miles west of here. The population is around eight hundred or so. We can drive out there if you want. Or, we can go seventy miles southeast and across the river and visit Stockholm, Wisconsin."

"Perhaps after I've settled in a bit."

In truth, Livy wouldn't at all mind visiting each of these Stockholms in the coming year. She was amazed that within twenty-four hours of arriving, she was so fully embracing her new home state, even though she couldn't be sure how long she would stay after she finished her Master's. She smiled. Would Jenny mind if she took up permanent residence in the basement apartment?

Yes, the basement apartment. Would she have felt as secure here in Minnesota if her apartment was in the attic or even on the main two floors of Jenny and Davis's house? She only knew it was such a pleasure being under the radar, as it were. So safely submerged. So snug within the womb. Livy assumed the feeling would last but a brief time, but she wasn't sure she really wanted it to end. If her little apartment had windows she'd keep the drapes drawn.

To her displeasure, Peter insisted that the interior of their places in California and Virginia be as exposed as possible. The drapes always opened—even at night—until they went to bed, when she insisted they be closed. Livy believed it was all part of his desire to be seen and remarked upon. Peter had already pushed his way onto several on-camera interviews freshman congressmen rarely procure. One talking head even noted after an interview that "the camera seems to like Representative Garner." It wasn't her husband's vanity per se she objected to. Rather it was his shameless courting of attention and positive press. His staff never had to encourage him to sell himself, either in California or now in Washington, for Garner took to that task with an exuberant fervor.

Jenny jabbed her index finger into the menu. "Livy, let's get the artichoke and spinach dip. It's the best in the city."

"I think I can handle that. But I'm not sure how much else I'll want to eat."

"You have to try their fish and chips or the bangers and mash."

Livy scanned through the menu. "I've never tried bangers and mash. No, I'll just have the dip and a bowl of the cream of tomato soup."

"Whatever. You can't go wrong with anything here, although I can't believe I've never tried the Guinness Pot Roast."

"Pot roast cooked in beer, you mean?"

"Cooked in Guinness, darling. There is a difference. And speaking of which, how about a pint of Guinness to start the festivities?"

"You know I'm not a beer—or Guinness—drinker, Jenny. I better stick to pinot grigio. I'm assuming you won't drink too many pints of Guinness and that we'll have something more slushy when we get back to your place."

"Feel free to call it 'our place' from now on. Yes, just one pint—that way I'll be just sober enough to tell you which turns to make in order to get us back safely. You do have a driver's license, I assume."

"It's out of state. Can I drive here in Minnesota?"

"We do allow it if you're sponsored by a resident."

Seeing that her friend was completely back to her old rambunctious self, Livy vowed to ask nothing about Davis's career or about Jenny's fears while they enjoyed themselves at Brit's.

After the server took the women's orders, Livy surprised herself by blurting out, "Okay, Jenny, what else do you want to know about my life as a congressman's disenchanted wife?" She took a sip of her water and grinned at her table mate.

"Well, did you find yourself disappointed by what you experienced in Washington—or had you expected to find what you found—if my question makes any sense to you?"

"No, I understand. Remember that my mind was made up to separate from Peter as far back as the end of last summer, so I wasn't really thinking of the life as Congressman Garner's wife as much as how I was going to get away from it and flee to the arms of my Minnesota soul-mate."

"Well, I can certainly understand that."

"When we first arrived in Washington, I hated even walking into our new place in Virginia, because I knew I should have already made my move here. I didn't tell you this, but I initially applied for admission at Minnesota for the January term.

"Well, you should have come. January is the ideal month to move. Ice fishing, polar bear swimming clubs, wolf hunting—all things that give California girls orgasms just thinking about."

"Stop. I didn't come then because I wasn't able to "have that talk" with Peter. He was knee-deep in campaigning. Then the election to the House. Right before Thanksgiving I finally told him I wanted to come here to continue my Master's. He did his usual patronizing thing—you know, 'Just wait until you get to Washington. Getting your Master's will then seem like joining the Girl Scouts.' Whatever he meant by that. Oh, thank you."

The server delivered their drinks and took their order—after which Livy continued.

"I admit with some shame that initially my head was turned by the entire experience of being in the city, and especially around the Capitol Building. Nothing has ever impressed me more. But all that stirring architecture is unfortunately cluttered with far less impressive human beings, and it didn't take long for me to regret my cowardice and desire to make the separation from Peter as painless as possible for him."

"I hope you have at least a dozen tales of Washington corruption and seduction to amuse me with. I want to be sure that my tax dollar is being put to good use."

"I don't think you'll be disappointed, Jenny."

"Then proceed. Start off with something brief, so I can enjoy it before the artichoke and spinach dip arrives."

"All right. This should serve you as a kind of salacious appetizer."

"Ah, my favorite kind."

"Do you know that a senior staff member of another congressman began massaging my spine—without an invitation to do?"

"Don't tell me you complained about an achy-breaky spinal column."

"I did not. What happened was I was waiting outside the office of a senior congressman who was chairing one of the committees Peter was assigned to. This congressman wanted to meet the spouses of the new members of the committee—but I was the only one who could make it that day. The congressman had at least a dozen members of the press inside his office suite, so his senior staff person came out to apologize for the delay. He had no sooner begun speaking to me when I had to scratch a spot in the middle of my back. It was right in that place where you can't quite reach it, you know?"

"Every summer out by Memory Lake. The mosquitoes head right for that same spot. Never fails. I end up rubbing my back along the edge of the bench. A sight most erotically comical, I must admit."

"I can just picture it."

"Good thing I read the *Kama Sutra* and know all the mosquito-bite-relieving positions. But go ahead. You had an itch that *he* just had to scratch for you, right?"

"Correct. He politely said, 'May I?' and rubbed me right where I couldn't reach. By the time I said thank you, his stubby fingers had made their way down my spine some three or four inches, and..."

Jenny pressed down on Livy's arms as the server came with the dip. Jenny grabbed Livy's wrist to prevent her from eating any of the appetizer before finishing her story.

"Okay, now finish your spine-jiggling tale. You were saying that this staff assistant had something that was stubby and three to four inches long. Go ahead. I'm dying to know how you handled it."

"You should be sent to a convent and have your mouth washed out with holy water. No, the man had stubby fingers and he began sliding them three or four—then five or six inches below where I had the itch. Wait, that didn't sound right."

"Maybe *you* should be the one gargling holy water—not me."

"So, he got to the spot on my spine just above the Mason-Dixon Line before I spun around and gave him a look I hope he never forgets."

"Then you slapped him?"

"No."

"Turned him in?"

"No."

"Told Peter?"

"Definitely no."

"But you gave him the look?"

"Yes."

"Poor man. He'll never be the same." Jenny released Livy's wrist and the women attacked the artichoke and spinach dip. Talking while she munched, Jenny gave Livy the once-over.

"Jenny, why are you looking at me like that?"

"I bet you have a whole bunch of stories about men touching and massaging you without permission, don't you?"

"Actually I do. I don't know what it is about me that invites that kind of behavior."

"When you get hugged, they hold you longer than normal for such a greeting or goodbye—eh?"

"How did you know?"

"When they kiss you on the cheek, they always get a little too close to your mouth, right?"

"Not always, but often, yes."

"And when a man sits next to you and carries on a conversation, he rubs your forearm, correct?"

"Occasionally."

"That forearm-rubbing thing is supposed to be a woman's move, not a man's. You should tell them that."

"I will next time. But, again, why me? And please don't say it's because I'm attractive. You are far more appealing than I am, and I bet you don't get gently molested half as much as I do."

"No, I don't. And do you know why?"

"No, and that's why I asked you why."

"They know I wouldn't put up with it. My 'aura'—for the lack of a better term—sends out signals that if they dare to run their stubby fingers down my spine, I would slap, knee, or bludgeon them—or at least turn them in."

"And would you do any of these things?"

"Depends. But if I'm in a good mood, I'd most likely just drench them with profanity. But that's not the point. You, my lovely Olivia, just have that rare combination of undeniable sex appeal..."

"Shhh. You're embarrassing me." Livy wanted to drape the napkin over her head.

"...and a palpable sweetness that makes men more confident and bold."

"So, I'm too nice for my own good?"

"I didn't say that. I think you're as nice as you should be. It's just that 'aura' thing I mentioned. It's everything about you. Your smile, your eyes, your hair, your shape, your voice. You just draw them in and then, unfortunately, have to swat them away."

"Jenny, I have another side."

"I know, I know. When you play chess or any board game, it comes out, but generally you don't intimidate—that's the word I was looking for—you never intimidate."

Livy looked intently at her friend but didn't respond.

"Livy, why the inscrutable look?"

"I'm just trying to intimidate you, Jennifer."

"Sorry, you're only inscrutabilizing me."

"Inscrutabilizing?"

"My word of the day. So, why the look? Ahh, you're trying to show me that you are a sexy tease, aren't you?"

"But not an intimidating tease."

"No, that's my bailiwick."

Livy looked over Jenny's right shoulder at a man sitting at the bar, whose eyes were trained on Jenny. "Jenny, when men wish to approach you and rub your back, how do they usually go about it?"

"I'm a married woman, Livy. I never invite them to do so, if that's what you mean."

"No, I didn't imply anything about your fidelity."

"Just so we're straight about that." Jenny flashed a big grin marred by specks of spinach from the delicious dip.

"Jenny, you've got some..." Livy made the familiar gesture of rubbing her mouth with her finger. Jenny deftly swiped her napkin across her perfect teeth.

"Did I get it?"

"All but one bit of spinach to the right of your two front teeth."

Jenny removed the spinach residue and leaned forward to answer Livy's question. "I get the stare downs from men who are standing across a room or sitting at a bar, or driving a car. I've developed a sixth sense about it. I can tell if they're staring at me when they're standing or sitting right behind me."

"I see. Can you tell if he's staring at you from a side angle—

actually to the side and a little behind?"

"Are you telling me that...?"

"Off your right shoulder at the bar."

"What's he look like?"

"Quite nice. Seems to be about Davis's age. In fact he looks a little like him too."

Jenny manipulated herself so that she would turn toward the bar without looking as if she was deliberately turning toward the bar. Her eyes met the man's. He smiled. She did as well. He lifted his glass of either bourbon or Scotch. She turned back toward Livy and jerked the pint of Guinness to her mouth. "He just lifted his glass."

"Perhaps he's going to buy you a drink." Livy was amused at Jenny's fidgeting.

"That's what I'm afraid of."

"Well then, you might have to bludgeon him or turn him in to the bartender."

"Don't be a wise-guy, Livy." Jenny laughed into her Guinness, sending a series of bubbles to the rim. She was of course flattered, but she was most pleased by the fact than the man reminded Livy of Davis Montgomery—appearing to be the same age. The man was therefore naturally drawn to the right woman chronologically, even if he would never even get to first base with that woman.

Grateful that the man sent no drinks to their table, Jenny didn't look back toward the bar until Livy's soup and her fish and chips were placed before them. When she did, her heart sank. The man had apparently found another female to interest him. She stood by his bar stool rubbing his forearm. The man who was about Davis age was being charmed by a woman who looked no older than twenty-two.

Chapter 11

Two teenage boys pushed off in a small rowboat on the other side of Memory Lake, fifty yards or so from where the Lockhart house used to stand. Looking slightly to his left, Nick soon lost sight of them, since they were directly in line of the setting sun. He was glad the Montgomery home faced a number of degrees away from the sun's downward path, just as he had as a boy enjoyed the fact that his room was in the front of the house and the rising sun didn't wake him on the weekends when he wished to sleep late.

The boys in the rowboat were now totally obscured by the sun's rays—their youth swallowed up, Nick thought, by the unalterable movement of time. He imagined the boys in a cauldron, their youthful expectations of life reshaped by the merciless heat. The inevitable crucible that awaited them. He remembered when he experienced the alteration of his own dreams and assumptions, when he was slightly older than the two lads who were enjoying several minutes of fun before they made their way back into the house for the mundane yet comforting activities of every night—the home-cooked meals, the homework assignments, television, and whatever else they managed to fit into their evenings before drifting off to sleep.

As he glanced toward the location of his old house, Nick took heart in recalling that this was at a time of day when as a boy he most enjoyed being outside hitting small rocks into Memory Lake with his baseball bat. The setting sun, always behind him, never interfered with his watching the rocks sail into the air, then briefly hesitate before changing course and finally dropping into the water. The supply of rocks in the vacant lot on the other side of his house seemed endless. How many times since he moved away from Memory Lake had he wished he could go back—just one more time—pick up his bat, and hit rocks into the water until the inside of his hands were rubbed raw.

From across the lake, Lockhart heard the sound of a woman calling the boys back inside the impressive home next to the even more impressive one that claimed the area where the Lockhart house once stood, as well as that empty lot filled with small rocks and stones. Nick imagined that with their fun cut short, the boys were presently engaged in a running dialogue filled with complaints about the responsibilities of school from which both lads wished they could set sail on Memory Lake and be free. Perhaps it was Nick's empathy with the problems of boys and young men that made him feel annoyance at the mother's command that they bring the rowboat back for the more mundane chores of eating and studying. Perhaps it was also this empathy that influenced Nick to arrange a face-to-face meeting with Paul Vanderkellen immediately after corroborating the tale initially told to him by Kaitlin Terry.

"Thanks for meeting me, Paul." At the end of January, Lockhart invited Vanderkellen to Gold Medal Park, a couple of blocks from the U.S. Bank Stadium, the new home of the Minnesota Vikings, where this past season the young quarterback had completely failed to impress the Viking coaching staff, front office, and the fans. Walking on one of the undulating paths, designed to mimic the flow of the Mississippi located a short distance away, the two men braved the cold weather as best they could, both satisfied that their heavy winter clothing greatly lessened the chance that either of them would be recognized and approached. Lockhart preferred not to meet in a restaurant, lounge, or at either man's residence.

"Mr. Lockhart..."

"Just call me Nick."

"Sure. Nick, you sounded pretty serious on the phone. I assume you have some inside information on what the Vikings plan to do with my contract."

Nick easily detected fear in the young man's voice, but he was certain it wasn't prompted by what the Vikings thought of his play. He believed instead that Vanderkellen feared the writer had learned something about his gambling ties.

"Paul, I talked with one of your teammates from college about the homecoming game your senior year."

Vanderkellen reacted immediately. "He's lying. I made a bad read at the end of that game and threw the interception. That's all it was. Rodney was just pissed that he didn't get another reception. He loved his stats, and he would have set a team record for most catches in a single game had I thrown it to him. It's just ridiculous. Why would I deliberately throw an interception? I had everything going for me. I was looking ahead to the draft. I'd be insane to risk my career on anything like that."

"Paul, I didn't say anything about deliberately throwing an interception at the end of that game or about your motives for doing so."

"Come on, Nick. That's what you were thinking. Don't bullshit me."

"Okay, Paul. I won't bullshit you. That is exactly what I'm trying to determine. Did you throw the interception to keep the score within the betting line?"

"As I said, why would I risk my career by doing that?"

Nick had heard the same line many times from athletes charged with drug-related crimes, steroid use, and domestic abuse. "I'm just trying to find out what happened, Paul."

Vanderkellen did his best to sound indignant. "A jealous teammate? That's what you base your story on?"

Nick wished to keep Kaitlin Terry's name out of it. "I have corroborative evidence beyond Rodney Sims. Another teammate, for instance, but also others."

Vanderkellen froze. He searched Lockhart's eyes for any indication that the writer had investigated the matter thoroughly. Trying to recover, Vanderkellen laughed. "Oh, so you've talked to Kaitlin." Nick refused to show his hand. "You do know she hates my guts because we were engaged and I broke it off, right? Or did she give you some bullshit story that she broke it off. She's got a very active imagination, Nick. She's accused me of being with other women I didn't even know. She's just out to pay me back for not wishing to spend the rest of my life with her." Not once during his characterization of the relationship with Kaitlin did Vanderkellen look directly at Lockhart.

Nick waited until an elderly couple passed by on the path. "Paul, I've learned that you're very deeply in debt to some big players in sports wagering."

Vanderkellen barely got the words out. "Kaitlin told you that story too? Jesus."

"No, I heard it from someone who's up on such matters. Someone in the business."

Vanderkellen shook his head from side to side, but Nick wasn't sure it was a deliberate attempt to deny the fact presented him or simply an involuntary reaction to having been found out by the city's leading sports writer. Unable to speak, Vanderkellen gazed intently at Nick.

Lockhart wasn't prepared for the young man's next movement. Vanderkellen reached out and grabbed Nick's shoulders and brought his face closer to the older man's. Vanderkellen's eyes welled with tears. He began to drop his head on Lockhart's shoulder. Could it be the troubled quarterback was about to weep?

Nick was undeniably affected by the Vanderkellen's behavior. He never saw anything like it from any professional or collegiate athlete he ever interviewed. But Nick felt uncomfortable and even threatened by Vanderkellen's incipient emotional collapse. He took the younger man's hands off his shoulders and backed away. Nick was in the process of advising Paul to get control of himself, when Vanderkellen's neck and shoulders slumped.

The young man stared at the ground. "It's all true. I deliberately threw the interception to keep the score within the betting line. I was forced...I mean I had to do it. But after college, I didn't learn my lesson. I bet money I didn't have. On several sports, including football. But not for Vikings to lose—I swear. I would never do that. There was just one game where I had to be sure we didn't win by more than seven points. But the way it worked out, we ran a punt and an interception back for touchdowns—so it wasn't anything I did. I played like shit in that game. But they blamed me anyway. Before I knew it, I was into them for six or seven hundred thousand. I just didn't have enough to pay all my debts."

"Paul, you got a million-four for your signing bonus two years ago, didn't you? Are you telling me with that and your salary, you didn't have seven hundred thousand left to pay your debt?"

Vanderkellen offered a sick laugh. "People don't understand how quickly someone can go through a million dollars or more. Other than the tax hit, I bet a lot and lost almost all of it. I ended up with other outstanding gambling debts besides the one I'm on the hook for with the Vegas people. I even had to borrow eight hundred dollars from Kaitlin to keep me afloat."

Nick kept his distance as the young man went on about his gambling history, adding that he hung out with the wrong crowd and didn't have proper guidance when he was in high school—his father having died when he was thirteen. "Nick, I needed someone strong in my life to kick me in the ass. If I had someone like that—a father or a big brother—I wouldn't have gotten into this mess. I needed someone to make my decisions for me when it came to the money. I wasn't emotionally ready to receive the contract I got from the Vikings."

Without moving from where he stood, Vanderkellen spoke of having his head turned by several boosters irresponsibly and illegally enticing high school recruits to sign with Vanderkellen's university. The confession wasn't stunning for what it said of booster involvement and the phenomenon of big-time sports wagering, but rather for how Vanderkellen delivered it. The weather was bitterly cold on that day, yet the young man stood immobile with his head still bowed as if he were some kind of medieval penitent, prepared for the suffering he would inflict on himself as well as that to be inflicted by others.

"Nick, I need help. I need someone to help me get through this. Please, please, can you help me? I want to get clean of all this and start over. If I can make things right enough for the next few months, I could begin over again in the spring and summer. Forget what I showed this season. I'm a damn good quarterback. I can lead this team. I just need some help right now. Can you help me, Nick?"

Lockhart assumed the young man was asking him not for money but for a promise he would bury the story. He grappled with conflicting thoughts of journalistic integrity, professional expectations, and his own humanity. He knew he wouldn't make any decisions standing in the January cold on one of the paths in Gold Medal Park.

"I don't think I can wait another day, Nick. I'm literally losing my mind with worry. I'm really afraid. Can you help me?"

"I need to go now, Paul."

Nick walked past Vanderkellen, dissatisfied with his response. He didn't look back until he was far down the pathway, and when he did, he saw that the young quarterback was watching him.

Nick was about to ponder further Paul Vanderkellen's on-air interview two night from now, when he heard the back door of the Montgomery house open. Jenny's voice soon obliterated all other sounds around Memory Lake.

"Who's down there? Is that you, Nick?"

"It's me."

"Alone or do you have a naked honey with you?"

Nick wondered if the two boys across the lake had heard Jenny's penetrating and voluminous inquiry. "Just me, Jenny—with my clothes on."

"Drats!" By this time, Jenny and Livy had made their way almost to the bench.

Fortunately, the bench by Memory Lake measured a full five feet across, rather than the usual four, making the seating accommodations for the three adults comfortably snug. Livy guided her friend to sit between her and Nick, even though Jenny had gestured otherwise. Now dark, the area was lit only by the torch lights Jenny and Davis situated at the back of their spacious backyard and behind the bench near the lake's edge. Whatever stars were in the late April sky had been obscured by clouds none of them could see in the darkness. After ten minutes of chatter about each other's day, Jenny excused herself "to see a man about a horse," although Livy wondered whether the bathroom break was intended merely to allow her and Nick Lockhart to get better acquainted.

"I'm not sure a woman should use that expression, Livy."

"I'm sure you're right, Nick. That's probably why she used it."

Nick took the occasion to ask about her nascent views of Minneapolis, to which Livy replied that she loved everything about the city she had so far seen.

"I know you'll enjoy taking classes and working on your Master's at the university."

"Can't wait to start." Not since her chess game with Evan Donnelly in Washington had Livy felt as comfortable with a man as she did at this moment.

Lockhart carefully sifted his thoughts, concerned he might bring up a sensitive topic—namely Livy's marriage, about which Jenny had earlier informed him. Still, he was curious to gauge her feelings on politics and living in Washington, although he understood she had been there but a few months. "There's no question you'll see a stark contrast between here and Washington D.C. But then that would be true anywhere else you lived."

Livy groaned in that exaggerated manner suggesting her willingness to express her opinion. "Nick, the city itself—the architecture and history, I mean—is beyond my ability to describe. If you'll excuse my naïveté, it felt almost like a privilege just to walk around and stand in front of those buildings."

"I know exactly what you mean. I've been there almost thirty times in my career and once when I was a boy scout. Let's see, you arrived in January, so you got to experience some cold days and some snow."

"Yes, more than I saw and experienced in all my years in California, that's for sure." Lockhart smiled. "Come on, Nick, don't look at me like that. You do think me naïve, don't you? Jenny has already filled me in on what awaits me here starting in the fall."

Lockhart cocked his head. "Then you really plan on being here for the fall and winter? I thought maybe Jenny was exaggerating and that you were just taking summer classes and then going back, working on your thesis in Washington." But whereas many men would add, "Well, I'm glad you'll be staying on, because that will give us more time to...," Nick simply nodded without enthusiasm but with visible pleasure nonetheless.

Livy looked out at the darkened lake, which she could now hear more than see, except for the shore line attractively illuminated by the burning torches at the rear of the other houses around the lake. Even given the cool temperature and lack of palm trees, she conjured one of her favorite images—that of sitting alone on some tropical shore line, listening to nothing but the surf splashing and running up to where she sat, the salt water lightly touching her feet but going no further. Never had she imagined being in this setting with another person. Memory Lake was hardly the Atlantic or Pacific, but it was coming close to satisfying the requirements of her favorite recurring image. Only she wasn't alone. There was an attractive and accomplished man sitting right next to her, even though there were some twenty inches separating them.

Livy understood that twenty inches wouldn't be far enough if another type of man was on the bench with her. Yet for some reason, Nick Lockhart made her feel more than relaxed; he also made her feel confidant. She quickly concluded that her wit was stimulated in his company, perhaps not to the degree it was in Jenny's but stimulated nonetheless. Such was rarely the case with others she knew—from her taciturn father to her wit-barren husband—and not even Jenny's husband Davis, for whom she had deep affection. For the first time she gave thought to Nick's love life—present as well as past.

"You know what, Nick. I bet you Jenny will come back and force me to move over."

Nick laughed. ""I was thinking the same exact thing. Except she'd be pushing me over, not you."

"Okay, it's a bet. I'll wager a free drink at lunch that I'll be the one she'll shove to the middle." Livy wondered how often Jenny had tried to set poor Nick up with one of her friends.

"You're on. One free drink it is."

"Nick, I'm not kidding when I say I'm most impressed by the many awards you've received in your career."

"You're too kind."

"I only wish I knew more about sports to have the full effect of being impressed." She smiled puckishly. "I'm as ignorant as they come, I would imagine. What I know of baseball I've learned from Jenny and Davis, and they understand I can only absorb the basics."

"Oh, you're just being modest."

"I wish my ignorance on the subject *was* modest—really."

"Your father wasn't into sports, then?"

"If he was, I never knew it. Crossword puzzles seemed to be the extent of his athletic endeavors."

"There see? I'm terrible at crossword puzzles. I only embarrass myself when I can't finish even the easy ones. As for Sudoku and the other advanced word puzzles, I'm completely lost. And I'm a journalist—go figure."

Livy didn't want to ask him if he played chess. If he did, it would come out that she did as well, and Jenny would surely suggest a match. Livy didn't even want to oppose Nick, let alone beat him. She knew whatever charms she had would be set aside as she applied the full powers of her concentration.

"Three more drinks." Jenny had quietly come down the steps neatly balancing a serving tray. Here you go, my dear friends." Holding her fresh drink in one hand, Jenny handed Livy and Nick their margaritas, took the empty glasses, placed them on the tray, took her own drink, and deftly placed the tray with the two empty glasses under the bench on Livy's side. "Move over darling, I need to sit on the end."

Livy grinned and looked at Nick and held up one finger and then made the drinking gesture, while Jenny's head was looking under the bench. Nick shook his head and threw up his hands.

"So what have you two been saying about me since I left to tinkle and then freshen up our drinks? Oops. I should have done that in the reverse order, shouldn't I...have?"

But she did more than that when she returned to the house. As soon as she made it through the back door, she lectured herself for fretting over the impression left by the man and the young woman standing at the bar in Brit's. Since she and Livy stepped out of the establishment and drove home, Jenny fought with the appalling image of her husband having a few beers with several teammates while fending off the attention of flirtatious women—many of them young—seeking autographs and attention of all kinds. Davis wasn't one to come home after a road trip and regale his wife with tales of teammates resisting or occasionally succumbing to the kinds of temptation that came with the career of a professional athlete, but never had he categorically denied that anything of that nature ever occurred, even though he was thoughtful enough to repeat, "Jenny, you never have to worry about me. I don't want any other woman's attention but yours. You know I love you and I'll never let you down."

Yes, he had said that or something like it whenever the subject came up, but on the drive home Jenny dwelled on the fact that with his pitching as shaky as it was at the end of last season and his concern about the deterioration of his skills—his "advancing age" as he called it—it seemed to her most significant that Davis hadn't reassured her in the familiar manner since the season began. For the first time she plainly visualized a scenario in which her husband would welcome the attention of another woman, especially one young enough to alleviate his growing concern about his "deterioration."

"Don't tell me. I know what the two of you were saying about me. You both reluctantly admitted to each other that things had gotten pretty dull since I went to the indoor outhouse."

Livy winced in reaction to the sudden stab of pain from the "ice cream headache" she experienced after taking in too much of the frozen margarita. Jenny was quick to exploit the reaction. "There— see? I exposed you for the Judas figure you really are, Olivia."

Nick savored the playful banter between the two women. At first he felt a little disconcerted because, whereas it felt good having Livy sitting close to him with their hips touching lightly, he also knew that she was still married. His logic could tell him Jenny was right about Livy's impending divorce from the congressman, but his better sense warned him that Livy could simply be exercising the freedom she now experienced being away from Washington and that a future with her was highly unlikely. But then the advice of his mother wedged its way into his thoughts: "Don't borrow either trouble or romance, Nick. They'll both come when they come." Since the women's energy was just what he needed, he decided to sit back and enjoy it. He refused to give any thought to what was really the main reason he had so long resisted a permanent relationship with a woman.

The three of them sat for another forty-five minutes, the two women sharing anecdotes about undergraduate life, with Jenny embellishing every tale of Livy's "wilder" college activities and punctuating many with "You see, Nick, she's a lot more wicked than she looks."

Livy countered by asserting that whereas Jenny was exaggerating considerably, there never could be any embellishment of Jenny's collegiate waywardness. "She majored in the liberal arts. All the romantic arts only liberals could talk about in polite company."

"Ha, ha, Livy. At least I wasn't asked out by a lust crazed, fifty year-old history professor."

"You had to bring that up?"

"Don't worry, Nick, she turned him down—when she remembered that he didn't make that much as a history professor. Had he taught in the business school, well...In any event, she just has this older man musk that draws them to her."

Both Livy and Nick looked out across the lake. Livy because of recent memories from her time in Washington—Nick because being around ten years older than either of the women qualified him as an "older man." His embarrassment was impossible to disguise. Livy rescued the moment. "So, Nick, since we've hogged the conversation about college, how about sharing some of your stories of life at the University of Minnesota—soon also to be my alma mater?"

Lockhart was grateful for the chance to move past the awkward interlude prompted by Jenny's jocular comment, but the transition wasn't as smooth as it could have been."

"I was an undergraduate in the mid-nineties. You sure you want to hear about ancient history?"

Jenny couldn't resist. "So, Nick, did you wear a Mohawk and M.C. Hammer pants while you listened to Duran Duran and Bananarama?"

"That was the mid-*eighties*, Jenny. I was in middle school at the time and had an impressive Mullet."

"Oops."

"Don't mind her, Nick." Livy was all smiles. "She got a D in fashion history."

Jenny sighed and put the margarita to her lips. "But Livy dear, you forget that I got a bull's eye in archery."

"What?"

Their collective laughter made its way over Memory Lake—perhaps catching the ear of the two boys on the other side.

Chapter 12

Livy placed her book on the nightstand and clicked off the bedside light. It had been quite a good day, annoying moments of guilt and concern regarding her marriage notwithstanding. She believed she wouldn't have to pull the covers up to her chin the way she did last night and for the past year or so. Of course she was aware that such a nocturnal habit testified to feelings of insecurity and fear, although she managed to avoid adjusting her body into a classic fetal position while sleeping. Perhaps tonight she could rest comfortably with the sheets and comforter pulled only to a point just above her breasts—where they always rested before she finally accepted that her marriage was a mistake she couldn't and surely didn't wish to rectify.

Adjusting her pillows, Livy also concluded that tonight marked only the fourth time since her marriage she and Peter hadn't slept in the same bed for two consecutive nights. Wishing to get her husband out of her mind, she thought of Nick Lockhart and the many sports statistics he surely committed to memory and the others he researched as part of his work. At least they had that in common, for she often came up with her own statistics and percentages relating to her daily life. Anything from calorie counting and travel mileage to investment and savings account interest and the hours and minutes until the beginning of some event helped keep her mind adequately exercised when she had no chess to play or puzzle to solve. She therefore couldn't wait to begin graduate classes and the research for her thesis. Allowing one more thought of Lockhart, Livy looked forward to interviewing him about his military experience, even though she sensed it wasn't a subject he spoke of freely.

Livy repositioned her body to take advantage of the spacious queen sized mattress. The previous night she had slept on the far right side of the bed, the locale ordained to her by Peter, who years earlier insisted he needed to sleep on the left side and that he didn't wish to feel her nestled against him. At first, her ego was bruised by his announcement, but in more recent years she was grateful he didn't wish to feel her presence in his "resting space," as he termed it. When he wanted sex, he slid to her side and performed the act without either of them encroaching on his space. She found his habit ungentlemanly and insulting for hygienic reasons, but for the past year she resented his trespassing on her side of the bed. It seemed she could find no place where her privacy was respected.

In short, sex with her husband became a distasteful chore she could from time to time postpone but never terminate, although she desperately wanted to. On rare occasions she refused his periodic advances, owing to genuine fatigue and health issues. Only once had she said no otherwise. The night before she left for Minnesota. Peter's look of incredulity was almost laughable to her.

"I don't understand. It's going to be a while until we're together again, you know."

"I'm getting up very early tomorrow morning, Peter. Besides, I'm too keyed up about the trip."

"You could have flown to Minneapolis. I would have sent your stuff right along."

"I told you I wanted to take my car."

"Jenny and Davis wouldn't lend you one of theirs if you needed to go somewhere without them?"

"Even though I'll be living with them, I need to feel as independent as I can possibly be."

"That makes no sense. You're going to be dependent on them for lodging and food—don't you see?"

"I told Jenny I'm chipping in for the food. But I can rent my own apartment, if that's what you want."

"No, no. Forget it. I want you staying with them for as long as you insist on playing co-ed. You've never lived by yourself, Livy. It's not as easy as you think."

She recalled the flush of anger that came over her after he callously delivered these tactless and offensive remarks. Profanity wasn't one of her weapons of choice whenever she was frustrated or indignant, but she thought her husband deserved whatever she could draw forth, especially since he punctuated his comments with a patronizing chuckle and an attempt to kiss her mouth. But she said nothing and merely turned her face enough to take his kiss on her cheek. She wouldn't curse Peter, not with her departure so imminent. Still, when he again asked to be inside her, she shook her head and turned away from him. Even so, she uttered an "I'm sorry, Peter" before he got out of bed and went to the living room to watch television.

That was three nights ago and she was disgusted with herself for having added the "I'm sorry." Why couldn't she have said nothing or just a simple "Good night"? Then she would have felt victorious. But with the soft apology she believed she lost, even though she had in truth won, the moment.

When she departed the Virginia residence at 6:15 a.m., Peter was still in bed. He seemed genuinely asleep, but Livy was almost certain he was refusing to wish her well on her trip. She left him a note saying she would call him in two days' time. Missing from the note was any closing. She hadn't written "Love, Livy" on a note or card to her husband for close to two years.

. . .

Jenny stood at the opened back door—half of her body inside the kitchen, half outside on the patio step. The lawn torches had been extinguished; the rear flood lights were turned off. The only illumination came from the light inside the kitchen, which washed forward over several feet of her stone patio, and from the sprinkling of lights from the houses across Memory Lake. The breeze had ceased completely. No sound accompanied Jenny's thoughts as she struggled to make out the features of the lake before her. She felt as if she had escaped into tranquility.

Livy had gone downstairs and was likely asleep by now. Jenny tried to follow suit, but she got no further than the removal of her shoes before she realized it would take another hour at least before she could climb into bed and expect to drift off. Instead, she fixed herself a cup of hot cocoa and debated how to spend the next sixty minutes or so. Reluctantly, she knew what she'd do, but first she wanted to take a few moments to stare at Memory Lake, even though she couldn't really see it in the darkness. But just knowing it was there was enough.

Finishing the mug of hot cocoa, Jenny returned to the kitchen and locked the door behind her. Her laptop waited on the kitchen table. Unhappy over having capitulated to her promptings, she dutifully typed into the search engine "Why a husband cheats—mid-life crisis" and opened several sites dealing with the issue and began skimming through the contents. Some of the sites relieved her concerns, since they dismissed the inevitability of cheating based on a male's reaching a certain age, usually between thirty-five and fifty. These sites blamed extra-marital affairs almost exclusively on a lack of understanding, trust, and communication between spouses, as well as other motives, such as revenge and low self-esteem. Jenny shaped a tepid smile, reassuring herself that she and Davis had none of those problems.

But other sites placed a considerable emphasis on the inevitable phase husbands entered at a certain age—whether flippantly called the "seven year itch" or something more clinical. Frowning as she read on, Jenny thought how she might re-channel the factors that encouraged such affairs into something she and Davis could survive without his seeking the affections of another woman. Yet not one of these sites had anything to say specifically about professional athletes and the unique lifestyles and sexual opportunities available to these men. Perhaps it was generally accepted that no other occupation was as fertile for extra-marital affairs as that of celebrities—including those in Davis's profession.

Completely frustrated and fatigued by her emotions, Jenny closed the laptop. She walked to the living room in search of the book she had been reading off and on for the past two weeks. As she turned on the light and sat in her favorite chair, she looked at the book shelves, which included framed photographs of her family at different times of her life. Making her way to the shelves, she kept her eyes on the photo taken when she was nine, with her parents and two older brothers. She picked it up and stared intently at the expression on her father's face, almost as if she wanted his image to express something other than the contented smile he wore in the shot. Jenny recalled that he was forty-one when the photo was taken, but by the time her father turned forty-two, she had already learned he had cheated on her mother— with a twenty-four year old woman.

Lockhart grabbed for his remote and quickly changed the channel. How could he have forgotten that ESPN would of course promote the forthcoming interview with Paul Vanderkellen scheduled for two nights hence? It would take a few weeks, Lockhart imagined, for the story to wear out its welcome as being current. He saw such a time-table so many times before relating to college and professional athletes, coaches, and front-office personnel. But it was rare for a sportswriter to be the subject of such intense scrutiny and public controversy. Lockhart was confident the networks and print media would offer him a chance to give his perspective on the matter. His attorney Hugh Martin advised him to preempt Vanderkellen's scheduled interview by setting up one of his own—"getting out in front of the story," as the popular expression had it. But Nick rejected the idea, as he did giving any immediate response to Vanderkellen's forthcoming appearance, now less than forty-eight hours away.

Whenever in his youth he escaped to his bedroom or down to Memory Lake, Lockhart role-played—whether he batted rocks pretending to be the Twins' Kirby Puckett or scouted his way around the lake assuming the identity of Daniel Boone or Davy Crockett. He was always careful on his scouting expeditions—checking his immediate surroundings for the likes of badgers, loose dogs, black widows, and timber rattlers that might have strayed north of where they were usually found. In fact, caution, prudence, self-examination, and temperance *before* taking action became a hallmark of Nick's personality. The formula failed him only twice. The second time occurred at age twenty-eight, when he was involved with a young woman whose physical charms completely suppressed all his caution and temperance. The relationship lasted but ten months before the couple's mutually agreed separation. But the first time the formula failed him was when he kept true to that formula during an event occurring when he was serving overseas in the U.S. Army—the event that had the most lasting and damaging impact on his life.

Flipping through the channels, Nick was grateful to Jenny Montgomery for not bringing up the forthcoming interview with

Vanderkellen. Jenny and Davis were aware their friend had infuriated his paper for withholding something about the young quarterback, but the Montgomerys didn't press Lockhart on the details. Instead, they simply offered their assurance that they were in his corner, supplementing their support with an encouragement for him to come by as often as he liked to be with them or by himself down at their bench by Memory Lake. Jenny in particular was sensitive to Nick's need to sit by the water and think. Lockhart felt comforted whenever he recalled the conversation they had a week earlier while sitting on the bench and drinking Jenny's cinnamon coffee.

"Jenny, I know it may be hard to understand, but I feel my mind more fully concentrates when I'm sitting down here than it does anywhere else."

"And you may find this hard to believe, Nick, but I understand completely. I've never been anywhere else that allows me to clear up confusion and make resolutions than right here."

"Maybe we're both waiting for the Lady of the Lake to reach up from the water and offer us our own Excalibur so we can slay all of our problems."

"Either that or we're waiting for Minnesota's answer to the Loch Ness Monster to raise its ugly head and dine on our flesh."

Finding nothing worth watching, Lockhart clicked off the television and headed for his bed, still grinning over the memory of Jenny Montgomery's exhilarating wit.

Chapter 13

Livy was cold, even though she had donned a long-sleeved pullover shirt and her heaviest sweater. The sun to her rear was only yawning, hardly awakened enough to dispense any warmth. Livy stood at the end of the Montgomery's back yard, at the edge of the steps that went down to the bench. She enjoyed this elevated perspective of Memory Lake and the houses across the way. The breeze flowed and ebbed as if it too were a body of water. Livy sensed the wind was in some way trying to communicate with Memory Lake. The morning birds chirped at various tempos but still in an exuberant harmony Livy found stimulating. She made a mental note to learn, from several books resting on Jenny and Davis's shelves, the names of the various species presently serenading her.

She already pulled one of the volumes down the previous evening and read that the males of the various species did almost all of the singing—the females warbling only occasionally. And contrary to popular believe, the male for the most part sang either to invite the female to his territory or to warn other male birds to stay out of it. Livy easily accepted that happiness or contentment didn't inspire the singing—for she hadn't felt either emotion, for any sustained period, for the past several years. As she listened to the birds, she played with the idea of invitation. Jenny had invited her to come to Minnesota, and now the birds were inviting her to remain—right here next to Memory Lake. Livy wished she could chirp an assurance that she truly wanted to stay—and hoped to stay for a very long time.

But the male birds might well be issuing as many warnings as invitations. There was something about the male of the species issuing those warnings, much as her father had done in several serious discussions about Livy's "misplaced interest" in cultural and historical matters. Richard Elman was a successful attorney who long embraced the notion that his only child would join him at his firm and ultimately inherit the most important of his San Francisco-based clients. As Livy approached her decision about college and the major she wanted to pursue, her father rebutted her defense of her interests with a series of warnings about unsatisfactory jobs she could expect to compete for, dim financial prospects for the long haul, and the clincher—the breach her decision would likely leave between them. Richard Elman offered all these cautions with gentility and sadness—he never browbeat his daughter—but his approach in this matter was no less hurtful. Still, Livy knew she had no choice but to give in. She couldn't live with herself if she disappointed her father and destroyed his dream of being partnered in the law with his daughter. She spent the summer after her high school graduation discussing with him the select law schools she would be applying to four years later—satisfied he had at least given in and supported her decision to attend Cal State Chico and study whatever she wanted at the undergraduate level. "It's really no big deal what you major in for the next four years," he said. "With the grades I know you'll get and with my assistance, you'll have no trouble getting into a first-rate law school."

She hadn't yet turned eighteen, but she understood she could better handle moving into a career path she initially judged with indifference than if she asserted her independence and ended up damaging her family and deeply wounding the man who did love her and who taught her so much about honor and integrity. But there were so many times she would have preferred that he dispense with the lessons on living morally and ethically and simply take her in his arms, squeeze her tightly, and say he would support whatever she wanted to do with her life. She felt during that summer that perhaps—just perhaps—she could express those feelings to him when she came home for the Thanksgiving break. But the late November visit back home was marked by a viewing and a funeral rather than a father-daughter heart-to-heart talk. Richard Elman died of a massive stroke in his office the day before Livy left Chico for the fall holiday.

The budding friendship with Jenny Lindstrom that autumn helped Livy survive the shock of her father's death. Livy couldn't wait to get back to school in January, for Christmas and New Year's were difficult to get through—especially for her mother, who nevertheless rejected

Livy's sincere offer to leave Chico for the rest of the year and remain at home. Her mother also expressed her wish that Livy alter her future plans to attend law school. "I know your heart was never committed to going your father's way. Just study what you want and let things happen as you feel they should. It's what I want for you, okay?"

But it wasn't what her father wanted, and even though she returned to Chico free from the future her father long planned for her, she still couldn't shake the guilt of deciding to go her own way. Livy had no idea then that she would end up attaching herself to another assertive man who dragged her from her intended course. Why had she continued to feel guilt about disappointing her deceased father and why did she allow herself to concede to yet another man's wish to guide her way? Even now, as she was about to return to the classroom, she couldn't believe she'd actually be permitted to finish what she was about to begin. Fortunately, she had several years earlier stopped actively imagining and dreaming about her father returning to show his disappointment and to demand she follow through on the promise she made to him before she went off to college. But that image was now replaced by a much more realistic one of her husband forcing her to turn around on her own path and make her way back to where, as Peter said often enough, she "really belonged."

During the past seven years, her husband had become quite insistent on educating her. Perhaps he had disguised the pedantic teacher in him before they wed and during the honeymoon period. Or had she been too much in love to notice his manner until all settled down and their life together truly began? At first, Livy found interesting his lectures about California politics—its history and contemporary applications. But as the months went on, her husband freely and often delivered his *ad hoc* lectures about every topic that appealed to him—from world geography to monetary investments. In every instance, he dispensed knowledge and opinion without ever assuming she might already know something about the topic. In addition, he often punctuated his lectures with admonitions about a host of consequences should his wife fail to heed the lesson he was attempting to convey. Livy found particularly disagreeable Peter's comments about food. He'd warn his wife of the damage she would do to her health or appearance if she continued to order a favorite specialty drink or fried appetizer at a restaurant. Each course and side dish came with an explanation of its health benefits and caloric content. Too many times she heard something to the effect of "What you've ordered has double the calories of my meal—and if you keep adding salt the way you do, you're inviting disaster. I have to warn you that by the time you reach forty your habits will be so ingrained you'll find it impossible to keep the weight off, and you'll be on your way to serious health issues by the time you're fifty."

Livy recalled that any time she offered him a disapproving look for his unsolicited advice he'd invariably counter with, "Hey, I don't want to make you mad. I'm just really concerned for you and how you'll look and feel in a few years, if you don't watch what you ingest. Garbage in doesn't always come out, you know." Making matters even worse, Peter frequently ended his dire predictions with "I just care for you, that's all"—as if that assurance justified anything he might say to wound or patronize her.

But other than shooting him a disdainful look or suggesting he change the subject—or reminding him he was gaining weight—Livy avoided whenever possible any heated exchange that would embarrass her in public or leave her with sensations of guilt over having attacked her "well-intentioned" husband. As her eye caught a formation of birds flying low over Memory Lake, she remembered the nights when she lay in bed lamenting a simple disdainful look she gave her husband. After all, he at least ended his lesson or warning with "I just care for you, that's all." She turned from the lake and gazed up at the rear of the house. Why couldn't she be more like Jenny in this respect? She couldn't imagine Jenny putting up with any of Peter's pretentiousness and patronizing ways. Yes, Jenny Montgomery—with that personality, assertiveness, and vigorous self-respect for which she had absolutely no need in her marriage, because she was fortunate to have found a mate who truly loved and respected her intelligence and privacy. Livy stared at the back door, feeling deep frustration for the way she'd always been. But might a summer here at the Montgomery's change her behavior enough so she might then feel frustration merely for the way she *used to be*?

Livy returned her gaze to Memory Lake. Now she had an urge to swim across the lake to the other side. Perhaps it was because Peter

Garner never learned to swim. Livy couldn't help laughing. Yes, a California native, whom some in the media called "Surfer Boy" because of his sandy blond hair and ever-present tan even in the middle of a Washington winter, had never learned to swim. Indeed, if she turned around now and saw him standing at the Davis's back door, she could jump into the welcoming arms of Memory Lake and he would be powerless to follow her. Yes, unlike Peter she had the ability to swim to the other side. She just had to get in the water and do it.

The birds recommenced their unrestrained though harmonious singing. Or had they been at it all along and she was just too preoccupied with other thoughts to realize it? Were the sounds a continuation of their welcome or did they see her standing on the ground above Memory Lake and only intensify their warnings?

"Hey, Livy!" Wearing a purple Minnesota Viking sweatshirt and gray sweat pants, Jenny stood in the rear doorway—her thick blonde hair piled on the top of her head. Livy couldn't be sure, but it looked as though she was holding a wooden spoon in her hand. Jenny the domestic goddess.

"Is breakfast ready, Jenny?"

"Come and get it, pretty momma."

Several minutes later, Livy marveled at the treat Jenny had placed before her. "Jenny, I never imagined you could make breakfast the way you do. Remember when we were roommates at Chico? A gun to your head couldn't have made you crack an egg or flip a pancake."

"But I made the meanest toast; you'll have to give me that."

Livy continued to admire the fluffy omelet on her plate.

"Are you going to worship or eat it?" Jenny was genuinely pleased that Livy was impressed.

"Can't I do both?"

"Eat it while it's still hot, angel breath."

Livy took her first bite. "Mmm. Mushrooms and spinach—right?"

"And feta cheese. It's my Greek side coming out."

"You have a Greek side?"

"Actually no, but I've seen *My Big Fat Greek Wedding* four times."

"Well, I guess you're qualified, then."

Jenny nodded but her mind was evidently elsewhere.

"Jenny, what's wrong?"

"Ask me later tonight."

"Okay, I didn't want to bring it up unless you did. Davis pitches at what time?"

"7:05 Baltimore time. 6:05 our time."

"Are you usually this preoccupied on the day he pitches?"

"Lately, yes. Before last year I was always pumped from the time I got up to the moment he threw his first pitch. Even if he didn't do well, I'd brush it off and have no problem maintaining my cheery disposition."

"And you can't do that now?"

"Big difference. Before, I always knew he'd get back on track the next time he pitched. But now I've lost all confidence that things will be any better when he takes the mound again."

"I know that must be disappointing to you."

"To *me*? Imagine what it's been like for Davis. If you think *I've* lost my confidence..."

Jenny pressed both her eyes with the meat part of each hand. But her effort failed to stem the tears that now freely came. "I'm sorry. I just can't seem to..."

Livy pulled at Jenny's arm. "Here, let's go down to the bench so we can talk."

"But our omelets."

"We'll heat them up when we come back in."

Partially dazed, Jenny stood and looked around the kitchen. "Let's take some coffee down with us."

• •

For the next forty-five minutes, after Jenny snapped off the top of her bottled-up emotions, she spoke honestly about her fears for her husband and their marriage. Livy asked not a single question nor uttered a single platitude. She just let her best friend run through a gamut of feelings—from understandable sadness and fear to surprising anger. At one point, Jenny stood, reshaped her hands into claws, and took several steps toward Memory Lake.

"I just want to strangle his goddamned bastard of an agent for suggesting they play golf the day Davis hurt his shoulder."

Livy had to sneeze. Now wasn't the time, she knew, but she couldn't prevent it. Jenny turned back toward her friend and burst out laughing.

"I have my one moment of rage—complete with a masculine profanity—and all you can do is sneeze? Didn't I frighten you just a little bit?"

Livy delivered her response with a straight face. "It was my fear that made me sneeze."

"I love you, Livy. You've always had such a wonderful way of letting me bitch and moan and then bring me back to planet earth with a look or a grunt."

"Or a sneeze, don't forget."

"I'm sorry I went on the way I did."

"No, no. I wanted you to. You should never keep suppressed your..."

Livy shut the door on the completion of her point. She was about to say "your emotions and concerns," but who was she, the queen of peace-at-all-costs, to offer such advice?

"Anyway, I'm calming down rapidly—so you won't have to worry that I'll pull an ax out of the closet and split your skull or anything like that."

"Thank heaven for small favors."

"You know I feel shitty about having emoted the way I did down here while we were sitting on this bench. Memory Lake is usually my tranquilizer—only this time I didn't let it perform its office."

"Does a tranquilizer perform an office?"

"Don't start flaunting your A in freshman comp, Olivia."

"Couldn't help it. I still owe you many more for your having humiliated me on all those tennis and handball courts."

"And especially on the lanes. How anyone can roll a 29 for ten frames is beyond me. So what do you think I should tell Davis to make him better understand that I don't want to leave this house?"

Livy was hardly prepared for this sudden return to the serious topic of Jenny's future. "I...I guess I would insist that he understand how badly you want to stay here. Just..." Livy halted. Again, what qualifications did she have to offer advice on how to be assertive?

"Go ahead, Livy. You were about to say?"

"Just...just make things completely quiet—look into his eyes—hold both his hands—and tell him how you feel as slowly and sincerely as you can." How often had she thought about speaking to Peter in that very manner. She now realized that although she had failed to do so before she left for Minnesota, there was still time. But that would mean seeing him in person—the very last thing she wished at this point.

"Livy, you look as though you're having second thoughts about that advice."

"Oh no—no. I'm only thinking about my own situation. *Selfishly* thinking about my own situation."

"Well, I'm right here. Both ears open. One bench—no waiting."

"Nuh, uh. This is your time. I want to listen to you and help if I can."

"You can help me by shifting roles. I'm very content when I'm playing Freud and listening to other people's problems. Okay, dear?" Jenny wore a wry smile as she patted Livy, Aunty Em-like, on the top of her hand. "Either that or let's go back to the house and heat up the omelets."

"Sounds like a plan."

"And speaking of plans, later this morning we'll taken another tour of Minneapolis and then meet handsome Nick for a late lunch."

"Does he know that?" Livy felt her spirits rise at the thought of seeing Nick Lockhart again, and this time didn't attempt to stifle them.

"Not yet. But I'll call him after we finish our breakfast and let him know."

"Might he not think the invitation was kind of sudden?"

"He won't say no. If he does, he knows I won't let him sit on this bench anymore."

"Come on. You wouldn't do that."

"No, I wouldn't. Besides, I already mentioned the possibility of the three of us having lunch. Don't you remember? You were there."

"Oh, right. But some breakfast before lunch, as I always say."

The women moved toward the stairs. Jenny turned back and took in a full view of Memory Lake. "Livy, I want this beautiful little lake to be both my now and my forever."

Chapter 14

Nick had to admit that Jenny Montgomery's luncheon invitation wasn't as welcome as it would normally be. He was hoping she and Livy would go out by themselves and again leave the bench by Memory Lake all for him. Today he wanted to indulge further recollections of his boyhood. The Montgomery property had two smaller houses on it back then—one belonging to a woman with a grizzled fisherman's face who had never hooked a husband—the other to her slightly younger brother and his decrepit bride. The Spitzler family—each one old and crotchety—each wishing to outdo the other two in cantankerousness. Taking a cue from the Marx Brothers movies Nick and his friends enjoyed, they gave each of the three Spitzlers a first name—the two women were Meano and Beasto, and of course Mr. Spitzler was Groucho.

The trek completely around Memory Lake could never be made because the Spitzlers hated kids and refused to allow them to pass through any part of their property, even though the boys had politely assured Beasto they would only walk right along the water's edge. But all attempts at negotiations were rejected, with a snarling Groucho adding that the cops would be called to haul the young lads off to "reform school" if they dared take a step on the sacred land belonging to the evil and hideous three-headed Spitzler hydra. In the weeks following, Nick and his friends drew up secret invasion plans reminiscent of the assault on Normandy in June of 1944. They would make their way at night across Memory Lake lying on large black inner tubes. They would all wear black clothing and their faces would be smeared with soot so their mission of stealth would succeed. The only problem was they had no idea what to do once they made their landing. Nick was the one who forwarded the plan. They would bring rope and kidnap Meano the spinster because she was the frailest of the old timers and would put up much less of a struggle than Groucho or his ogre of a wife Beasto. But when the night for the planned mission arrived, discretion proved the better part of valor and the boys went back to the drawing board for a better plan—which they could never devise.

Lockhart appreciated that sitting on the bench also delighted him because of this history. It was the same feeling, he believed, that others felt throughout history who inhabited the palace of an evil tyrant after that tyrant had been dispatched. As for the Spitzlers, all three survived for another two decades after they first confronted young Nick and his chums. In fact, they made a financial killing by being the last of the original homeowners to sell their property to the outfit that built the upscale homes—including the Montgomery's—all around Memory Lake. Lockhart liked to argue the Spitzlers were still alive ruining the fun of a new generation of rambunctious boys, even though now they would have to be in their tenth or eleventh decade of life.

Still, no amount of time could efface the significance of Memory Lake to his life. Jenny once asked him if he regretted he wasn't doing his sitting and thinking on the other side—on the site of his old house.

"Well, it's a moot point, Jenny. There's no bench over there."

"You can buy a bench, you know. Davis will lend you his truck and help you place it down there—that is if you can get permission of the present owners."

"I doubt whether they would appreciate that. I understand they're transplanted Chicago White Sox fans, so Davis's pitching for the Twins wouldn't help matters any. In any event, are you hoping I'll go and sit somewhere else?"

"Heavens no. I just wondered if you wish you could be sitting where you used to live."

"Jenny, I don't. I think I'd feel as though I was sitting on a gravestone or crypt—right on top of a loved one."

"Good analogy. Vivid, to the point, and deliciously ghoulish."

"No, I mean it works better if I'm looking across the lake to where I once was, rather than looking out from where I once was to where some very bizarre people used to live."

"You mean those decayed child-haters the Swizzlers?"

"That's the Spitzlers."

"Whatever. But you might be missing out on something incredible by not sitting over there rather than here."

"And that would be?"

"Every morning, I open all the blinds at the back of the house and dash madly about—buck naked. I've done it while you've been sitting on our bench, but your back is turned so you don't see me."

Lockhart stepped out of his car still grinning from the recollection of Jenny Montgomery's naughtiness. As he made his way to the restaurant to meet her and her best friend for lunch, he comprehended for the first time that he might benefit from talking to someone—not so much about his looming professional crisis, but more about his personal history and the effect it continued to have on so much of his life. Jenny wouldn't do because she'd get him laughing. Nor would Davis because he was, well, a man. But perhaps Livy Garner might listen.

•   •   •

"Hey, Nick. Over here."

Lockhart made his way to Jenny and Livy's table inside Vincent, one of Minneapolis's finest restaurants. Nick found the food and ambience splendid, and in summer he always preferred sitting in the outside patio area. In another month, he'd ask to sit out there—that is, if he still had a job in the city.

He hugged Jenny and extended his hand to Livy, even though his first inclination was to hug her as well. "I see Jenny wants to spoil you by bringing you to one of the city's best spots."

Livy remembered to put enough squeeze in her hand to make the handshake worthwhile. She hated the way women—and some men—held out their hands like a wilted rose—to be lightly taken and weakly shook. She never squeezed overly hard, as if to make some statement about the strength of her sex, but she truly enjoyed the firm exchange between herself and a man or a woman, although she often had to laugh at the looks on the faces of female acquaintances who didn't expect such a solid grip from one of their own.

"I meant to tell you earlier that I like your handshake, Livy. I wish more men would shake the way you do."

Jenny interjected with "Well if you like her shake, you'll really love her shimmy."

Livy gritted her teeth in momentary embarrassment, but she couldn't have been more pleased if Lockhart had complimented her about her clothes. "Thank you, Nick. But not you, Jenny."

Nick ignored Jenny's naughty contribution. "You'd never guess how many professional athletes have limp or wilty handshakes."

"Really?" Livy was genuinely surprised.

"Yes, really. Perhaps it's because some of them are so large and well-built they don't feel they have to prove their masculinity with a firm handshake, but still..."

Jenny refused to be left out of the conversation. "The first time I shook hands with old Livy here, she dislocated one of my knuckles. That's why she was known to her sorority sisters as 'The Knuckle Buster.'"

"She's lying, Nick." Livy took a delicious pause. "I was never in a sorority."

"Bravo, Livy." Jenny literally applauded, causing three tables' worth of eyes to look their way. "That was genuinely funny."

"I learned from the best."

Jenny took a seated bow, dropping her forehead so that brushed against the table top. "I do what I can."

Livy tapped her on the shoulder. "But it should be 'Brava,' not 'Bravo,' since I'm a woman. The feminine ending is required, you know."

Jenny raised her head and shoulder back to the normal positions. "But you shake hands like a man—so correction not accepted."

Sitting directly across from Livy, with Jenny between them, Lockhart solidified the view he had begun to form when he first met the congressman's wife down by Memory Lake. Whatever the reason, he just felt comfortable in her company. Yes, she was a most attractive woman in her early thirties, with dark eyes beautifully shaped. Yet eyes that seemed to reveal only part of all she was. Lockhart liked to think that most women had eyes that either complemented the rest of their facial features or fully revealed their personalities, whether the woman was intelligent, friendly, honest, deceptive, predatory, or insipid. But some women, like Livy Garner, had eyes that kept the curious unsatisfied, leaving all evaluation of character and personality incomplete.

Nick had long ago dismissed the notion so popular when he was a boy that men and women had to act, think, and dress differently when they reached certain "plateau" ages—thirty, forty, and fifty. He remembered his favorite uncle mentioning that when Frank Sinatra and Dean Martin hit fifty, they were still—at least apparently—doing all they did hedonistically when they were in their twenties and thirties. Nick enjoyed seeing a woman past one of those plateau ages still wearing her hair long and her dresses on the short side. Now that he had passed forty, he wasn't about to change the way he dressed or how he wore his hair, but he had begun wondering if women Livy's age thought a man eight to ten years older not the best match. He could immediately think of dozens of couples in the celebrity world and among those he knew who exceeded a ten year age difference, but he couldn't shake the thought that he was too old for a woman as attractive and charismatic as Livy Garner. Or was this yet another manifestation of the guilt he felt over his actions twenty years earlier?

"What are you going to have, Jenny?"

"You sound just like my mother, Livy. She can never decide what she wants when we go out, so she always asks me what I'm having. Then she announces, 'I'll have that too.' Is that what you're trying to pull here, little lady?"

"For your information I've already decided on the Saffron Risotto."

Jenny scanned further down the menu. "Yeah, I think I'll have that too."

Lockhart nodded. "It's very good. You'll enjoy it."

Jenny affected mild disgust. "So, Nick, you're going to follow my lead and have the Risotto as well?"

"No, actually I'm ordering the Vincent Burger."

Jenny dropped her disgusted persona and replaced it with her aggrieved one. "I invite you to join us at this wonderful restaurant, filled with masterful selections in the French style, and you walk in here and order a burger? A burger?" She hammered her finger into the table as she read down the menu. "When there is Pasta *Coq au Vin*, *Escargot*, Steak *Tartare*, *Foi Gras*, *Nicoise* Salad, and a *Croque Madame* sandwich on the menu?"

"I like their burgers."

"I'm moving to another table." Jenny had already made the switch back to her "affecting disgust" persona.

Livy took the opportunity to come to Nick's defense. "I'm sure a burger here at Vincent isn't like a burger anywhere else."

Jenny shook her head. "And to think that I was going to pay for his lunch."

Enjoying Jenny's feigned indignation, Livy volunteered to pay for Nick's burger, but he put up his hand.

"No, no, Livy. I'll pay for it." Livy dropped her eyes remembering the bet she won the first time they met on the bench. Nick wore a mischievous smile. "Do you know the last time I was here I had lunch with someone who also ordered the Vincent Burger? Would you know who that was, Jenny?"

In her best blue-blooded haughty voice, she replied, "Sir, I wouldn't have the slightest idea or interest."

"It was a gentleman by the name of Davis Montgomery—who raved on and on about the burger."

Livy and Nick stared at Jenny, wondering what kind of response she'd come up with. After a momentarily delay, she didn't disappoint them.

"The hell with the Saffron Risotto, I'm having the burger."

Livy followed suit and they were ready to order. She smiled at Nick, who seemed genuinely pleased about the entire exchange about ground beef.

.   .   .

Livy couldn't remember when she enjoyed a hamburger more. The three of them were in perfect synchronization throughout the hour they spent at the table. One would hold forth while the other two would eat, although Jenny had no trouble conversing with food in her mouth. Livy recalled how her college roommate had perfected the art of chewing with one half of her mouth and chatting with the other. The only awkward moment came when Jenny reached over and wiped an inch-long clop of mustard from the side of Livy's mouth—followed by the obligatory "Can't take her anywhere" squib.

Livy fought off the reminders of all the joyless meals she had taken with her husband, either at home or at one of his favorite eateries. Other than his lectures on her caloric intake, he invariably restricted the conversation to himself—his political career and all the reasons why he'd likely never get enough breaks to run for even higher office. He had no sooner won the Congressional seat than he complained about how the cards were stacked against him in a future U.S. Senate run. California's two women senators, he opined, were at least one too many. Even when his wife pointed out that the senior senator was in her eighties and might not run again in 2018, therefore opening up a seat in less than two years, Garner complained that the state would only want yet another female senator—so what would be the point of running? For her part, Livy began the marriage with the firm belief that her husband needed her unqualified support and thought the best way to insure it was to dismiss as much political business from her own conversations as possible. She never talked politics with her friends—not even Jenny—and made it a habit to walk from the group or the room when the discussion turned to the subject. What she grew to hate as the months went by, though, was Garner's habit of co-opting her endorsement when she had never given it. When she was in his company, he would often punctuate informal political discussions with "My wife agrees with me that we can't continue to throw money at this problem" and "Even Livy will tell you that this issue isn't going away anytime soon."

It was the prefix "Even" that bothered her the most. Anyone who heard him speak in this manner must have thought that she hadn't a brain in her head—that at best she was smart but completely unsophisticated when it came to understanding the nation's problems. And now here she sat, an equal member of a trio, with both Jenny and Nick Lockhart honestly interested in her opinion and not a patronizing bone in either of their bodies. And what made it sweeter was that neither of them treated her or looked at her as though she was a woman running away from her marriage—even though that's exactly what she was.

Livy understood she'd soon have to stop running and then turn and face her major problem. Metaphorically, she wanted to do it in an open field rather than with her back against a brick wall. But the question remained: when could she count on being ready to do so? Shaking the thought from her mind, she dropped half a teaspoon of real sugar into her coffee and twirled it around with the spoon. She liked the image of the sugar dissolving into the blackness of the coffee. Yes, if she could just gently stir and have her problem simply dissolve. Still, she reveled in the fact that she didn't have Peter taking the sugar away from her and pushing forward a packet of artificial sweetener as a replacement.

"I'm curious, Jenny."

"Good trait to have, Nick."

"I've written several stories over the years about some of the more peculiar superstitions of professional athletes."

Livy couldn't help butting in. "*Peculiar* superstitions?"

"Oh yes—especially baseball players. Surely you've heard about athletes not changing socks or underwear during a winning or hitting streak, haven't you?"

Jenny put her hand over Livy's ear. "Surely she's not heard. Livy grew up in a convent and didn't date a man socially until she married...umm, old what's his name." Again, Jenny couldn't believe her *faux pas*. But Livy saw the expression on her friend's face and got her off the hook by getting her on another one.

"Tell us, Jenny. Does Davis have such unhygienic superstitions too?"

"Well, I don't give a damn about his socks, but I insist he keep his drawers clean. I can't vouch for his jock, though. It may hold something more deadly than his package—if I may speak freely among mixed company."

Livy dropped her head several inches toward her coffee, which she began stirring again. To the casual observer, she must have looked as though she was watching a bug swimming laps in the cup.

Nick tried not to laugh at Livy's reaction but he wasn't successful. "Jenny, I recently talked to a manufacturer of such things and he told me that members of the younger generation aren't following in their father's footsteps." He felt his choice of terms wouldn't embarrass Livy further. But he didn't count on Jenny's editing.

"'Not following in their father's *footsteps*'? You need to aim a lot higher to get the biology right, Nick. You mean that they're not incarcerating the old pencil and marbles the way their dear old dads used to do, don't you?"

"Something like that—yes."

Jenny honed in on her droopy-headed and silent friend. "So what do you think, Livy? To jock or not to jock? That's one question Hamlet didn't have to deal with."

Livy spoke but without lifting her head. Nick saw that her eyes were closed as well. She uttered soft "Can't we get back to discussing simple superstitions?"

Lockhart was about to talk about one player's insistence that while he was hitting well he never deviate from the routine of putting on his socks before his underwear—but Jenny was too quick and got in before Nick pushed out the first syllable.

"Nick, forget the professional athletes, you ought to write about the superstitions of their wives."

Livy returned her head to the normal upright and locked position. "Okay, so what are some of your superstitions, Jenny?"

"All right, since you asked. I never wear panties when Davis pitches."

Nick looked away toward his right—Livy to her left. Jenny was delighted that she had them right where she wanted them. "Hey, it beats never changing your soiled underwear as a superstition, wouldn't you agree, Nick?"

He wasn't about to give her a "yes"—not even a nod. "And another of your superstitions would be?"

"You're such a party-pooper, Lockhart."

"Blame my generation."

"What? You of the MTV, Michael Jackson's Thriller, androgynistic, Super Mario, experimental-sex generation?"

"Something like that."

Livy kept her gaze toward the confluence of the far wall and the ceiling right above it, but she was nevertheless intrigued by Lockhart's possible experimental experiences.

Jenny's torso bobbed up and down with glee. "Wow. I can't wait to drag you back down to the bench by Memory Lake and have you spit out exactly what you mean by engaging in experimental sex." Nick tried to protest that he didn't mean that he had indulged in such things, but Jenny wouldn't let him speak. "You're interested to know—aren't you, Livy?"

As she turned back toward her friend, Livy prayed her face bore no evidence of her embarrassment. "I was just admiring the surroundings. What did you ask me?"

"Forget it. Finish your coffee and let's head to the movies. Ah, here you go." Jenny gave a cursory glance at the bill and handed over her debit card to the server. Both Livy and Nick protested but Jenny waved them off. Then in unison, both of them said, "I'll get lunch next time."

Jenny smiled broadly. "My, my, aren't we of one mind today. Livy you get the next lunch. Nick you get the next dinner."

"It's a deal." Once more Nick and Livy shared a look and a smile. Trying to push matters way from sexual experimentation, Livy asked to hear one of Jenny's genuine superstitions relating to Davis's career.

"Okay, Livy, I'll give you one for the road. Whenever Davis is pitching I keep my hair piled up on my head the entire day—the way I do now."

Livy wondered why her friend hadn't let it down. "Why do you do that?"

"The first time I went to a game and watched him pitch for the Giants, the weather was especially warm. I just pinned it up in an attempt to stay cooler. Davis pitched a shutout that day and I of course took the credit, saying that piling my blonde tresses on the top of my noggin' gave him good luck."

Jenny knew it would come to this—one reason she didn't wish to press her luck and stay too long at Vincent. But her eyes had already begun to glisten. She wanted to be sitting on her bench, sharing her thoughts with only Livy. At least she trusted Nick to keep to himself whatever she might reveal and how she might reveal it. She hadn't given any thought to how she would articulate her distress. The words just came out.

"I suppose I should start keeping my hair down when Davis pitches, because pinning it up hasn't done him a hell of a lot of good lately." She stared at Livy and Nick and sighed in exasperation. "I'm sorry. I'm just worried about Davis, and I don't know why I'm all upset like this."

Nick told her it was okay. "We understand."

She reached out and took his hand. "Come over later tonight and we'll all sit down by the lake and chug-a-lug some margaritas."

"No, no. You and Livy need to be alone. You don't need to have me—"

"Nick, you know I'm not genetically wired to take no for an answer." Jenny laughed as the tears dropped in the crevices between her cheeks and nose. Livy thought she looked pathetically beautiful at this moment.

Nick glanced at Livy, who was nodding her head, encouraging him to come over later. "Okay, I'll be there around 8:00 or 8:30. Can I bring something?"

Jenny noticed and then removed the spoon from Livy's cup. "Whatever you want, Nick. Just none of those cheesy things that stain my nails orange."

"And if you don't mind, I think I'll go over to your place and sit by the water while you two are at the movies."

Not quite in command of her thoughts, Jenny placed Livy's spoon back into the cup. "I'll leave the key to the lake for you under the bench, Nick."

After Lockhart left, Jenny added the tip and signed the receipt. She signaled to Livy she was ready to leave. "Look around, Livy. Is anyone staring at me?"

"Not a soul, Jenny."

"Honest?"

"Honest."

"Hmm. What does a girl have to do to get attention around here?"

By the time they reached the door, Jenny's looked exactly as she did when she came through it over an hour earlier.

"Livy, let me tell you something about Nick Lockhart."

"And that would be?" Livy was certain her best friend was about to say that the sports writer had a thing for the congressman's wife.

"He needs to unload."

"In the sense of?"

"In the sense of Freud, *meine freundin*."

Livy sighed. "There seems to be a lot of that going around, Jenny."

"Tell me about it."

Chapter 15

"Livy, I must apologize for doubting you. *Unaccompanied* was an excellent choice. I'm glad I saw it."

"And you really wanted to see *Hot Tub Zombies 2* at the Dollar Movie?"

"I was just kidding about that. Besides the dollar translates to $3.99 at that place. But, honestly, I didn't think I'd like *Unaccompanied*. I was afraid it was all about a lonely guy who couldn't get a date but who wasn't about to be denied the pleasures of the flesh."

"Jenny, you're bad—you know that?"

Livy was happy Jenny responded so well to a movie centered around the lives of singers, but her bawdy joke about the lonely guy wasn't far off from what Livy was imagining three-quarters' way through the film. She always had to fight a propensity to daydream—whether she was sitting in school, watching a movie, or listening to music. The benefit of this habit was that it facilitated her ability to tune out whatever she didn't wish to hear. On the other hand, part of her mind seemed always to remain on guard—invariably warning her whenever someone asked her a specific question, so she would be able to respond even though she hadn't been truly listening. This skill was more finely developed throughout her marriage to Peter. She even trained herself to nod periodically as he was pontificating so he could believe she was hanging on every word. How often she had chided herself for not telling him she wasn't at all interested in what he had to say. Yet she knew she could never do that. But during the film, she dismissed what was happening on the big screen and took a few moments to ponder a future devoid of sex.

Again, she had for many months desired to be free of her husband's touch, although she never articulated that wish. Instead, she took perverse pleasure in imagining a time when this desire would be satisfied. Still, she rarely allowed herself to fantasizing about making love to another man—not even in a harmless scenario with any celebrity or literary hero whose sex appeal earned her approval. And to imagine being in the arms of someone she knew, either back home in California or in Washington, filled her with anxiety—and not only because such a concession to fancy would be adulterous. She now lacked confidence she could satisfy an ardent lover, regardless of how well he treated her. And it mattered little that two other congressional wives admitted extramarital affairs to her and assured her that finding a lover in Washington wasn't much of a challenge for someone as attractive as she was. No, she would see no other man until she was either divorced from Peter or in the formal process of getting a divorce. A simple separation wasn't going to be enough—even if that separation was in one way or another leading to a permanent parting of the ways at some unspecified time.

But during the movie, with Jenny gorging on buttered popcorn, Livy feared she might never find a man with whom she could be sexually intimate. To find the man of her dreams wasn't even considered a remote possibility. At the moment she began recalling events from her short time in Washington, she abruptly stood up, sat back down again, and nabbed a handful of Jenny's popcorn.

"Have to go potty, Livy?" Jenny whispered.

"I thought I did, but I don't."

After they left the theatre, they made their way to a coffee shop Jenny occasionally patronized. The women continued their discussion of the film and how parts of it had relevance to their own experiences.

"You still play piano, Livy?"

"I haven't played in over a year."

"That's too bad. You were pretty good, as I remember."

"I was functional. But what about you? I can't remember your ever playing an instrument."

"Oh, I have many talents you aren't aware of."

"Or *want* to be aware of. But, seriously, did you ever play an instrument?"

"When I was growing up, the only music in my house came from a big ugly boom box—the one that played my cassette tapes and then

CDs. It was kind of neat, though, because it had two tape decks so you could record from one tape to another and from the CD player to a cassette tape. I made about fifty potpourri tapes that way."

"No you didn't."

"Yes I did. I had all these albums from which I recorded the songs I wanted in the order I wanted. I always got bored listening to full albums in the same order time after time."

"Have you done the same thing with your CDs?"

"I had someone do it for me. He put all of my cassette tapes on CDs. It used to be you had to cultivate a lawyer, a physician, and a plumber as friends. Now you have to add a tech nerd to the list."

Livy replied that she always listened to her albums—whether they were on cassette tape or CDs—all the way through, never skipping a song when she could have easily done so with a CD. "So you never played an instrument, Jenny? Not even in high school?"

"No, but seeing that movie has inspired me. I couldn't help visualizing myself playing a violin while sitting on the bench by Memory Lake. Maybe I'll get a second-hand Stradivarius and teach myself 'Chopsticks' or whatever."

Livy judged the last part of her friend's remark as facetious, but Jenny's expression as she spoke of sitting on the bench playing violin was far more thoughtful. Livy visualized her best friend in flowing night dress, playing something haunting and exquisite, while the wind blew across Memory Lake billowing Jenny's gown and beautifully long wavy blonde hair.

But Livy's reverie was interrupted by the Mozart coming from her cell phone. She checked the caller's number and looked almost grief-stricken. "It's Peter."

•   •   •

Before Jenny and Livy came out of *Unaccompanied*, Lockhart made his way down to the bench by Memory Lake. Placed next to him on the bench were his cell phone, a coffee thermos, and of all things his high school yearbook. He was almost amused by his decision to stop at his condo and retrieve the yearbook, which had for years been wedged on the bottom shelf of one of his several bookcases. He had last pulled it out several years earlier, soon after he received his invitation to join others from his graduating class for their twentieth reunion. He returned the yearbook to the shelves as soon as he decided not to attend the event. Would it be possible to explain exactly why he stayed away from the tenth and then twentieth reunions? Could anyone really understand, even if he made the attempt? Besides, to explain his reasons would be exposing the part of him he wished to keep forever hidden. Then why did he choose today to open the old yearbook and look back on what life was like over twenty years ago? Perhaps it was because his life was about to be changed significantly with the broadcast of the Paul Vanderkellen interview the following evening.

Opening the cover of the yearbook, Lockhart gazed at the message in overly large script taking up the entire inside cover and the first page. The author was Virginia Edens—the love of his senior year.

Dearest Nick, will never forget all our fun times together this year. You've made my life so exciting and meaningfull." Lockhart smiled at the misspelling of "meaningful." She went on, "*Someday when we're living in Colorado, we will remember the great football season, when we fell in love with each other, the "pains-in-the-you-know-whats" Mrs. Janacek and Mr. Yarborough, and the rings we got each other. What can I say? You're EVERYTHING to me. Love you forever, Ginny."*

The "forever" made it almost another three months from the time Ginny wrote in Nick's yearbook. They broke up and he knew the fault was all his—no matter how many family members and friends told him otherwise. He immediately felt guilty about breaking her heart and never stopped feeling remorse. He even blamed himself for her tragic death at the age of thirty-one—in an automobile accident up in St. Cloud—tormenting himself with the thought that if they had gotten married she wouldn't have been at the wheel, since he never let anyone else drive when he was in a vehicle other than a taxi or limousine. Now he recalled a major reason why he was adamant about missing his ten-year high school reunion. She was going and he couldn't bear to see her. But this wasn't the only reason, because he didn't want to see *anyone* so connected to his past.

He knew his classmates assumed he was too high and mighty for their company once he became successful in sports journalism. And Lockhart dismissed his mother's suggestion, right before she passed on, that he see someone about why he seemingly turned his back on his past, because he knew the reason—and there was nothing any professional could have said to enlighten him any further. And now he faced the fact that many of those he met *after* high school would surely turn their backs on him once Paul Vanderkellen appeared on ESPN.

Nick's attorney pleaded with him to prepare a series of responses to the questions that would soon come from a multitude of media—especially those dealing with why he decided to keep Vanderkellen's nasty secret to himself—even though the young man admitted his gambling addiction openly to Lockhart without asking that it be kept "off the record" and even though Nick followed up on the quarterback's admissions and found them all to be true—corroborated by research as well as anecdotal evidence. But Nick sat on everything he learned—surprising Vanderkellen, who acted as though he was offended that the sports writer hadn't broken the story immediately after they spoke in Gold Medal Park.

Since that meeting a few months earlier and in the context of Nick's reluctance to publicize what he knew, Vanderkellen got himself deeper into debt with some serious individuals. In addition, he was hit with charges of property, identity, and credit card theft prompted by his attempt to gather enough cash to earn a reprieve from those to whom he owed money. He was at present awaiting a resolution of the charges, but was now even more in need of funds, given the quality of his legal representation.

As he stared out at Memory Lake, Nick shifted his eyes to the left and right—not wishing to look across the water to where his house once stood. He had never expected Vanderkellen to react to his silence the way he did. After all, shouldn't the young man have thanked him profusely for keeping it all quiet—that way giving him some kind of chance to extricate himself from his dire predicament?

The former quarterback either came up with the scheme on his own or more likely it was suggested to him by his new lawyer. In short, it was to blame Nick Lockhart for keeping the secret of Vanderkellen's gambling addiction, rather than revealing it to the world and thereby forcing the young man to seek the help he so desperately needed. But sadly the renowned sports scribe had chosen discretion when revelation would have been the better course. Had he written about the athlete's situation, Vanderkellen would have been too ashamed—and exposed—to have committed the felonies for which he was subsequently charged. Vanderkellen was still a young man. His immaturity only made him vulnerable to the allure of sports wagering. He needed a guide—a guardian—a parental or avuncular figure—and he approached Nick Lockhart without guile or subtlety, doing all he could to persuade the sportswriter to perform that role—at least for the short term—so that he would help make possible the troubled young man's finding the help he so desperately needed. Why else would he have confessed his sins to the older man? But for some reason, the acclaimed sportswriter sat on the story, and Vanderkellen's felonies were the tragic result. All this was what Vanderkellen and his attorney would no doubt say during the forthcoming interview on ESPN.

Nick poured all the liquid from the thermos on the ground in front of the bench. He had no taste for coffee now; he only wished he had something to wash out the sour taste in his mouth. Perhaps the coffee reminded him of how his editor at the paper, Bob Walton, had drunk three full mugs of it as he articulated his confusion and disappointment over what his star sportswriter had failed to do. The paper's lost exclusive contributed only partly to Walton's dismay.

"Nick, why the hell didn't you at least tell *me* what Vanderkellen admitted to you? We could have talked about why you were reluctant to break the story—which you still haven't explained. God damn it, Nick, what's going on here? Have you forgotten the business we're in? Have you lost your fucking mind?"

As an explanation, Lockhart offered only his reluctance to pursue tawdry leads about players' personal lives.

"No one asked you or expected you to stake out some adulterer at a cheap hotel or find out what on-line sites some athlete's fond of, Nick. You know I don't want any of that crap for this paper. But this is a genuine story—a big story, damn it, that we should have broken. Now we not only have to explain why we weren't first but also why you wouldn't break it. I hate to say this, but you've embarrassed us and you've embarrassed yourself. Damn it, Nick, you've embarrassed our whole fucking profession."

Chapter 16

Livy signaled to Jenny that she would take the call outside. Jenny flashed a quick "Don't talk to him" gesture but then accepted that her friend should speak to her husband. Doing so, she reasoned, might prevent Peter from bothering them later that evening. Then again, it might not.

Livy walked down the sidewalk. "Peter, I'm sorry but it's hard to hear you with all the street noise."

"Can't you go inside somewhere?" he almost shouted into the phone.

Her husband's agitated request reminded her of one of his calls when she was having lunch with another congressman's wife inside a Washington bistro. There too she found it impossible to hear him. Then he barked, "Can't you go outside so I can hear you?"

She blurted it out before she had time to think. "Peter, you can call me later, when we get back to Jenny's." No, no damn it. That's not at all what she wanted. She didn't want him to call her there—at all—for any reason. "Wait, Peter." She came to a side street, turned, and briskly headed down a narrow access lane between two buildings. The new location muffled the sound of pedestrians and traffic adequately enough for her to hear him clearly. She couldn't believe she was standing in an alley talking on a cell phone to her husband. And yet it all seemed so appropriate. She was in essence hiding from the normal world of movement up at the street—in a reluctant and almost surreptitious communication with the man she was running away from.

"Can you hear me now?"

"Yes, go ahead. Why are you calling me, Peter?"

"So how are you?"

She let out a depressing sigh. She didn't want to give him even a cursory answer to that question.

"Peter, I've left Jenny in a coffee shop. I need to get back to her. Is there something wrong? Why are you calling me?"

"All right, all right. I'll keep it short. I'm flying back to California. They think it best I attend a fund raiser they've got scheduled for the day after tomorrow."

He paused, waiting for her reply. Livy feared what he was likely to suggest. But she was determined not to be manipulated—not this time.

"Peter, I'm sorry, but I'm not leaving Minneapolis to go back to California."

"Wait, wait. I'm not asking you to. Damn it, Livy, why are so defensive all of a sudden?"

All of a sudden? Hadn't he been paying attention to her the past several months? If he wasn't going to ask her to accompany her, then why the call?

"Livy, I was just thinking that I can fly to Minneapolis tomorrow afternoon, get a hotel room for the night, and then fly out to San Francisco the following morning. That way, we can have dinner and have a nice leisurely chat."

Livy looked up at one of the brick walls forming one section of the access lane. The wall seemed so high. The blue sky above it was barely visible. How could she climb it and escape?

.   .   .

Jenny paid the check and stepped outside the coffee shop. She scanned the sidewalk up the street to her right and down the street to her left. Failing to see Livy, she did a full sweep of the sidewalk-storefront area across the road. Could her friend have darted into a shop either to talk to Peter or to examine a potential purchase? Jenny understood that if she began searching for Livy the two of them might completely miss each other.

"You idiot." Jenny finally realized her cell phone was resting inside her fingers. Looking up the street to her right, she punched in Livy's number, fully expecting it to be in use. That jackass Peter never spoke in sentences when he could pontificate in chapters, she thought. But

Jenny was surprised to hear the melody from Mozart rather than the indication that the phone was busy.

"I'm right behind you, Jenny."

Livy wore a smile that seemed plastered on by a fully committed curmudgeon. "You okay, Livy?"

"That's a relative term. Yes and no."

"Okay—which do you want to hit me with first? The yes or the no?"

"Peter said he was flying in to Minneapolis tomorrow and he wants to have dinner with me."

"And you said the yes or the no?"

"The no."

Jenny's mouth unhinged and her lower row of teeth jutted forward as though she was a former denizen of Jurassic Park. "You told him *no?*"

"I told him no." Livy face was flushed, as though she had done something unsanctioned and thoroughly enjoyed it. "I reminded him that we agreed not see each other until September at the earliest. I also reminded him that he had agreed to that."

Jenny couldn't have been prouder of her best friend. "And what did he say?"

Livy's awkward smile gave over to a sullen frown. "He wasn't happy about it. He said he was flying to Minneapolis anyway."

"Oh, fuck."

"He said he'd take a cab to your place if I didn't at least meet him at the airport."

"That shit."

"Yeah."

"So how did you respond to that bit of blackmail?"

"He didn't give me a chance to respond. He made his announcement and hung up."

"He didn't even tell you when his flight was coming in—so how could you know when to meet him?"

Her nerves having been wrung out thoroughly, Livy expanded her eyes at Jenny's observation and then began to laugh. Jenny didn't want her to guffaw all alone—especially not on a Minneapolis sidewalk, so she joined in. Within fifteen seconds they had two other passer-bys laughing as well and at least a dozen others on the sidewalk smiling broadly.

·   ·   ·

As they neared Jenny's, Livy asked if they could take a short detour and look at the other houses surrounding Memory Lake. Jenny cheerfully acceded to Livy's wish and provided a tour-guide's narration of the other properties. They made it to the house across the lake from the Montgomery's—just two houses to the left of where Nick Lockhart used to live—before Jenny commented on one of her neighbors.

"In this lovely domicile lives a Latino couple—both big-shot dermatologists The husband's also an avid cross country skier, and the wife's in perpetual training for the over-forty Olympics. I hate her, actually. One morning I was jogging around the lake—well, half jogging and half gasping for air—and Valeria the Super Latina blew by me without even a 'hello-how-the-hell-are-you.' I was right then in the middle of one of my gasping moments. The least she could have done was slow down and offer me a free skin exam before going on her merry way. But no. Instead, I swore I could hear her thinking, 'This Swedish babe has fair skin that will soon bubble over with cold sores, boils, warts, eczema, shingles, and ringworm. Ha, ha."

Livy drank in every exaggerated detail. "Jenny, I bet you're good friends with Valeria, aren't you?"

"Truth be told, we are indeed friends with the Velasquez-es—or whatever the plural of Velasquez is. For the past three years we've been invited to their outdoor whole-pig orgy on *Cinco de Mayo*. As luck would have it, each of those years the wind has cooperated and we've been treated to the most extraordinary smells wafting across Memory Lake. The pig cooks all day—so it's heavenly beyond description."

"Wow. I can only imagine."

"Well, in about a week you won't have to imagine. You'll be joining us in the best hog culinary orgasm you've ever experienced."

"Oh, Jenny, I wouldn't feel right going over with you and Davis."

"You've been invited."

"You can't invite me to someone else's party."

"I sure as hell can. Do it all the time. But in this case, I didn't. Valeria did. And she'll be stopping by in a couple of days to do it in person."

"And you said you hated her."

"I can suspend my contempt if I'm getting great pig."

Jenny's reference brought to Livy's mind the night during the previous spring when she and Peter had their big discussion about her working full time. Insistent that she have the freedom to accompany him to his political functions, Peter made clear how "devastating" it might be to his election chances if his wife were committed to her job, which at the time consisted of proofing scholarly monographs and preparing indexes for several university and small presses on the west coast. But she was then offered full-time employment by the University of California Press, and she was inclined to take it. But her husband's aggrieved expression was only a prelude to his argument against her accepting the job.

"Livy, you know I hope to win in November, don't you? But to do so, I need you with me, sometimes at a moment's notice. Anyway, it wouldn't be fair to the people at the press if you worked only a few months and then moved to Washington. And why do you have to work anyway? My parents have seen to it that we'll never lack for anything the rest of our lives. You can do so much more good for me if you're not committed to a full-time job. I know you want to use your mind, and you're probably the only woman on the planet who actually likes preparing indexes. Why don't you wait until we get to Washington and then you can take a couple of classes if you wish— just to challenge your intellect? I don't know. I'm just hurt that you would willingly risk my chances in the fall for a full-time job you don't need."

Painfully aware she would have to turn down the full-time offer, Livy groped for a weapon she really didn't have in her arsenal. "Sure, Peter. Perhaps when we get to the Nation's Capital, I can find a part-time job working in a barbeque joint."

Failing to recognize his wife's sarcasm—or refusing to acknowledge it, Peter responded with "Livy, eating barbeque reflects a lesser intelligence. It wouldn't do to have you work in one of those places. Just think about taking some classes, okay?"

Ironically, then, his patronizing suggestion led her to Jenny's and the bench by Memory Lake. She smiled thinking what he would say if he knew she would be dining on a whole pig cooked in someone's back yard.

"Jenny, do they use an apple?"

"What?" Jenny was presently in the middle of a monologue about the romantic habits of the Holimans—the recently married middle-aged couple two houses away from the Montgomerys. Jenny remarked that they were both married previously to persons of the cloth, were both in their fifties, and with their second marriages were making up for lost time—sexually. Therefore, Livy's question about the apple completely startled her.

As they pulled into the Montgomerys long driveway, Jenny yawned. "So now that we've all had lunch together, what do you think of Nick Lockhart?"

Livy didn't answer until they pulled into the garage. "Jenny, the way you phrased that seems again to be asking me how I'd feel about him as a potential love interest."

Jenny shut off the engine and turned her body, as much as the steering wheel would allow, in Livy's direction. "Look. To be completely serious for a moment."

"Ha."

"Okay, so it won't be a long moment, but I think Nick is worth getting to know more in..."

"Intimately?"

"No, I was about to say 'more intensely.' But really, he'd be—"

"Jenny—stop."

"Listen to me. After your divorce from Peter and after a reasonable time to enjoy a life of licentious irresponsibility..."

Livy was stunned by Jenny's matter-of-fact "After your divorce from Peter." There it was. A flat-out statement about the inevitability of her marriage dissolving. Her "divorce from Peter." She wasn't sure whether she was so affected by the word "divorce" or by the follow-up "from Peter." Perhaps it was both. She had once remarked to Jenny that no one in her family had ever gotten a divorce. The women on both her paternal and maternal sides ended up widows and not ex-wives. Didn't her mother once sit her down when she was seriously dating a boy in high school and remind her that her aunts, cousins, and grandmothers all married only once—except for Aunt Harriet, who outlived two husbands and died married to a third? Was that why Jenny's simple remark started winding the knot in her stomach? So where did the accompanying feeling of excitement come from—the one that electrified certain nerve ends on her cheeks and just under her nose. It had to be the "from Peter" part. Could it really happen? She just couldn't imagine it as a reality. For too long it had only been in the realm of momentary fancy.

"...you'll find someone who respects and admires you for who you are—who loves your little idiosyncrasies, who supports whatever the hell you want to do with your life, and...and...oh, yeah, who can't keep his hands off you—but only when you're in the mood."

Livy laughed as they entered the house. "And you're sure you're not suggesting Nick Lockhart as that 'someone?'"

"No, God love him, he's too handsome and virile to be a candidate for you. I know you have your standards, and..." Jenny winced at suggesting even inadvertently that Livy's judgment, as far as men went, was flawed—the proof being Peter. "Anyway, you need someone older."

"How much older exactly?"

"Hang on." Jenny opened one of the kitchen drawers and pulled out a calculator. She started punching the keys—with her tongue hanging partially out of her mouth—her signature "I'm concentrating on something" facial expression.

"Jenny, what in the world are you doing?"

"There!" Serpent-like, Jenny slid her tongue back inside her mouth. "He needs to be exactly forty-nine."

"And just how did you figure that?" For once Livy was more intrigued than amused by one of Jenny's familiar antics. That it included math was fascinating enough.

"It's the old rule written down in the Bible—or in the Dead Sea Scrolls—or somewhere. To find the ideal age for a wife, the man—at the time of marriage—should choose a woman who's half his age plus seven years."

"Come again."

"All right, I'll give you an example. A forty year-old man should marry a twenty-seven year old woman."

"Because...?"

"Because of what I just told you. Half of forty is twenty—right?"

"It used to be, I'm pretty sure."

"Half of forty is twenty—and then you add seven years to that and you have twenty-seven. See?"

"So if he's thirty-six, she should be twenty-five, then?"

Jenny furiously pressed the keys of her calculator. "Uh, wait. Yes—yes—that's it."

"And if he's forty-four, she should be twenty-nine?"

"Livy, can't you stick to the easy ones—forty—sixty—eighty?"

"Okay, then a seventy year-old man should marry a forty-two year old woman."

"Jenny pondered the math. "Yes, yes. You've got it."

"Okay, so if the man is now forty-nine, I take half of that—which is twenty four point five and add seven, which would then be thirty-one point five."

"And that's you!"

"Actually, I'm closer to thirty-one point six than I am to point five."

"Stuff it, Livy."

"Sorry."

"But, Jenny, that's all from the male perspective. Isn't there a scale from the woman's point of view?"

"Yes. You just do that math backwards and it comes out the same."

Livy marveled at how seriously her friend was taking these calculations. "Okay, Jenny, so if a man wishes to marry at twenty, he takes a seventeen year-old bride."

"That seems right."

"And if he's one hundred, she must be fifty seven."

"Wait. Really?"

"According to your formula she does."

"No, that can't be right. At fifty-seven I intend to be the same as I am now—with perhaps an additional smile line and a few visible crows' toes around the eyes. No way am I getting into bed with any human gargoyle with barely working lungs."

"There are some other strange pairings." Livy frowned when she calculated that Nick Lockhart, at forty-three needed to find a woman twenty-eight point five to fit the old Biblical formula. Livy could always do math in her head with ease. Peter long ago pitched a fit when she figured out an eighteen-percent tip in about a second. "So Jenny, the only time a male and female can marry at the same age is when they're fourteen."

"Okay." Jenny was going to trust Livy to get the math right.

"If it's a case of royalty, and the king of one country wants his eight year-old daughter to marry, the young prince she's about to walk down the aisle with has to be two—or the union is doomed."

"Yikes. No wonder the history of Europe is filled with lunatics and opium eaters."

"So the bottom line is that I need to find a man who's about to turn fifty."

Jenny scrunched her lovely face thinking of someone older than Nick Lockhart. "No, early forties—no older."

"That age doesn't fit the formula."

"Screw the formula, then."

"If you insist."

.   .   .

After freshening up, Jenny and Livy enjoyed the last twelve minutes of one of Jenny's favorite series running on HBO. As the credits rolled, Jenny once again engaged in jarring transition.

"When the time comes, you should marry a man between, oh, forty-one and forty-three, because men at that age have jumped the mid-life crisis hurdle and are finally ready to learn from the example of their previous romantic failures and treat their love interest the way she ought to be treated." Jenny paused. "Wow, that sounded profound, didn't it?"

Livy knew what her friend was trying to pull, but she played along regardless. "Ah, but Henry VIII was about to turn forty-two when he married Anne Boleyn and he ended up chopping her head off—so there's a flaw in your counsel."

"Right—I guess. But he wasn't forty-two when he chopped off her head, was he?"

"No, he was about forty-five, if I recall correctly."

"There—see?" Jenny licked her finger and drew the imaginary line in front of her face. "Score one for the gorgeous blonde." She then leaned over and hugged her friend.

"Why the hug, Jenny?"

"Because you so cleverly brought me back to that weekend you and I worked on my Six Wives of Henry VIII history project at Chico. Remember the wine—the cheapest on the face of the planet? We drank all five bottles over a two-day period."

Livy laughed. "Do you remember how shocked you were to learn that Henry the Eighth only had six wives?"

"I thought he was called 'the Eighth' because of all his weddings."

"But you were even more astonished to learn that he only killed two of his six wives."

"I know. He wasn't one-quarter the man I thought he was."

Livy was warmed by the memories, regardless of the present hyperbole. Yet, she felt some envy over Henry's six wives. After all, they all got out of their marriages, didn't they?

"Okay, Livy, let's plan dinner and then check the tequila supply for our margarita fest later out on the bench by Memory Lake—joined by you know who."

"Yes, the man who seems to like me but is too young for me—or I'm too old for him. That is, if I weren't presently still married." Livy stared at her friend and felt her spirits sag.

"Change the subject, Livy."

"You're right. Subject changed. But I do have one question relating to what you've told me about marriage."

Jenny offered a timid "All right."

"Just what are those 'little idiosyncrasies' of mine my next husband is supposed to love?"

Chapter 17

Livy couldn't have been more pleased by how well her Veal Piccata turned out. Jenny had planned to boil some pasta for dinner, but her friend insisted she be allowed to cook. "I want to earn my keep," Livy noted.

"When was the last time you actually prepared a meal?"

"I cooked one for myself about a month ago. I last cooked for Peter over three months ago—right after we got settled in our place in Virginia."

Settled? She was anything but settled in January. The lemon chicken was dry and bland, and she couldn't really blame her husband for suggesting they eat out or call in for meals after that. She already began to disdain any kind of domestic activity—anything, really, that contributed to the state she wished herself out of. Peter of course failed to read anything into her reluctance to play wife on any level.

Jenny assumed her skeptical pose. "So you're saying you haven't cooked for anyone in over three months, and you expect me to play guinea pig?"

"That's exactly what I'm saying."

"I know I'm risking a lot, but all right, for the sake of our friendship, you can cook."

As the women loaded the dishwasher following the meal, Livy glanced at the kitchen clock. It was 6:25. Didn't Jenny say that Davis was pitching tonight in Baltimore at 6:00 CST?

"Jenny, isn't Davis's game on now?"

Jenny rinsed the dinner plates before putting them in the dishwasher. "Yes."

"It's being televised, isn't it?"

"It is."

"Don't you want to go in and watch? I'll finish up here and join you in a minute."

"I'm not going to watch the game."

"Why not?"

Jenny wiped her hands with the dish towel and drew in a long breath exclusively through her nostrils, and Livy could see she was making every effort to control her emotions.

"Pitching well tonight is so very important to Davis, as I told you. Maybe I'm thinking that since my watching hasn't helped much this year, my not watching just might work to turn his luck around."

"Jenny, you don't believe that."

"All right, it's because I'm *afraid* to watch him pitch tonight, Livy. I've been more uncomfortable watching him the past year, but it's been nothing like this. Am I crazy?"

"You're not crazy, Jenny. You just love him and hurt for him, that's all."

"I wish that's all it was. But I know I'm hurting for myself too."

"I'm not sure I know what you mean." Livy took Jenny's hand.

"I don't expect you to. It's just that I'm afraid I'm going to lose so much if he...Oh, hell. I'm not making sense, am I?" Jenny stepped away from Livy and looked out toward Memory Lake from the kitchen window. "I'm sorry, Livy. I'm speaking in illogicalities." She laughed. "Is that a word?"

"Actually, I believe it is."

"Really? Then I have no earthly idea where that one came from. Anyway, let's just get ready for the escape to Margaritaville. I'll get Nick to check on the score of the game when he gets here. I'm sure I'll watch Davis's next start. But for some reason tonight is too...well...let's just forget what the blonde chick just said. She's suffering from temporary fits of incomprehensitivenss. Is that a word too, Livy?"

"Afraid not."

"Good, then I'm back to normal. Let's proceed with the party prep."

"You got it." Still, Livy remained curious about Jenny's comment that she was hurting for herself as well.

Livy had always admired Jenny's special gift for moving at the snap of a finger from an agitated state to one completely serene or bemused. And she was presently demonstrating that gift once again, as she left the kitchen and headed for the bar in the den, humming what sounded like something from *Hamilton*.

"I had a hunch I'd find the two of you down here."

At 8:05, Lockhart arrived, holding a cloth sack into which he had placed a large bottle of Cuervo Gold. It was a beautiful late April early evening, and as he drove up to the Montgomery's, Nick's car thermometer read a balmy 52 degrees. Perfect light sweater weather, he believed, although Livy Garner's double-sweater look complete with one of Jenny's quilts belied such a "balmy" assessment of the evening.

Jenny opened the bag. "Thank you for the offering, Nick. It's about time you showed up. Livy and I were about to go skinny dipping in Memory Lake."

Livy knew she had a long way to go before becoming Minneapolisized, as Jenny might have said. "Of course we were."

Jenny dropped her smile and stared at Nick. He immediately understood.

"It's been a good game so far, Jenny. I checked on the radio before I got out of the car. It's now the bottom of the sixth, and he's still on the mound. The Twins are losing two to nothing, but Davis has only allowed four hits—one being a two-run homer—and he's struck out three, walked only one. I think he'll go this inning and then they'll take him out."

Livy's eyes darted between Lockhart and Jenny. She thought the news was good, although she barely understood the ins and outs of baseball. "Jenny?"

"No, no, it's good, Livy. It's very good. He's pitching well. One bad pitch—the home run. He's got his control. Three strike-outs is below what he used to average, so...No, no, but it's good. It's good. If he can just get them out this inning without any more damage, he'll feel good about his outing." Jenny slapped both her thighs with the palm of her hands. "Look, I'm going up to see if I can mix up another batch of margaritas."

Lockhart laughed. "Looks like you've been practicing." The two empty glasses were on the small fold out table positioned in front of the bench.

Jenny bounced up the steps with the tequila and headed for the rear of the house. "I'll light the lawn torches."

"Don't ignite yourself, Jenny." Livy was relieved her friend was in good spirits following Lockhart's report on Davis's pitching. "Nick, I'm so happy you had good news to share." Something told her that Nick was the kind of man who liked to share good news, not hoard it, as Peter had so often done.

"Livy, I'm just a little surprised she's not watching. She always watches every game he pitches when the Twins are in the road."

Livy grew anxious at Lockhart's apparent concern. "Nick, please don't think she's not watching because I'm here. Or that I don't like baseball—or sports. As I hope I made clear earlier, I'm not exactly an expert, but..."

Nick smile told her he saw her defensiveness as charming. "Livy, I never thought any such thing. I just realized that I've failed to consider adequately how difficult it's been for her, given Davis's problems of late."

"You must have seen so many in similar situations during your career as a sports writer."

"True. I've seen far too many cases of the deteriorating athlete and the effect that deterioration has had on the athlete himself, but also what it's done to the families—especially to the wives. It's been one of my major failings that I haven't devoted enough space to that issue—one the public rarely, if ever, considers. Certainly, it's hard to make the case given the salaries many of these pro athletes receive, but there's more to the life than just financial advantage. Raw emotions and personal insecurities aren't really lessened by the amount of money in a checkbook."

Livy listened attentively—not only because the topic involved her best friend or because she had never given any thought to the matter—but also because she felt herself admiring the man sitting next to her on the bench. She thought it so wonderful she could talk to this handsome and intelligent man and feel so comfortable—neither worried about the impressions she was making nor the possibility that he would come on to her. She fought a smile as she recalled the hilarious description of Nick Lockhart Jenny earlier volunteered at the dinner table.

"Livy, he's not like a father figure to me but rather like one of those way older brother types—you know, the brother whose child—who's your niece—is as old as you are."

Nick interrupted her thought, "Are you still enjoying Minnesota?"

"I am. But I lag a bit behind in cold toleration." She playfully pulled at the sleeve of Lockhart's light sweater. She had already come somewhat out of her quilt cocoon and was braving the elements in just her two-sweater ensemble.

"I'm sure you'll like the university. Have you been over there yet?"

"No, not yet. Jenny promised we'd head over tomorrow. I can't wait to see it."

"We'll make a Gopher out of you before you know it."

Livy's head jerked forward, her jaw opened, and her tongue attempted to articulate English but to no avail. Lockhart laughed.

"The gopher is the university mascot—the name of its sports teams—the University of Minnesota Golden Gophers."

"Oh. There see? I told you I was deficient in my knowledge of sports."

"But you're not doing a Master's in Sports Studies, so you'll be all right."

Livy spoke about her planned thesis. "Nick, when I begin work on my proposed thesis—provided I'll get my committee's approval—would you mind if I interview you about your time in the Army?"

Lockhart turned his head and looked directly across darkened Memory Lake, catching Livy off guard. She hadn't expected him to hesitate replying to her request.

"Nick, I'm sorry. I know you're very busy with all you have to do, so..."

Still gazing across the lake, he answered, "Livy, I'll talk to you...at least about some of it."

His remained silent for several long seconds. Livy believed he was presently in the middle of making a significant decision of some kind. What that had to do with her request, she wasn't sure. And why did he say "some of it"? Finally, he turned his head back toward her. He seemed in part relieved.

"I see no reason to wait until you start classes and get the approval of your committee for your thesis idea. If you don't mind, I'd like to talk to you about my experiences as soon as you'd like. But I can promise to go only so far and then...Well as I said, whenever you'd like."

"Nick, are you sure? I would really appreciate your time—and I'd like to learn about both your experiences and your perspective on how those experiences tie in with your outstanding success as a writer."

"I understand."

Once more his demeanor suggested to her that he would be reluctant to talk about everything. Of course she knew that many who have fought in war have little inclination to speak about the atrocities and other horrors they witnessed, but she wasn't sure he had actual combat experience. Had he served in the Iraq War? As she tried to do the chronology, Nick's face regained its social and pleasant demeanor.

"Livy, how about sharing some of your experiences at Cal State Chico? And start with some Jenny stories. Just hurry before she gets back with the margaritas." Lockhart dropped his eyes and realized for the first time that Livy wasn't wearing her wedding ring.

Delighted by Nick's request, Livy quickly made a judgment on which of her favorite tales she could tell that wouldn't violate her promise never to betray Jenny's confidence. "Did Jenny tell you about the time the cable guy came to our apartment to install service and she ended up punching him in the mouth?"

"She did what?"

"Well, the cable guy was on the floor running the wire—or whatever they do—and he called Jenny over. He was on his hands and knees, and when she walked over, he reached out and ran his finger up and down her shin bone." Livy swung one leg out from under the quilt and demonstrated. "Right like this. And Jenny wasn't wearing jeans. She was barefoot and had on shorts."

"Did she tell you this?"

"I know what you're thinking, Nick. She might have exaggerated. But I saw the whole thing. I was standing not five feet from where he rubbed her shin.

As soon as the cable man did that, he lifted up his head and smiled at her. She then sort of bent down from the waist and slugged him right in the mouth."

They heard Jenny in the back yard. "Let me light these torches and then I'll be down with the margaritas. Anyone want something to munch on? Never mind, I'll bring to some chips and salsa."

As Jenny went about setting up the lawn pyrotechnics, Livy lowered her voice and finished the tale—emphasizing that Jenny followed the assaulted cable man down to his truck, vowing to turn him in to the police.

"Did she, Livy?"

"No, she was laughing too hard to make the call." Livy and Nick had leaned toward each other to avoid being heard, and Livy could smell the breath mint or breath spray Nick had obviously taken before arriving to the bench. She had a visceral reaction to the minty smell, which startled her.

"Well Livy, I hope you haven't been forced to slug anyone in the mouth."

"Who me? I've never even slapped anyone, let alone punched them."Yet how many times had she wanted to show aggressive tendencies the last several years, especially when her husband was at his condescending best. Since her marriage to Peter, she willingly entertained the occasional fantasy of responding aggressively, if not violently—not merely to his insufferable behavior toward her but in other situations as well—whether they had to do with surly behavior by fast food cashiers or insulting taunts from an impatient drivers. But she had never engaged in any kind of verbal skirmish when these situations arose. Instead she was left to berate herself for her inaction with a catalogue of epithets—including "spineless," "coward," "wimp," and even "fraidy-cat." She often wondered why she couldn't shake free from the grip of "Peace-at-all-Costs" Olivia.

But hadn't she said "No" to Peter's request that she fly to California with him for the fund raiser? Wasn't that enough to silence her self-criticism? Unfortunately, she knew the small victory would be forgotten if she didn't tell him she wanted out of the marriage and take the legal steps to end it. She looked at Nick Lockhart and regretted he wasn't a lawyer.

Chapter 18

"And here we are." Or at least that's what Livy thought she heard. But the articulation of those four words was considerably compromised by the top of the unopened bag of tortilla chips Jenny had clamped in her mouth. One hand was gripping the handle of the large pitcher containing the freshly blended frozen margaritas. The fingers of the other hand were entwined around the stems of three clean margarita glasses—complete with salt on the rims. Under one arm was a small stack of red and green napkins, and barely pressed under the other arm were three plastic party plates. A long plastic stirring spoon rested under her shirt between her breasts, and squeezed into the waistband of her jeans were two jars of salsa—one mild and one hot.

"Why didn't you call for help, Jenny?"

"I didn't want to interrupt your conversation with Nick. Besides, I know how much you hate doing common labor. As long as you do everything for her, Nick, she'll be your friend."

Nick stood to help disencumber Jenny of the food stuffs, but he wasn't about to reach for either the long plastic serving spoon or the jars of salsa. Fortunately, Livy was on more familiar terms with Jenny and pulled out the items with surgical deftness from the tall blonde walking convenience store.

With the lawn torches illuminating the area behind them and the patio lights cutting into the darkness at rear of the houses all around Memory Lake, Jenny, Livy, and Nick sat on the bench in perfect contentment. Davis's solid six innings of work gave Jenny hope that he might be turning things around. For the moment, she felt less anxious she would have to leave her house and all those sublime sunsets while sitting on her bench. As for Livy, she felt protected sitting between Jenny and Nick, imagining that they might somehow shepherd her through the most difficult time of her life. And Nick gave no thought to how such simple pleasures would soon end two night's hence when Paul Vanderkellen appeared on camera for ESPN.

"Nick, don't you think Livy would have made a terrific waitress at Hooters?" Jenny's interruption of the blissful silence couldn't have been any more jarring. But of course she knew that and spoke accordingly. Both Livy and Nick jerked forward on the bench. But Livy was the only one who could push out a response. Even so, it wasn't much.

"Jenny!"

"No, no, I mean it. You're just the right height. You have a very cute butt and killer legs—so you'd really show your assets in panty hose and those orange shorts—and your upper body is..."

Livy reached past Nick and clamped her open hand over Jenny's mouth to prevent the embarrassing finale to the descriptive flourish. "I'm not letting go until you promise to shut up."

In mock helplessness, Jenny nodded her promise, which Nick feared would be immediately broken upon the release of Livy's hand. He didn't know who was embarrassed more—Livy or himself.

Livy slowly and reluctantly took her hand off Jenny's mouth. "Remember—nothing about my...you know whats." Livy felt the residue of margarita salt on her palm.

"I won't, Livy. I said I promised. But can I at least say how great you'd look in the Hooter white socks and white gym shoes?"

Livy shook her head in exasperation and poured another margarita from the pitcher resting on the portable table, now next to her side of the bench. She didn't want to look at Nick. He'd probably been to his share of Hooters. No way could she compete with those girls. Maybe ten years ago when she was in her early twenties. Then she recalled how Jenny had begun her catalogue.

"What do you mean I'm 'just the right height,' Jenny? Don't they have women in all heights at Hooters—even yours? Say, wait just a minute." How could she have forgotten? Jenny had in fact worked the summer between her sophomore and junior year at a Hooters knock-off on the Deer Creek Highway outside of Chico. Because Livy's aunt had taken her on a summer jaunt to New York and Boston, Livy wasn't aware until the fall term of Jenny's three-week failed experiment in serving wings, burgers, and draft beer. "And should I tell Nick about your outfit when you worked at The Demon's Dip—Chico's

Ultimate Hot Wing Emporium?"

Jenny roared. "By all means tell him. Better yet, I'll do it myself. Nick, you would have loved this place. I'd come up to your table and say, "Hi! Welcome to The Demon's Dip. I'm Devilette Jenny. Here's the menu. Now what can I get you to drink?"

"'Devilette Jenny'?" Nick's imagination began sprinting past his better sense.

"That's right. I was in a flaming red one piece made out of faux satin. Red fishnet hose and heels. A little beret contraption on my head with two devil's horns sticking out of it. The owner was naturally inspired by the Playboy Bunny look."

Nick corralled his imagination. "And you quit after three weeks? Why am I not surprised?"

"No, no. I didn't mind the outfit. I quit for two other reasons. One because we didn't exactly lure in the classiest of clientele, and I spent too much time trying not to act disgusted or indignant by the looks and propositions I was getting. And two—and this may have been the bigger reason. Because Danny, the owner, had all the girls at the top of each hour line up in front of the bar and announce that we were beginning 'another hot hour' at The Demon's Dip, after which we all had to put our finger on our ass and make the sizzling 'ssssssss' sound." Jenny looked perplexed. "How the hell did I last a whole three weeks?"

Fifteen minutes later they noticed the margarita supply running low. Jenny smugly announced she had already prepared a second pitcher, which was now in the fridge. "I'll be back down in a flash."

Livy cheered her on. "Go get it, demon lady."

Nick wouldn't hear of it. "I'll get it. I need to avail myself of the accommodations anyway." He looked at Jenny, who immediately understood.

"You do that, Nick. Forgive me. I forgot to raise the seat. And while you're in there will you...?"

"I will."

As soon as Nick made it into the house, he turned on the television to see how Davis Montgomery had fared in the seventh inning.

•   •   •

"Having fun, Livy?"

"Jenny, I am, I really am. If I had my way, I'd want this night to go on indefinitely."

"And look at you. You're no longer under the quilt."

"My body's acclimating to spring time in Minnesota."

"Nick seems to be enjoying himself too."

"I think so." This time Livy didn't demand that Jenny cease her indirect suggestion that her two bench-mates get better acquainted. Livy now wanted to hear Jenny say something along those lines.

"He's in some trouble, Livy." Again, one of Jenny's fender-bending transitions.

"Trouble? What do you mean, Jenny? Legal? Personal? Medical?"

"Nick probably doesn't know that I know, but Davis found out from one of the writers covering the Twins that Nick is in hot water with his paper for sitting on a big story that's about to break big time. It has to do with one of the former Minnesota Viking football players, who has a serious gambling problem. Davis said this player is going to accuse Nick of not helping him when he could have. I'm not up on the specifics, but it looks bad. Davis thinks Nick might have to leave Minneapolis if he wants to keep writing."

"Oh Jenny, I don't know what to say. I could tell that Nick was distracted when we were down here together—and at moments he seemed to be dealing with some kind of problem—but I never would have thought it was professionally related. I was fearful he had received the results of a medical test and that the news wasn't good."

The women's conversation was interrupted by the sound of birds flying very low over Memory Lake. Livy was startled. "What was that?"

"Probably ducks. They usually buzz the lake just before it gets completely dark."

"But it's now completely dark, Jenny."

"Yeah, it is."

Livy suddenly thought of the darkness as a metaphor for all of their situations. "Then they're late."

"Yeah, they are."

"I'm looking forward to feeding the ducks out here."

"Yeah, and they're looking forward to you feeding them, Livy."

Was it knowledge of Nick's professional crisis that lowered their spirits? Or was it Livy's growing concern that Peter would make good on his threat and come to the Montgomery's and ruin everything? And just what would she do if he did indeed show up? Her initial impulse would be to run down to her basement apartment, lock the door, and let Jenny kick Peter out the house, after a quick warning not to bother her best friend again. But Livy knew that wouldn't do. Again, if she was going to have any kind of life on her own, she would have to face Peter and make him understand she wanted out of the marriage. Long periods of silence or indirect communication through intermediaries or brief phone conversations wouldn't be enough.

Livy assumed she'd have to assure Peter that, since he was so new to Washington, their divorce wouldn't affect him politically. But then he would most likely try to negotiate a delay until the next election won him a second term in the House. Were she to agree, he would only ask for another delay after that. Livy imagined a nightmare scenario in which she would live out the rest of her life hiding in Jenny's basement apartment—physically separated from Peter Garner but never divorced from him. But the truth was that she'd have to be as cruel as she never imagined herself being if her husband wouldn't agree to the divorce. She hated the position she was in. She just wanted everything to end without any trauma. And she hated that she couldn't entrust Jenny or anyone else to do the dirty work for her.

Livy recalled a discussion with her mother right before her marriage to Peter. They were talking about Livy's general temperament and how that might cause her difficulties in her marriage. Her mother reached for the hackneyed "band aid" image to make her point.

"My darling, you always took forever to remove a band aid from one of your cuts. I timed you once. You took a full two minutes to take it off. But me? I just yank it off in a second. It may sting a little, but it's done with."

But then her mother admitted she had employed the band aid metaphor far too often when it came to her daughter's delay in making difficult decisions.

"No, let me change that reference. Remember how you used to like it when I put hydrogen peroxide on your dirty cuts? How you liked that fizzy effect, knowing that is was cleaning the dirt and killing the germs? You see, Livy, you're the type of person who wants her problems to melt or fizz away. I'm afraid that will make you endure problems for much longer than you should."

Livy also recalled feeling so sad that her mother seemed to expect her and Peter to have difficulties in their marriage. Her mother was right, of course—just as she was spot on about her daughter's desire to have things melt and fizz away. Livy even laughed at herself for one of her "idiosyncrasies," as Jenny would call them—the one that made her stare at pats of butter as they melted slowly in the frying pan over low heat. She never turned away from the melting process; it was too pleasurable to watch.

"Ducks do fly at night, though."

"What, Jenny?"

"Ducks do fly at night. They follow the stars and the magnetic fields."

"What are you saying?"

"I read that somewhere."

Jenny delivered her ornithological factoid with such a serious face that Livy wondered if the margaritas had already gone to her head.

"Special delivery." The voice came from behind them. It was Lockhart with the new pitcher of Jenny's weak margaritas.

"About time. I was about to call in a complaint." Jenny was back to her teasing self.

"As Nick poured the refills, he started whistling a tune neither woman recognized. Jenny knew him well enough to understand he had a happy announcement to make. She hoped it had something to do with the lessening of his professional crisis. Perhaps matters had been resolved at his paper or with the ex-Vikings quarterback.

Jenny extended her hands, palms up. "What is it, Nick?"

"Oh, nothing much. I just found out that Davis Montgomery pitched a scoreless seventh inning."

Jenny was startled. Her assumptions about the news were wrong.

Nick continued, "He gave up two hits in the inning, but he pitched out of trouble. And to make it all the sweeter, the Twins scored two at the top of the next inning, so Davis won't be the losing pitcher of record even if Baltimore wins."

"Yes!" Jenny leaped up and hugged him forcefully—almost knocking the pitcher of margaritas out of his hand. Livy wasn't sure she completely understood the "losing pitcher of record" part, but she was thrilled the news about Davis was good.

Again seated between the women, Nick understood that such a joyful reaction to a decent to solid pitching performance merely testified to the deteriorating state of Davis Montgomery's career, but he nevertheless took pleasure in Jenny's exuberant reaction. Still, he wondered how short-lived her enthusiasm might be, because Davis would pitch again in five days. Nick had seen it so often during his many years in the profession. The joy over the momentary evidence that an aging professional athlete might again be finding the sharpness of his prime—that a serious injury would not affect the skill set as initially feared and the success would continue unabated for many years to come. And yet it rarely worked out that way. Nick so admired athletes who recognized they were on the down side of their peak and called it quits before facing the embarrassment and ridicule the hangers-on always experienced. It was one of the satisfactions of his own profession that he could go much longer—easily twenty or thirty years beyond the time span of the athlete—without any erosion of skills and that, as often as not, death rather than retirement signaled the true end of a sportswriter's career. Even so, as he sat on the bench by Memory Lake, he knew he was facing the end for an entirely different and far more painful reason.

With the tip of her finger, Jenny curled the remaining salt residue from the rim of her margarita glass and placed it in her mouth. "Livy, do you know what they call Minnesota?"

"A state?"

"Yes, a state—but that's not what I mean. Do you know the familiar motto of the State of Minnesota?"

"Not sure I do."

"It's called the Land of Ten Thousand Lakes. You've never heard that before?"

"I know Land of Lakes Butter. But are there really ten thousand—or is that an exaggeration?"

"Not an exaggeration." Jenny turned to Lockhart, "How many are there exactly, Nick?"

"Memory Lake here is just one of 11,842."

Livy was impressed. "And the Mississippi River starts in Minnesota as well."

Nick added, "And don't forget our other 365 rivers—including the Artichoke, the Little Gooseberry, the Dead Moose, the Rat Root, the Egg, and my favorite, the Little Sucker."

Jenny laughed. "Nick, we ought to go into the tourism business together." Immediately, Jenny regretted the jocular remark. Poor Nick might well be looking for a job any day now, if the reports Davis heard were correct. As always, she escaped her verbal predicament by changing the subject without adequate transition. "You asked about my major pet peeve, Livy."

"I did?"

"Nothing makes me more ill than looking on the toilet-paper holder and finding that little cardboard insert staring back at me. I can't even stand to change them. I detest the feel of that cardboard thing on my fingers—and so I have to wait for Davis to come home before we can put a new roll of toilet paper on the roller contraption. And if guests come while he's on a road trip, well you can just imagine the embarrassment I have to endure."

Vintage Jenny, Livy thought. Hilarious. Utterly hilarious. And yet Nick wasn't smiling.

"Livy, I should have mentioned this as soon as I came down with the margaritas, but there's bouquet of flowers for you in the front room of the house."

When Nick went up for the pitcher of frozen margaritas, he first headed out the front door to retrieve his cell phone from his car. As soon as he opened the door, he saw the bouquet resting on the stoop. There was a handwritten note on the door handle saying that delivery was attempted and that the instructions were to leave the flowers at the residence if no one was at home. When Nick picked up the bouquet, he assumed that Davis Montgomery sent them to Jenny— perhaps calling the local florist as soon as he was replaced on the mound after the seventh inning. But the addressee on the card read "Olivia Garner."

Because Nick was aware that Livy had come to Minnesota in part to facilitate the end of her marriage to the congressman, the flowers suggested to him that Peter Garner was having second thoughts about the forthcoming divorce. Nick could well understand why the congressman wouldn't wish to lose someone as lovely and warm as Livy, but it was evident she wasn't regretting her decision to come and live at the Montgomery's. Assuming the flowers wouldn't be welcome, Lockhart didn't wish to mar Livy's evening by mentioning the arrival of the bouquet. In fact, for one brief instant he toyed with the idea of placing the flowers in his car so Livy wouldn't know they had arrived. It was an absurd idea of course, because he had absolutely no business getting involved in the couple's marriage—doomed or not. Yet, he couldn't help wanting to intercede—wanting to protect her. He hadn't felt that way about a woman for quite some time. But now he felt the impulse palpably. All he knew was that he was drawn to the congressman's wife and was quite comfortable in her company. He believed if he could open up to anyone, it would be to Livy Garner, regardless of the brevity of their relationship.

By the time he headed down with the margaritas, he thought he'd just let her find the flowers when she and Jenny returned to the house. He placed the bouquet on a table in the front room so it couldn't be missed. But the longer he remained sitting next to Livy on the bench, the more he conceded to the internal argument that he should tell her the bouquet had come. After all, the flowers couldn't have gotten to the table without his putting them there, and if he said nothing, Livy might wonder why he didn't inform her. It just didn't occur to him that he could have left them on the front stoop.

"Flowers?" Livy's face made it clear she knew who sent them. "Oh."

Jenny got up and took several steps toward the stairway. "Livy, I'll trash them so you won't have to see them."

"No, Jenny. I need to see them."

"Really?" Jenny was confused by her friend's calm demeanor as well as by her response.

"I'll be right back." Livy moved up the steps neither slowly nor rapidly. Jenny thought her walk looked confident—although that seemed odd given the reason she was going into the house.

"Nick, that bastard Peter is pulling the same shit he always pulls when he thinks he's pushed Livy too far."

"What do you mean?" Nick knew what she meant, but he wanted to hear more of the indictment against Livy's husband.

"He's the kind of thoughtless and selfish jerk who was raised to believe that any demonstration of rudeness, insensitivity, or ignorance on his part can be covered over with a grand promise or gift of some kind. Livy's told me time and again about the jewelry he purchased for her—or the gift certificates—or the spa treatments. And then there are the promises. 'I promise not to do it again' or 'I promise to make it up to you' or 'I promise that after I get back from wherever, I'm taking you to wherever you'd like to go.' She tells me he always has either the incredulous 'Did I do something wrong?' or the little boy "But I didn't mean to make you upset with me' look on his face when she informs him—too gently, I might add—that he's hurt or offended her." The grating call of a common crow traversing Memory Lake provided proper punctuation of Jenny's account.

Nick took another sip of his margarita. Although he enjoyed the concoction, at this moment he really craved bourbon. "What you say about Livy's husband sounds so much like many athletes I've covered over the years. More often than not, when an athlete makes a controversial, insulting, or politically insensitive comment, he'll insist that he was taken out of context or that he was only attempting to be funny or that the reporter set him up to make the offending remark. Jenny, I hope I'm not being nosey, but to your knowledge has Peter Garner ever cheated on Livy?"

Jenny's face tightened as it always did when she was especially angry. "Hell no. And it makes me so mad. Peter probably hasn't even glanced at a centerfold or been to a strip club in the seven years they've been married."

"Can you be certain, since you don't see him that often?"

"Livy is sure he hasn't strayed, and we've often talked about Peter's Mr. Puritan personality."

"That may be just for the voters. And we know how often the Puritans fail to live up to their principles."

"Not in this case, Nick. It's my theory that Peter's fidelity is just one of his manipulative tools."

"How do you mean?"

"He thinks he's made it utterly impossible for Livy to leave him.

He's Mr. True Blue. He buys her nice things and never resorts to any kind of physical violence. I mean, he won't even raise his voice to her when they disagree. He's confident that everyone who knows the both of them—except for me, that is—thinks he's the model husband, worthy not only of his wife's love and devotion but also that of his constituents. Think how well all that would serve him when he runs for the Senate or the Governor's office. You can bet your sweet hind end, he thinks that."

As Jenny offered her blistering assessment of Peter Garner's character and motivations, Livy stood before the luxurious bouquet in the Montgomery's front room. Having worked part-time in a floral shop during her teenage years, she was well versed in the symbolic value of each flower. Before her were a mix of asters, carnations, red tulips, red chrysanthemums, and seven red roses. During their brief engagement, Livy informed Peter that these flowers signified love and passion. It was a lesson Livy now deeply regretted teaching him. She knew the seven roses in the present bouquet stood for each of the years they were married. When she received a single red rose on their first anniversary, Peter announced that each year he would add another rose to her floral gift. At the time, she thought the gesture was romantic, and it did much to lessen her anger and hurt over Peter's patronizing treatment of her—over what she couldn't now recall. Their eighth anniversary wasn't until September, and Livy didn't want to see that eighth red rose. Could she do enough to make sure the next anniversary bouquet never came? Would she have enough time to convince him that the marriage was over before then—or at any other time?

Livy held the unopened card as she recalled a few other floral associations, especially with her own life. The blue hydrangea denoted loyalty and faithfulness—qualities both she and her husband honored in their marriage but inharmoniously, for how often had she wished Peter would find a mistress to endure his little cruelties—someone he could teach and patronize with impunity. Livy also thought of the peonies, which suggested riches, prosperity, romance, and honor. The first two qualities she could always have with Peter; the third both of them could always agree to do without, just as long as the trappings of affection would be apparent enough for him. As for honor, Peter believed strongly he could have it and with more authority with Livy remaining his wife, whereas she knew she could have none of it if she allowed herself to remain Mrs. Peter Garner.

Livy slid her finger under the seal and pulled out the note Peter had dictated to the florist over the phone—or had he left that up to one of his staff? She took the note to the kitchen window and glanced out at Memory Lake, partially and most intriguingly illuminated by the lawn torches Jenny had ignited earlier. Livy tore the note into pieces and deposited it unread into the trash can.

Chapter 19

"No, my darling, of course it's not too late. I'm happy you waited to call until you got back to the hotel. Livy's already gone down to bed." Jenny was curled up in her favorite living room chair, a thick crocheted blanket forming a comfortable cocoon around her. For some reason she came back into the house chilled after Nick left. It surprised her, since she had developed a fairly good tolerance for the cold—at least for a California native. It had to be her emotional state, she figured, caused by her worry over Davis's pitching performance but also by Nick's professional crises. Mixed with the concern was her agitation over Peter Garner and what he had done to make her best friend so unhappy.

After she told Davis how proud she was of him for his seven good innings, she took a breath and articulated what she decided only a minute earlier not to tell him. "Davis, I didn't watch tonight. I couldn't. I'm so sorry, but I was becoming afraid I was bringing you bad luck."

"What do you mean, Jenny? You've always been my lucky charm."

"That's just it. I feel as though I failed in my duties. Maybe they found out that I'm Swedish and not Irish and took away my powers." Jenny smiled, so gratified to hear her husband laugh.

"Jenny, I understand why you didn't watch the game tonight—I do. Did you listen to any of it on the radio?"

She hesitated before answering. "No, it would have made me just as nervous or even worse. You know how I feel about listening to games on the radio. It makes me feel as though I'm eavesdropping while locked in a closet blindfolded."

Davis's continued laughter made her feel confident he was genuinely relaxed. "Well, Jenny, we wouldn't want that."

"Anyway, Nick Lockhart was over and he told me how well you

were doing after six innings. And then he found out that you had a successful seventh as well."

"Did he tell you that I gave up a two-run homer early and got out of several jams after that?"

"Yes, he told me. So what? You still pitched magnificently."

"Jenny, I'd hardly call the outing magnificent."

"Don't contradict your wife, darling."

"Sorry."

"Davis, I was so happy that I wanted to run all the way to Baltimore and attack you in the shower."

"That would have been good. I showered with two other guys tonight—both of whom think you're gorgeous. Well, actually, the whole team does."

Jenny was as content as she'd been in days. Davis sounded very upbeat and hopeful that he might be on his way back to that special place he had inhabited before his shoulder injury. After informing his wife he didn't see Peter Garner at the game, his voice took on a more serious tone.

"Jenny, I heard a little more today about the situation with Nick."

"Please tell me. He didn't talk about it tonight."

Davis shared what he heard about Paul Vanderkellen's gambling problem, the meeting the young quarterback said he had with Lockhart, and the claim that Nick refused to reveal the truth through the newspaper or through his connections with sports television, local or national. "It's Vanderkellen's position—as far as I've been told—that he wanted Nick to help him by revealing the story, and he's claimed that he wouldn't have gotten in further trouble with the law if Nick had exposed his problem at that time. Vanderkellen's going to play it all out during a live interview with ESPN two nights from now."

Jenny wriggled out from the blanket and repositioned herself on the sofa. "How can he blame Nick for his own problems? It doesn't make any sense."

"I know. But if he portrays himself as little-boy-lost, he could score some points of sympathy and make Nick look like he didn't care enough and all that crap."

"But Nick cared enough not to out the little bastard, didn't he?

He's not his keeper, is he? Nick can't be seen as being responsible for what happened to Vanderkellen—no way."

"Jenny, you know how these things go—some will paint Vanderkellen as the hapless victim turned away by the 'establishment figure'—the older and decorated sports writer. Many see gambling as a disease, you know."

"Disease, my fanny."

"Jenny, you know that's true. We've talked about this."

Indeed they had and Jenny had showed far more sympathy for the gambling addict than she was doing now. As always, the closer something like this came to home the less philosophically she approached the matter.

"But the worst part is that Nick sat on a major story his paper would have broken. Now it looks as though the paper, as well as Nick, failed to do its job. They lost the chance for an exclusive interview with Vanderkellen. What I'm hearing doesn't sound good for Nick's keeping his job."

"As honored as he's been. As high a place as he holds in his profession?"

"Jenny, we've seen it happen so many times before. One big mistake—or perceived mistake—and all that came before it doesn't matter much. True in politics; true in sports. Anyway, I didn't mean to get you so riled up."

Jenny realized her indignation over Lockhart's situation had taken away from the special conversation she was having with her husband. "Oh, Davis, forgive me. I just hate what's happening to Nick. I didn't mean to make you think I didn't want to hear more about your night."

Davis again laughed, but this time with appreciation. "Jenny, that's one of the major reasons why I love you so much. You are the most loyal person I've ever met. You're the lioness, always ready to pounce and protect those closest to you."

"Hey, that should be the motto of the Minneapolis Police: 'To Pounce and Protect.' I'll give them permission to use it."

"And that's another major reason why I love you so much. You're the funniest person I've ever met."

As she headed up the staircase to her bedroom, Jenny was disappointed in herself for allowing her anxiety to return. It had nothing to do with Nick's problems—or with Livy's. She had sufficiently purged her anger over both those matters during her long talk with Davis. She knew she should have been almost giddy hearing the optimism in her husband's voice as well as his familiar unruffled manner, which so endeared him to her when they first met. Yes, he admitted his shoulder was sore, but that wasn't at all uncommon. But with his optimism over his pitching came the reminder that his next outing might not be as successful and their discussion after that, which would likely take place in their bed since he would next pitch a home game, might reintroduce a more pessimistic Davis Montgomery. And then he would speak of the possibility or likelihood of the Twin's parting ways with him after the season. And after that he would speak of moving to another team—to another house in another town.

Jenny turned around on the staircase and headed to the kitchen. Not to get a glass of water or check the back door, but rather to open that door and look out toward Memory Lake. Did she hope to hear something comforting from the water, a sliver of which the crescent moon permitted her to see, or did she simply want to assure herself that it was still there?

Livy sat on the edge of the bed holding her cell phone in both hands. Why hadn't she turned it off earlier? Better yet, why did she need to turn it on at all? Upon her arrival at the Montgomery's, she had spoken to her mother and assured her that she would call again in a few days. No other friend would contact her—at least no one she needed or especially wanted to talk to. The only reason she kept her phone on was in case Peter called. How could she possibly feel obligated to keep it on for his benefit? Livy assumed he didn't wish to call Jenny's house and wouldn't have the night she arrived had her cell phone not been down in her basement apartment with her bags.

Peter had been so insistent, especially during the last ten months, that she always be available to take his calls. "You never know when I might need you to join me for political reasons," he repeated often enough. But Livy wondered now if she had all along felt something other than obligation when it came to leaving on her cell phone.

Certainly, it was easier to concede to Peter's wish just for the sake of avoiding another elongated sigh or lecture about the matter. But was it really pragmatism that influenced her concession on this point? Might it also have been fear?

Livy kicked off her shoes and sat on the bed in a lotus position—just as she did as a girl when she was dealing with a difficult math problem or, as she thought then, a momentous decision about one of her boyfriends. She pondered the word—fear. She accepted that for all this time she was afraid to turn off the cell phone. She knew Peter would never harm her physically—he never had—and she was dead certain she would have left him if he ever did. But still she dreaded some kind of repercussion if she violated this ridiculous "command" of his.

Livy surveyed the room and noted the wall color she knew her husband wouldn't approve of. Here she was all alone in her own burrow, over a thousand miles away from Representative Peter Garner, for the first time examining rather than dismissing her conduct and psychological state as they pertained to her seven years of marriage. She smiled and almost laughed. "It's that Memory Lake," she muttered. Every time she sat on that bench, she felt pushed toward self-examination of a kind she had never engaged in before. She refused to believe she would have had such promptings if she were anywhere else than right here just outside of Minneapolis—no matter how far away she was from her husband. At least she hadn't brought to her basement apartment the flowers Peter sent. She had given Jenny permission to dispose of them as she saw fit. But even here in Minnesota, Livy couldn't physically place them in the trash herself. The note she could, but not the flowers.

She checked the menu on her cell phone. There were four numbers she could call to locate Peter—their residence in Virginia, his cell, his House office, and another number at the Capitol at which he could be reached. Livy scrolled to the Capitol number and deleted it. She immediately felt charged by a sense of triumph. It was absolutely silly, but she couldn't help her reaction. This the smallest of gestures—far less significant than her packing her things and leaving for Minnesota, but still an important one, for Peter expected her stay with Jenny to be brief and not at all the beginning of a lasting separation or a divorce.

But this elimination of a single phone number was something she had done just for herself without telling him. That was it. A refreshingly satisfying gesture of assertiveness.

Livy scrolled next to the number of their Virginia residence. Many of her clothes and personal possessions remained there and would have to be collected when she and Peter agreed on a permanent breech. She hated the thought of having to go back and pack up all these items. Much of it she could simply leave behind, for her husband to keep, donate, or trash. As for the rest of it, Jenny had volunteered to fly to Washington by herself, rent a car or small van, and haul all of Livy's stuff back to Minnesota.

Still on the bed in her lotus position, Livy decided she wouldn't go back to Virginia to inventory her remaining possessions. She'd just provide a list of what she wanted shipped back to her and hire someone to do the work. But then what would Peter say or do to prevent that from happening? Discouraged by the image of Peter standing at the door refusing to allow anyone to move his wife's belongings, Livy got off the bed and headed for the bathroom and a shower before calling it a night. She no sooner felt the hot water spatter against her body, than she turned off the water, jerked the towel from the rack, made an attempt to dry herself, and walked back to the bed where the phone still lay. She quickly got to her menu, scrolled down to her and Peter's home number, and pressed delete.

Once more emboldened, she stared at the phone as if it were an opponent she was about to hammer into submission. She was therefore totally unprepared for the jolt of surprise she received when it lit up and played the Mozart ring tone.

"I hope I didn't wake you, Livy."

"You didn't."

"I'll be quick, because I want you to get your beauty rest before I see you."

Livy didn't need to be told what was coming next.

"I have all the flight information, which I'll send in just a minute by text—so you don't have to search for a pen and paper. But let me just say now that I'm flying out on Delta at 11:50 a.m. and will arrive at 1:35 your time there. I then catch the flight to California at 4:10. So that gives us well over an hour together before I have to go back through security. I understand that Jenny will have to drive you to the airport, but can you work something out with her so we can be alone? Just suggest that she do a little airport shopping or something. Okay? Livy?"

"What?"

"Did you get all that?"

She closed her eyes, as she always did whenever she was about to lie to her husband. "Yes, but I'm not sure I can make it, Peter." She wished she could just leave it at that, but she couldn't. "Jenny's made some plans for the entire afternoon."

For fifteen seconds, she heard nothing but the sound of his breathing on the other end. Finally he cleared his throat. "I'll send you the flight information now by text. Explain to Jenny that it's important for you to be at the airport. She'll understand. Oh, wait. I'm just wondering. Did you get my flowers?"

.   .   .

"Look, I just don't think I'm going to do myself any good by going on the air to explain why I kept Vanderkellen's admission to myself."

"Nick, I don't mean to push you on this, but you can't simply remain silent and take the consequences lying down." Hugh Martin, who also doubled as Nick's agent, was having a difficult time maintaining patience with his client. Fortunately, they were speaking on cell phones and Nick couldn't see the frustration on his lawyer's face. "Nick, promise me you'll give this some further thought. We've still got two days. ESPN's offering you on-air time to rebut."

"Rebut what? What Vanderkellen says is true. He told me; I checked out his story; and I sat on it."

"All right, then you're being offered on-air time to *explain* why you chose to sit on it. I think we can arrange things so you can appear on the air while Vanderkellen is being interviewed and confront him about whatever else he alleges regarding your responsibility for his subsequent arrest."

"Hugh, if some want to make that cause-effect connection, then there isn't much I can say to change their minds, is there?"

The lawyer hesitated before playing his final card. "Nick, you have to think about the Hall of Fame."

Nick's fingers tightened around the short glass of bourbon—his third since leaving the bench by Memory Lake. The Hall of Fame. He was presently a member of the Baseball Writers' Association of America, an organization committed to enhancing and protecting the relationship between the press and Major League Baseball. The BBWAA had the honor of electing retired players into the National Baseball Hall of Fame, as well as voting on the annual awards, such as Most Valuable Player, Rookie of the Year, and the Cy Young, which was given to the year's outstanding pitcher. Soon after he passed the ten-year threshold as a member of the BBWAA, Nick became eligible to vote on these honors and twice had the pleasure of voting for his friend Davis Montgomery and seeing him presented the Cy Young Award.

That Nick had stopped covering the Twins on a daily basis wasn't held against him by the national media or the BBWAA because he broadened his focus to cover all of Major League Baseball. And there were also his award-winning history of the Twins franchise and other highly respected books on baseball and college basketball. He genuinely felt honored to cast votes on each year's class of possible Hall of Fame inductees, but there was another Hall of Fame he now contemplated as his mind reeled from Hugh Martin's comment. Elected National Sportswriter of the Year on three occasions, Nick looked forward, perhaps when he was in his late fifties or sixties, to his election into the Hall of Fame of the National Association of Sportscasters and Sportswriters. Because he was so well respected by his peers, he anticipated ultimately receiving the high honor. But now he faced the distinct prospect it would never happen.

"Nick, are you hearing me? You have too much to lose by remaining silent or stoic—or whatever the hell you're doing. Think about that, all right? Have a few drinks and get a good night's sleep. We'll talk again tomorrow."

Nick took another swallow and balanced the glass of bourbon back on the wide arm rest of his favorite living room chair. He couldn't get his body into a comfortable position, so he stood and did a tour of his den and surveyed the many framed photos, awards, and plaques hanging on the walls. Other than this tangible evidence of a highly successful career, Nick also had the satisfaction of knowing, in spite of his relative youth, that he was one of the most acclaimed and popular sports writers of his generation. He was equally welcomed by players and management, who found his journalism fair and respectful. He never added a cheap shot to his critiques of athletic performance or reached for a biting allusion, metaphor, or parallel to punctuate a point. He saved his sharp edges for the occasional and necessary scathing article directed at the worst of professional or collegiate sports—lingering racism and sexism, the abuse of young athletes, and management's periodic lack of concern for the average fan's financial situation. But would all the good will he had justifiably earned throughout his career make any difference once Paul Vanderkellen had his say?

Over the years, Lockhart received a number of job offers from other cities. He refused them all, choosing instead to remain in the state of his birth—as close as possible to where he grew up. Only once did he venture far from home and the experience had been utterly devastating. For over twenty years he fought off every urge to speak to someone about that experience, deciding that he deserved to live with the memory of what had happened—a form of penance he believed he could never satisfy. All that kept him afloat, he firmly believed, was a connection to his boyhood and to the place where he spent what he now saw as an idyllic period, which did little to prepare him for the most serious choice he ever made—the choice he made incorrectly—the choice that would without question haunt him for the rest of his life.

But his old house was gone, torn down and replaced by a much larger home nothing like the modest residence that made up his world—in his room, with his books, records, and baseball cards. Yet Memory Lake remained. Unchanging. Still serving as the silent keeper of his past.

.   .   .

Nick turned on the bed-side lamp and reached for the novel he had been plodding through whenever sleep wouldn't come. But this time he only got through a page and a half before he closed the book. He checked the time. 2:50 a.m. It was clear to him that he'd have to make a decision of some kind before he'd be able to close his eyes and drift off. He got out of bed and pondered his options. Regarding the matter of an on-air response to Vanderkellen's assertions and accusations, Nick resorted to long habit and imagined how he'd feel if he did respond and then how he'd feel if he remained silent. Should he simply offer a public statement and nothing more? But what could he say? "I chose not to reveal Mr. Vanderkellen's admissions to me because I didn't wish to embarrass him"? Or "...because I didn't wish to destroy whatever chance he had at a career in pro football"? Or "...because I felt the whole matter too sordid to share with my readers"? Nick understood he'd then be expected to answer the obvious follow-up: "But, Mr. Lockhart, didn't you sense that Vanderkellen was in essence asking for your help? And if so, why didn't you help him? You could have written the story sympathetically and even called on others to assist the young man." No, the only way he could answer any of these questions was to explain the true reason why he chose not to reveal Paul Vanderkellen's admission. But to do so would cost him dearly. Too dearly. It was impossible.

Nick slipped on a sweatshirt and headed into the other room. He pulled a clean glass from the cabinet and unscrewed the top of the bourbon bottle. He barely poured a finger's worth before he decided he really didn't want another drink. If he could just talk to someone he trusted and who would understand, he could at least relieve some of the mounting pressure he'd been experiencing, especially during the past week. If he didn't seek an outlet, he couldn't be sure how he'd get through the next several days.

If it were any other subject than this, he believed he could talk to both Jenny and Davis Montgomery. They were genuinely close friends; he trusted them; and they would support him vigorously. But given the admission he'd have to make, the Montgomerys wouldn't be able to feel the empathy he believed was necessary if he were to entrust them with such a revelation. Sympathy, yes. But not true empathy. Nick long ago ruled out going to a professional. He guessed that part of his rationale for not making an appointment might have been some archaic sense of the stigma for talking with a "shrink," but it had to be more than that. For all the advantages he or she could bring to bear, a professional couldn't provide that empathy Lockhart believed he needed from a confidant.

But Livy Garner was in an unpleasant situation herself. She had apparently made mistakes—at least in having married a man she no longer loved and must have wondered how she ever could have loved. More than that, Nick just saw something in her—or felt something about her—that made him believe she would hear him out and understand. She possessed such gentleness, and he couldn't fathom how she could ever be petty. She would hear what he revealed and keep it to herself, honoring the trust he had placed in her—regardless of how briefly he had known her. He had no choice but to trust his instincts—that is, if he truly wished to speak about his past and the real reason why he remained silent about Paul Vanderkellen. Nick left the small amount of bourbon in the glass and headed back to bed.

Chapter 20

"I'm glad you slept in, Livy. I'm afraid I've set too fast of a pace for someone as delicate as you. We've been on the go ever since you arrived. Perhaps we'll just stay here all day. I'll have the caterer deliver all the food, and tonight we'll be entertained by Minneapolis's finest male strippers. We'll go down to the bench with our drinks and line the boys right up along the edge of Memory Lake. How's that sound?"

Livy couldn't be sure her friend was being facetious. "I like the going 'down to the bench with our drinks' part, Jenny. But I'm not quite ready for male strippers, I'm afraid.

"Okay, we'll wait until summer. Besides, they'll look all the more impressive in July, with their hot bodies glistening with perspiration."

"It doesn't get that hot in Minnesota, does it?"

"Another myth about my beloved adopted state. Did you know that in 1988 it reached 105 degrees at the end of July?"

"You're kidding."

"Look it up. And in the 1930s it reached 108, which, I'll have you know, is hotter than the hottest day ever recorded in sunny Florida."

"Really? I just thought that with rare exceptions the summer highs up here were constantly in the mid-70s."

"I wish. We have our share of days in the 90s in the summer, and I have the sweat soaked panties to prove it."

"Jenny, don't be vulgar."

"Of course we do have a temperature swing of over one hundred degrees in the winter."

"Can't wait."

Livy stared at Jenny, who smiled broadly. Both women thought the same thing—that Livy would indeed be living in Minneapolis when the snows came.

Livy poured them both a cup of coffee. "Any other fascinating facts about Minneapolis or Minnesota that I should know?"

Jenny took the milk from the refrigerator. "Well, since you asked. Did you know that Minneapolis has been determined to be the most literate city in America and that Minneapolis has the most live theater seats per capita than any other city in the country—with the exception of New York?"

"I didn't know either of those facts." Livy was delighted by Jenny's playful boasting about her adopted home town.

"And the first shopping mall ever built in this country is right here—the Southdale Mall—is a little south of the city."

"That I think I knew."

As Jenny regaled her with further facts about Minneapolis, Livy looked at the kitchen clock. 9:45 a.m. She reasoned she had two hours—perhaps a little more—to make her decision about whether to go to the airport and meet Peter or to stay where she was and by her absence let him know she wasn't pleased by his assumption that she would be there. Finally, Jenny finished dispensing information about Minneapolis and announced she was going to get cleaned up.

Livy refilled her cup. "I'll take my coffee down to Memory Lake then."

"I'll join you as soon as I'm presentable. It's five degrees warmer this morning than it was yesterday morning, so you might not need a comforter."

"I'll just slip on one of your sweatshirts and take my chances."

"That's the spirit, little lady."

Livy opened the back door and headed to the bench, feeling confident she'd make the right decision down there. Appreciating that the breeze was whispering more than speaking this morning, she sipped her coffee and thought the taste, enhanced by some ground cinnamon, was far superior to anything she ever brewed at home. Peter liked his coffee strong, whereas she preferred it "wimpy," as she and Jenny called it when they long ago settled on an acceptable blend that satisfied them both. Evidently, Jenny continued brewing her coffee the same way ever since—perhaps convincing Davis that the spoon didn't need "to stand up in the black muck," as she used to say it. Or did Jenny remember how her best friend preferred it and adjust the measurement just for her? It would be just like Jenny to make such a thoughtful gesture.

Seven years earlier Jenny had serious reservations about her friend's decision to marry Peter Garner, and Livy's defensive reaction caused a breech in their relationship—of about three days. But Livy couldn't bear harboring her disappointment over Jenny's lack of enthusiasm for Peter, and she decided to face the matter head on and come to a resolution. She invited Jenny to join her for a visit to the Japanese Tea Garden in San Francisco, which neither had ever gotten around to seeing. At first Jenny balked; she was still upset by Livy's apparent decision to end the friendship, when in fact all Livy had done was slam the phone down in response to Jenny's recommendation that Livy wait at least a year before marrying Peter. But Jenny too hoped for a reconciliation and agreed to meet.

Livy recalled that when they had mounted to the top of the distinctive curvaceous bridge in the garden, Jenny turned to her and offered a heart-felt promise that she would never bring up the matter again unless Livy wished to and would never again be on the other side when it came to anything her best friend decided to do. Gratified by Jenny's expression of friendship, Livy was able to share with her several of her concerns about Peter Garner's less than admirable quirks and habits. Jenny listened without interrupting and simply told Livy to remain who she was, regardless of any difficulties she might face.

How ironic then that Livy soon came to solicit Jenny's perspective on Peter and how he treated his wife. At first, Jenny reminded her friend of the promise made at the Japanese Tea Garden and refused to comment, even though Livy assured her she would no longer mind Jenny's frank assessment. But during the third year of her marriage, Livy broke down on the phone and said that she now truly *required* Jenny's perspective. That was all her friend needed. From that point on, Jenny lamented over, advised, and at times lectured Livy regarding her marriage to Peter. Livy purged so much of her frustration and hurt through her conversations with Jenny—either in person or in more recent years mainly by phone. It wasn't that Jenny's advice or commiserations led to any specific action on Livy's part. But Livy came to depend on these frequent "sessions" with Jenny, and without her friend's aggressive advice on how to make an initial break from Peter—namely, by coming to Minnesota to work on her Master's—

Livy believed she might not have taken any action, at least not for some time.

Listening to the soft sound of Memory Lake cavorting with the edge of the shore, Livy pressed the still warm coffee mug against her face. Thank God she had a confidant. Perhaps one day she could flip the dynamic and be the one offering sage counsel—or at least a sympathetic ear—the way she did when Jenny expressed concern about leaving her home and Memory Lake. Yet, she couldn't imagine the person needing frequent sage counsel being the indomitable Jenny Montgomery. At least not the Jenny of recent years.

Livy heard laughter across the lake to her left. Two women stood in the spacious backyard of one of the houses, apparently tickled by something they had seen or remembered. The laughter triggered Livy's memory of a similar moment ten months earlier when she was still living in California—the very night before she called Jenny and told her she had to separate from Peter—the night before Jenny insisted she come to Minneapolis.

Attending a late June wedding shower for one of her friends, Livy left the festivities and went into another room to watch her husband address a Veteran's group—as part of his campaign for the House seat. She had promised him she would watch and knew he would ask her pointed questions about his speech just to be sure she had seen it. Had her father been alive, he would have probably been there to hear Peter's speech in person, bragging that his son-in-law had served in the military. Livy sincerely respected her father's view of military service, and she decided to honor that respect by choosing the thesis project she did.

But during his talk to the Veteran's group, Peter Garner ruined the one virtue for which she still admired and respected him. In the summer of 1999, when he was twenty, Garner joined the Army Reserve. As he later told his wife, he felt he needed a service record to help him if he pursued a political career. Besides, his first two years at Cal Berkeley weren't distinguished, and he thought a break might help him concentrate on his studies when he returned to the classroom after undergoing basic training. He also told Livy that during the Iraq War, his reserve unit was supposed to be called up—which might then have taken him to the Middle East. But his unit was never called to active duty and Garner remained in California, finished his degree work at Berkeley, and embarked on his political career.

Livy stood alone in the room watching her husband walk to the microphone to address the Veteran's association, as someone off camera concluded his introduction of Peter as "a proud veteran of Operation Iraqi Freedom," the familiar euphemism for the war that began in 2003. Garner stepped to the microphone and nodded at the warm applause. Livy felt embarrassed for him, but she was sure he would correct the false impression that he had served in the conflict. But her husband did nothing of the sort. Instead he awkwardly ad-libbed his opening comment, "I don't believe General Schwarzkopf could have introduced me any better than that." Even Libby knew the late Norman Schwarzkopf had nothing to do with the Iraq War but was the commander during the brief Persian Gulf War over ten years earlier and retired soon after.

Livy turned off the television and went outside to the backyard to regain her composure before rejoining the other women at the wedding shower. As she stood outside, she heard two women laughing at the back door. Livy couldn't help thinking they were laughing at her for giving Peter credit for the one virtue she believed he still possessed. Peter failed to clarify the matter during the rest of the speech and when a member of the press finally brought it up three months later, Peter made a lame attempt to attribute the misconception to having believed the introducer had said, "an Iraqi War-*era* veteran." But by that time, Livy had told him that she'd be going to Minneapolis.

Livy took another sip of coffee and imagined attending a backyard party in the coming summer months. She would enjoy meeting Jenny and Davis's friends and looked forward to new discussions about new topics, instead of the same tired political themes that made up the bulk of the conversation to which she was exposed. It was enough that Peter used her as a sounding board, knowing she wouldn't contradict him. It's not that she agreed with everything he said; rather, she chose to remain silent, nodding every thirty seconds or so to give him the impression she was listening carefully and agreeing. Jenny would gladly battle over every sentiment she didn't concur with, but not Livy. She hated the physical feeling of agitation—the humming numbness that coursed throughout her body on those rare occasions when she had to do battle—with surly salespersons, pestering phone callers, and even more rarely her husband. And even though she was presently removed from these aggravations, she knew she would continue to feel the physical effects of such anxieties until the matter of her marriage was fully resolved.

Livy finished her coffee and for some reason felt compelled to wash out the mug with the water from Memory Lake. Without hesitation, she complied with the urge. As she knelt at the shore line and submerged the mug, she took pleasure in feeling the cold water cover her hands and wrists. She anticipated that come summer she would swim out and submerge her entire body under the surface of the lake. But was the image intoxicating only because it represented escape—hiding under the surface of Memory Lake—away from the unpleasant realities awaiting her on shore? Or might the image instead signify a baptism or rebirth? As she twirled the water with her fingers inside the mug, Livy whispered the two words "baptism" and "rebirth." For all the comfort these words implied, she also recalled the familiar phrase "baptism of fire" and the fact that a rebirth can only come after a death.

"Don't drown yourself, Livy. It's not worth it."

Jenny was back, freshly scrubbed, running a thick comb through her wet blonde hair.

"I'm just washing out my coffee mug."

"Really? Did you also park your covered wagon around front? Be careful. The Dakota Sioux are still pissed about the crappy land deal we made with them and are seeking the scalps of pretty dark haired California frontier women as proper compensation for their pain and suffering. I have a dishwasher, remember? You loaded it last night."

Livy was amused by Jenny's reaction but still embarrassed by her impulse to dip the coffee mug in Memory Lake. "Don't ask me why I did that."

"Do you know what kinds of things I've seen floating by while sitting on this bench?"

"Not sure I want to know."

"Dead things, Livy."

"Frogs, I hope."

"No. Corpses. Human corpses."

"I'm not listening to this."

"An entire family—the Egberts—all mutilated, with their skulls split open by a chain saw."

"I bet you're a riot to be around at Halloween."

"You'll find out in less than six months." Jenny walked menacingly up to Livy, contorting her face into her best approximation of a blonde, wet-headed zombie.

"Think I'll be here for Halloween?"

Jenny returned to the land of the living. She smiled supportively. "Why not? You'll still be working on your Master's—and even if you want your own place by then—but you better not—you're definitely coming to my annual Halloween bash. I'll alter my old Cher costume and you can wear that."

"I want to be there, Jenny. I really, really want to be there."

"Come on, sit back down with me and tell Aunt Jenny what's on your mind."

Livy finally told her about Peter's late night phone call and his assumption that his wife would meet him at the airport. Jenny sucked in both her upper and lower lips—the familiar gesture when she knew she shouldn't say what first came to mind.

"All right, Livy. What do you think you want to do?"

"I'm not sure."

"Okay. Have you thought about it from both sides—how you'd feel if you meet him and how you'd feel if you didn't."

"Yes—and in both cases, I'd feel terrible."

"Why?" Jenny was confident that Livy wanted her to pose direct questions more than offer sympathetic nodding and embracing.

"If I go, I'd feel that he won. He insulted me by assuming I would show up. And you'll love this. He said I should convince you to go shopping so he and I could talk alone."

"Did he now?"

Not so oddly, Livy thought of Mauna Loa, watching Jenny maintaining her composure. "Jenny, if I don't go, I'll feel somewhat petty and immature. And that won't stop him from calling me again— or worse, driving to your house and insisting we talk."

Jenny smiled. "Let him. Davis bought me a new shotgun for Christmas and I'm dying to give it a test run. Well, it sounds to me as though you're leaning toward meeting him at the airport."

"Does it? I can't stand the thought of going, Jenny. But..."

"But you feel you must—or that you have to—or that you ought to?"

Livy understood the subtle distinctions among the three possibilities. The first meant she needed to if she wished to open wider the breech between them; the second that she still felt under Peter's control; and the third that she would concede to her kind nature and go because she didn't wish to hurt him by not going.

"Jenny, it would be that I *must*."

"I understand. But knowing Peter, if he sensed you wanted to push on toward divorce, he'd change the subject and you'd find yourself in an airport listening to his latest take on the political scene. Didn't you say he always falls back on politics whenever the conversation begins to get away from him?"

"Yes, always. I know you're right, Jenny. He'll just ignore any attempt of mine to talk honestly about our marriage and my need to get out of it."

"Can't you make the same attempt on the phone? Call him when he gets off the plane. That way, if he refuses to acknowledge the problem, at least you didn't lower yourself by meeting him face to face."

"I still have half an hour before I need to make up my mind. I'm trusting that Memory Lake will provide me with the right answer."

"Don't laugh, Livy. This old lake has assisted me more times than I care to remember. Do you want me to leave you alone while you and Memory Lake do your thing?"

"No, stay here with me. I want to talk to you about something I've kept from you for a couple of months."

"Jesus on my knees, don't tell me you're pregnant."

Livy thought the look of horror on her friend's face trumped the zombie-like countenance a few minutes earlier, because this visage sprung up involuntarily.

"Uh, no. You know Peter's and my agreement. No children until he got firmly established in his career. I just didn't realize that 'firmly' meant a seat in the United States Congress." Livy sported a painfully twisted countenance. "I'm afraid he'll want to talk to me about starting a family. Nothing looks better on a campaign poster than a candidate, his adoring wife, and three lively children."

"Whether they're his or not—I know. Well, that's another reason why you shouldn't meet him at the airport. I wouldn't want my best friend attempting to conceive a child on a baggage carousel."

"Jenny."

"I know—completely insensitive—but funny, you'll have to admit." Jenny grabbed for her friend's hand. "Let's get back to what you've been keeping from me for a couple of months. It's not something to do with your health—please tell me it's not."

"No, I'm as healthy as a bull."

Jenny grinned in grand mischievous style. "Then it can only be that you have a lover lurking in the halls of Congress, and he's about to enter his conquest of you into the Congressional Record—correct?" Livy merely stared at her. "Wait—it's not a he, then? Oh, Livy, you naughty girl. Don't tell me she's one of the female senators." Livy's eyes dropped. "Damn it, Livy, you're scaring me. Are you telling me I'm right?"

"It's not a female."

"Then who is he? Does Peter know?"

"No, I'm sure he doesn't—although I think he almost wanted it to happen."

"What?"

Livy couldn't hold it any longer. "I'm sorry, Jenny. I couldn't resist. You really believe I've had an affair?"

"Well, what else could I think, you little unpredictable hussy?"

"Actually, you're partly right, but it wasn't an affair."

"Boob fondling then?"

"Wrong part of my anatomy."

"You mean your feet?"

"No."

"The sweet spot?"

"You're being vulgar again. But no, not there."

"Ah, you mean the thing you sit on. Is that non-vulgar enough for you?"

"Yes and yes, but only half-right."

"Come again?"

Livy enjoyed these rare moments when Jenny Montgomery was completely stumped. "Jenny, you still seem to think it was consensual on my part. I can assure you it wasn't."

"Okay, okay. I'm getting it now. So, who was the creep, and why did you say that Peter almost wanted it to happen?"

Livy informed Jenny of her initial meeting and subsequent chess matches with Congressman Evan Donnelly.

"How many times did you go to his office, Livy?"

"Just twice. You know me. I went with my first impression of him, which was all positive. He was charming and witty and he didn't seem at all concerned about his inability to beat me in chess. I enjoyed talking with him."

"But he wanted to put his money where his mouth was—am I right?"

"But when I went to his office for that second time, for the purpose of teaching him a few advanced moves—*chess* moves, Jenny—he stood up, after we were done, to escort me out and he began helping me on with my coat. He then brushed what he said was some lint from my back and let his hand stray below the waistline, where he began to brush off some more 'lint.'"

"And the length of your coat was lower than your tushy, so he could claim that he was simply playing housecleaner and had unfortunately lost his sense of geography. Yes, yes. I can visualize it plainly. So, he was just like the old 'itchy-spine-scratcher' you told me about earlier."

"But Congressman Donnelly didn't keep his hand there, Jenny. Perhaps he wanted to gauge my reaction."

"Which was?"

"Nothing, really. I guess I was waiting to see if he would apologize for touching me there."

"So, come on. You answered 'yes and yes, but only half right' to my question about where he touched you, so I'm guessing he moved his hand elsewhere on your body, but not to your breasts, feet, or pudenda."

"I appreciate the clinical terms this time. No—to none of those three places."

"Then...where?"

"He then said there was lint and specks all over my coat, and before I knew it, he had taken it back off me and asked one of his staff to brush it completely clean."

"Well, that was sure nice of him." Jenny's expression came complete with the rolling of her eyes and a sour-lipped sigh to suggest her disapproval of the congressman's supposed gesture of chivalry.

"Then he asked me to sit on a leather two-seater sofa in his office."

"Which you refused to do, right?"

"Well..."

"Okay, you sat down and told him off, right?"

"Not exactly." Livy's memory of Donnelly's words was still distinct. "He said, 'Livy, I have to admit I'm quite surprised your husband seems not to appreciate you the way you deserve to be appreciated.'"

"Oh, boy." Jenny was certain of what was coming next.

"He then dropped his left hand to his leg, and..."

"Your leg, you mean, right?"

"No, Jenny, his leg. He told me what it was about me that was attractive to him, adding 'And I'm sure I'm not the only one who thinks so.'"

"Did he mention body parts in his catalog of your attractive qualities?"

"Just one—my 'incredible eyes,' to quote him exactly. The rest of the catalog consisted of inanimate virtues he believed I possessed."

"Well, he was right, you know. You do possess them, and Peter has never appreciated...never mind. Go ahead."

"Then he put his hand on my leg."

"The sofa leg, you mean—or your leg?"

"Stop it. *My* leg. Right above the knee. He told me he wanted to see me—asked if I could get away for a weekend with him. Let me know he would treat me the way I deserved to be treated. And..."

"And...?"

"That he wanted to adore me and give me pleasure."

"And how hard did you slap him? Hey, do you remember the time I punched out the cable guy?"

"I vaguely recall it. But no, I didn't slap him. In fact, I didn't even remove his hand—at first."

"What? But you told him to remove it, right?"

"Again, not at first. I think it was because I was wearing pants. Had I been wearing a skirt, I'm sure I would have jumped up and said something."

"That's my Livy. Why slap, when you can jump up?"

"It just took me a few moments to realize his hand shouldn't have been there."

Jenny shook her head. "You probably let his hand remain there for those few moments because you really appreciated what he said about you."

"Maybe. Wait. No. It was inappropriate for him to say what he said—let alone put his hand on my leg." Livy was startled by her response. She realized she said it without a hint of indignation over what Donnelly said to her.

"So did you attack him—verbally, I mean?"

"No, I just stood up and told him I shouldn't come back to his office anymore."

"Did you turn him in?"

"No."

"Tell Peter?"

"No. I only let the congressman get out a quick "I'm sorry, I didn't mean to offend you" before I let his office. He seemed more crushed by my reaction than regretful he had touched me and told me how he felt. He avoided me the several times I saw him after that day. I really think I hurt his feelings. I even left my coat, but it was returned to me later that day."

"Lint free, I hope. Sorry. So you never told Peter?"

"I had already set the date for driving to Minnesota and I didn't want anything to interfere with that. I didn't want to hear Peter tell me either that I shouldn't have so reacted to Donnelly's 'innocent' touching of my leg or that I needed to see Donnelly again and assure him that I was no longer angry. Even if Peter reacted like a normal man and confronted Donnelly, it would still cause *me* problems, don't you see? I wanted nothing to jeopardize my leaving Washington and getting away from Peter."

"Okay, I understand. As for your congressman friend, how old did you say he was?"

"I think late fifties."

"There it is. Every man has to make one final and feeble effort to grope a younger woman before he reaches the big 6-0. Part of the right of passage. That and an enlarged prostate."

After a quick chuckle, Livy turned her head back toward Memory Lake. She closed her eyes and took in a deep breath.

"Jenny?"

"Yes, precious?"

"I've made up my mind."

Chapter 21

Lockhart unwrapped his sandwich as he pondered the thirty-two foot mound in Gold Medal Park. He returned to the place where he and Paul Vanderkellen earlier met. Nick once read that men and women often return to the "scene of the crime" not only better to understand what had happened but also as a symbolic pilgrimage of penance. Or was it that he held some absurd belief that he could relive what had happened and make another choice?

But what would he have done differently if he could begin that day over again? Would he have cut Vanderkellen off when the young man began his confession? Should he have made very clear to Vanderkellen he wasn't going to use that information? How ironic that he was in this professional mess not for something controversial he wrote but for the controversy that was about to explode publicly for what he didn't write.

Quickly finishing his sandwich and soft drink, Lockhart felt utterly disheartened by the prospect of leaving Minneapolis for another job—likely in a much smaller market, since he'd surely be damaged goods after the televised interview with Vanderkellen tomorrow night. Nick headed up the spiral walkway to the top of the mound inspired by the many Dakota Indian burial mounds throughout Minnesota. Since its opening a few years earlier, Gold Medal Park had become one of Nick's favorite in-city destinations, especially since it was so close to the notable Guthrie Theatre, where he had attended many classical stage productions. Part of the constant teasing he endured by his colleagues was prompted by the number of allusions and quotations in his columns taken from the likes of Plato to Tennessee Williams.

Lockhart reached the summit of the mound and contemplated the city that had been his home his entire life. The Mississippi River, not far from where he stood, served now as a metaphor for his likely having to leave the city. He imagined loading his possessions onto a raft and then pushing out, ending wherever the river might take him. Yes, he would deeply miss Gold Medal Park and the Mississippi and so many other places he loved to visit in the Twin Cities area. And the Montgomery's bench by Memory Lake might just be the place he'd miss the most.

As he headed back down the spiral walkway, Nick momentarily felt a flush of enthusiasm and something else he might at another time have called hope. He had made up his mind he'd soon be sitting on that bench and talking to Livy Garner. But his elevated mood quickly dissipated by the time he started out of the park. Once he began relating what had happened so long ago, she might well ask him to stop and limit his conversation to the subject of her proposed thesis— namely, how his military experience contributed to his professional success. As soon as he made that experience's connection to his impending failure, she could simply end their talk. If not, it was also possible she might listen but fail to understand. He had convinced himself that she would, but how often lately had he been wrong?

．　　　　　　．　　　　　　．

Jenny hoped Livy would understand. She found it impossible to remain at home as she promised and therefore got in the car and headed southeast, ending up at Washington Park, a stone's throw from the Minneapolis-St. Paul International Airport. Jenny felt better being close to where Livy was at present, although she was concerned about her friend's navigating her way through the huge Lindbergh terminal, which Livy had never before visited. As much as she hated the thought, Jenny hoped Peter would be right where he said he'd meet his estranged wife. Jenny didn't want Livy feeling any more lost and alone than she was certainly feeling now.

When Livy announced down on the bench that she made up her mind and would drive to the airport by herself, Jenny knew better than to insist she accompany Livy for support. When they were college apartment-mates, Jenny learned that on those rare occasions when Livy insisted on doing something in a certain way, there was no way she would budge, regardless of any sensible arguments to the contrary.

When they walked back up to the house, Jenny went over with Livy the online map to the airport and the use of the GPS in Davis's car, which Livy would be driving instead of her own. All Jenny could get from Livy was a promise that when the meeting with Peter concluded and she was on her way back to the parking area, she would call Jenny's cell.

But Jenny reasoned that if everything went wrong at the terminal, Livy would need her friend at her side as soon as possible. If it did and when she called, Jenny would therefore be only minutes away from joining her at the airport, even though she swore she'd be waiting at home for the call. As Livy got into Davis's car, Jenny tried to brighten the mood by reminding her to visit the terminal bathroom where a certain United States Senator was once arrested for lewd conduct.

Jenny now found herself walking around Washington Park with a large cup of Chai she purchased right off Cedar Avenue. She was so agitated thinking about Livy's decision to meet Peter that she feared her fingers would crush the nearly full paper cup and burn her hand and wrist with the hot tea. At least Livy's demeanor upon leaving didn't suggest she was passively conceding to the wishes or demands of her husband. If anything, Livy looked as though she was headed off to war—ready to fight valiantly for a cause she believed in. But would she hold up when the bullets started flying? Again, Jenny was glad she was nearby and ready to serve as the cavalry or a medical evac unit if Livy found herself in distress. But Jenny knew a large part of her agitation stemmed from flat-out jealousy. Livy was now all hers and she didn't want to lose her again to Peter Garner. Even if all went well and Livy dispatched her husband at the airport, she would still need her best friend to get her through all the difficulties that lay ahead.

And Jenny appreciated how much she owed Livy for helping her through her own painful period right before moving to Minnesota, when Davis was pitching for the Giants and when Jenny had her second miscarriage in four years. It seemed so long ago now—the bouts of tears and anger after the first one—and the lifeless acceptance of the second. Even the diagnosis of an "immune difference" between her and Davis left Jenny's spirits more vacant than devastated. But right before the end of Davis's last season with the Giants, depression finally replaced resignation—and Jenny took to consuming those "men's drinks" to get her through the self-blame and self-pity. She cut short her luxurious blonde hair, and refused to wear any of her skirts or dresses. But these reflections of her depressed state abated once she moved to Minneapolis and formed her bond with Memory Lake. She placed her miscarriages on a shelf she never wished to disturb again. As she recovered her spirits and personality—and the length of her hair—she decided she wouldn't attempt any further medical tests or treatments, and she knew why. She was frightened she would suffer a third miscarriage and lose all she had regained of herself upon the move to Minneapolis and to the house she adored. She and Davis agreed that adoption would be their course, although not until he stopped pitching.

And through all of the trying moments, Livy Garner was there. She allowed Jenny to express whatever she was feeling without offering criticism or platitudes. No, Jenny thought, there was no way Livy was going to pass through her own crisis without Jennifer Montgomery by her side.

Jenny took another sip of her Chai and watched a family of five admiring the landscape of the park, especially the tall evergreens that stood like sentries watching over all below. Jenny felt comfortable here, and the fingers clutching the cup of Chai relaxed. She felt more confident her friend was going to handle the meeting with Peter just fine. But there was no need to take any chances. Jenny took her phone out of her jacket pocket and checked to be sure it was powered up.

"Come on, Livy. Give me a call." Forty-five minutes later, Jenny's cell phone rang. But it took another fifteen seconds before she answered. First she had to find the phone in the Washington Park grass after it had leaped out of her hands.

"Livy?"

"I'm heading into the parking area. I told you I'd call."

"Well, how—?"

"Jenny, can you have a frozen margarita waiting for me when I get there?"

"Uh,...sure. Of course. Yes, you know I will. So tell me. What happened?"

"I don't want to talk about it on the phone. I'll tell you everything when we're sitting on the bench by Memory Lake with margaritas in our hands. See you in a little bit. Bye."

"Livy? Livy?"

Jenny dropped the cell phone in her jacket and headed out of Washington Park on a dead run. She had to beat Livy home and get a pitcher of frozen margaritas ready to pour. As she reached her car, Jenny thanked her stars she had run track in high school and was still in decent enough shape. The cool rush of air made her look up. Rain clouds. She devoutly hoped it wasn't an omen.

The rain had already begun before Lockhart pulled into the Montgomery driveway. He waited only another two minutes before putting his car in reverse. No need to go down to Memory Lake now. The weather report informed him that the shower was simply passing and the sun would return in about an hour or so. Soon after that, the bench would be again dry and perhaps then he'd be able to sit with Livy Garner and tell her everything.

Since he left Gold Medal Park, Nick entertained no doubts about his decision. If anything, he was even more anxious to share what he had experienced so many years ago. Still, why did it take so long for him to arrive at this place emotionally? Yet he couldn't imagine having told anyone any sooner than right now. Perhaps he was simply waiting for the right person to come along. Perhaps she had—finally.

His cell rang before he completely backed out of the driveway. It was his lawyer. Lockhart placed the car in park and turned off the ignition. "Yes, Hugh."

"Nick, are you anywhere near my office?"

"I can be there in twenty minutes—half an hour at most. What is it?"

"An interesting offer by Paul Vanderkellen. I just got off the phone with his rep. It's something we should discuss."

"Be honest with me. Is it really *worth* discussing, Hugh?"

"It is, Nick."

"All right, I'll be there as soon as I can." Nick assumed Vanderkellen wanted something from him—an admission of some kind—in exchange for holding back some of his criticism or accusations when he sat for his ESPN interview. Lockhart believed he'd judge the offer as unacceptable; still, he had little choice but to consider it. He turned the ignition back on as the rain pelted his windshield.

.　　.　　.

Livy gripped the steering wheel tightly, extending her forearms as if she were about to experience a head-on collision. She hated driving in the rain, and now she was in an unfamiliar car on an unfamiliar road. Even though she reminded herself that she had only to double back over the route she had taken to the airport—and that she had set the GPS for the Montgomery residence before she left her parking place—Livy still fretted she'd miss a landmark and would have to call Jenny to come get her. Dwelling on the rainy conditions and the trip back, she had suspended her concentration on what had just happened inside the Lindbergh Terminal.

When she arrived at the pre-designated meeting spot—Houlihan's Restaurant in the pre-security area—Peter was already seated. A cup of coffee had just been set at her place on the table and a bottle of imported beer at his. Livy was surprised he hadn't ordered her a cocktail. It would be like him to assume he would melt her resistance with alcohol. Instead, he likely wished to be on his best and most thoughtful behavior, a conclusion immediately confirmed by his gentlemanly greeting.

"Livy, please sit. I took the liberty of ordering you some coffee instead of a drink. I want you to be safe driving back to Jenny's."

She couldn't believe her first words to him. "Thank you, Peter. How was your flight?"

Given the placid flow of traffic traveling north on Cedar Avenue, Livy's forearms and fingers lost some of their rigidity, while at the same time her stomach tightened from the fresh memory of her meeting with Peter. How confident and reassured he seemed after she asked how his flight went.

"As you and I have often said, flying isn't the pleasure it used to be, but it went well. I was the only one seated in my row. I think it was a sign you should have been with me."

Livy felt like a fish contemplating an unappetizing piece of bait—which she now refused to take. Instead of responding, she merely twirled her coffee with a spoon.

Peter offered a half smile and continued. "I was of course so looking forward to seeing you when I landed. It's the next part of the trip that will be the most difficult. I really wish you were going with me."

Finally, she had to respond. "Peter, we went over this already."

"Come on, Livy. Call Jenny now and tell her you'll be gone for a couple of days. I've already checked. My flight to San Francisco isn't full. We can get you on it, but I should try and reserve the seat now. You can buy clothes and whatever else you need as soon as we land. I really want you with me."

Livy stared at her coffee. It still seemed to be moving from her vigorous stirring of a few seconds ago. Was it possible she at one time delighted in Peter Garner's spontaneity? Once during their brief engagement period, when she was suffering from an annoying cold, he slipped two airline tickets to Vancouver into her purse without her noticing and then waited patiently until she reached for a tissue. His sustained smile at her discovery had so charmed her that she actually took his hand and kissed it—not to mention that later in the night she thanked God for permitting Peter Garner to come into her life.

"Peter, I'm sorry, but I can't go with you." She now wondered why she didn't say, "but I *won't* go with you" or at least leave off the "I'm sorry." In any event, she was totally unprepared for his response.

"Livy, you used to be much more spontaneous."

There he sat nursing his beer, seemingly oblivious to the fact that their marriage was all but over—completely forgetful of everything his wife had said to him since the previous summer. Had he misconstrued the reason why she agreed to meet him? He acted as though she was merely reluctant to go because she had no luggage or because she would upset whatever plans Jenny Montgomery had made for them.

A minivan made a sudden swerve in front of Livy—squeezing into the space she had left between her and the car ahead of her. Once more her forearms tightened, and her fingers pressed more deeply into the steering wheel. She began trembling at the converging sources of agitation—the intruding minivan and the fresh memory of that cup of coffee in the Lindbergh Terminal.

Ignoring the matter of Livy's accompanying him to California, Peter launched into an account of his latest attempt at self-aggrandizement on Capitol Hill. At this point, Livy picked up the coffee and lifted it to her mouth. She kept the rim of the cup against her lips as if she were hiding behind it and avoiding the stare of the man she no longer loved and would never love again. She felt a rising contempt for every exuberant word he spoke regarding his burgeoning career. Presently, she loathed every one of the Washington images that marched through her mind. The army of grey and blue suits ornamented by their same blue and red ties. The flag lapel pins worn for the most past not out of true patriotic prompting but rather out of political necessity. The cacophonous clatter of heels as members of the media rushed forward with cameras and recording devices in the hope of chronicling the latest non-answer or empty platitude. The insincere smiles and greetings to those waving or expressing well wishes to the public. The smugness and opaqueness that seemed to go along with the job of working for the United States government. The daily assertions of what "the American people" want, believe, or will accept. The utter hypocrisy and mendacity. All at this moment embodied by the man sitting across from her with the bottle of imported beer lifted to his mouth. Or was it the other way around? Was everything she loathed about Washington simply a reflection of her husband? Had she never married him, would she have felt the same?

"Livy, when do your summer classes start?"

She was again unprepared for his apparent change of tact. "In about three weeks, why?"

"I promise I'll leave you completely alone after two weeks. I won't interfere with your getting started. You'll have orientation to go through, I suppose."

She knew what he was doing. It had become his habit in the past several years to push her beyond where she said she didn't wish to go—when it came to travel plans, large purchases, or social and political obligations. When she balked at giving him all he wanted in these areas, he would back off—offering a compromise as if he had never caused her grief or concern in his hammering arguments for what he initially desired from her. If he wanted her to fly with him to San Diego to meet some prominent state political operatives—and she resisted strongly enough—he would invite her to drive over to Santa Rosa or Yuba City for an event of less consequence. Just the previous year, Peter's fervent arguments for buying a luxury Audi couldn't change her view that the purchase of an automobile listing for over seventy-five thousand dollars wasn't at all prudent. He then started talking up a BMW he could get for just under fifty thousand—as if he had never made the passionate case for the Audi. He had to create an environment in which he appeared to win without compromise. And now he was attempting to do so again.

"I guarantee that you'll be back at Jenny's in plenty of time to begin the summer term without missing a day."

Livy put down her coffee cup. "Peter, what is it about my decision that you don't understand?"

She knew he'd ignore the direct question. He was always quite adept at that. His one-year flirtation with law school evidently had its influence. But once more he surprised her—to a point.

"Livy, I understand perfectly. Okay. I'll accept that I'm flying to Frisco by myself. But it's fine—it really is. This way you can go back, talk to Jenny, and get your bag packed."

She was almost as much curious now as she was disgusted. "My bag packed for what?"

"Well, I wanted to surprise you by telling you at the French Laundry, but since you're not going with me—"

"You made a reservation for us at the French Laundry?"

"I did. I know how much you loved going there on our fifth anniversary." And she had. Eating at such a superb restaurant was the one thing that made her feel in a celebratory mood on that occasion, because even then she knew she didn't want to spend the rest of her life as Peter Garner's wife. She heard so much about the French Laundry from Jenny and Davis, who had dined there at least a dozen times when they lived in the area. Livy never recalled approaching a dinner reservation with as much anticipation. And she wasn't disappointed. Everything she tasted was exquisite. But the next day, she painfully concluded that Peter took her only because he finally sensed his wife's disenchantment with him and their marriage. The reservation was just another of his many manipulative tricks. How could he possibly believe he could succeed with the same enticement now?

"But our going there tomorrow is no longer a possibility, so I'll have to tell you my surprise here." He checked his watch. "I'm going to address our party's other freshman House members when I get back to Washington. We'll be at the Willard Hotel, which is about as historical as it gets in the city. I know you love the place and I'd love having you there—sitting right next to me." Peter quickly finished his beer, keeping his eyes on his wife waiting for an answer or some positive reaction from her. Instead, Livy stared at his hands, which were now resting on the table. Her mouth was slightly open; her breath seemed suspended. His wedding ring was on his finger; hers was not. Had he noticed?

"Livy, you don't have to answer now, but it's going to mean a lot to my career, so if you don't want to come back to Washington for yourself, think about coming back for me."

She really expected him to add "or if not for me, then for your country." But instead he spoke of their going over to Mount Vernon and perhaps down to Monticello for further historical sight-seeing, assuring her once again he'd have her back to Minneapolis in plenty of time for her "first day of school." How like him, she thought, to employ such juvenile phrasing. The traffic continued its smooth pace, and her fingers and forearms again relaxed. But the tension in her stomach failed to ease. Why couldn't she get the words out before Peter stood up and dropped the money for the coffee and beer on the table? She still had time to speak before he cleared his throat and offered his quick farewell.

"I'm off, Livy. I'll call you tomorrow night and you can tell me if I can make the reservation for you to fly back to Washington with me. Then we can sit right back here, and I can buy you a real drink rather than coffee." He gave her a platonic peck on the cheek and headed back through security. Her body refused to cooperate, and she failed to intercept her husband and tell him why she wouldn't be joining him at the Willard.

Livy looked at the sky through the windshield. At least the rain had stopped. She wondered if it would start again before she made it back to Jenny's.

Chapter 22

Nick believed he couldn't make it if he waited to drive home or over to the Montgomery's. He was in need of a drink and quickly.

He stepped into the Pint Public House on 1ˢᵗ Ave. North, a short walk from Hugh Martin's office. The bar area of the pub was much to Nick's liking, with its dark wood tables and chairs and bar front and its walls covered with vintage photographs and HDTVs. He and Davis Montgomery liked to meet here in the afternoons during the off-season. Earlier in the year Jenny joined them with a recently-divorced "friend" she wanted Lockhart to meet. "No pressure," Jenny whispered to him when the woman excused herself for a visit to the ladies room. Much to Jenny's chagrin, Nick and thirty-seven year-old Natalie Wilcox didn't hit it off. But one thing Natalie said struck Nick as worthy of remembering. She observed that, with the rarest exceptions, human relationships came with a "shelf life"—marked in days, months, or years—but end they would. He had to admire Natalie for being true to her stated philosophy, although he found her too philosophically morose to ask out on a date.

Yet he didn't come into the Pint Public House today to reminisce or to second-guess past decisions about his empty love life. He just needed a stiff drink while pondering the offer made by Vanderkellen. According to Hugh Martin, the young man's representatives agreed to cancel the quarterback's planned criticism of Lockhart in exchange for Nick's public acceptance of responsibility—the exact wording to be "I should have done more to prevent Mr. Vanderkellen from taking the final steps that led to the charges brought against him." No further language would be required, although it was hoped Lockhart would also say that Vanderkellen's Gold Medal Park confession demonstrated Paul's contrition and hope of turning his life around. In addition, as Martin informed him, Vanderkellen's side would appreciate Lockhart's punctuating his remarks with a heart-felt regret over the intense pressures and temptations college and professional athletes face in the modern era. After all, hadn't Lockhart written passionately about that very topic in a number of his columns and in one of his books? Finally, Lockhart had also to agree to appear on camera or have his statement quoted *before* the formal interview with Vanderkellen commenced.

Lockhart ordered bourbon neat and appreciated the relatively sedate mid-afternoon atmosphere in the pub's bar area. He had heard that the place "really rocked" at night, when a far more youthful and exuberant crowd filled the establishment. He smiled and took another swallow of Jack Daniel's. Now he replayed his response to the offer as articulated earlier by his lawyer.

"Hugh, you know damn well what Vanderkellen and his reps are trying to pull, don't you?"

"Just think about this for a moment, Nick, okay?"

"If I do what they want and announce my complicity before Paul's interview airs, then he can present himself as the victim—the gifted athlete taken advantage of by the system."

"But that's true at least to a degree, Nick."

"Look, I've made the point in everything I've written on the subject that the responsibility rests foremost with the athlete who fouls up, even if others had a share of the blame."

"I know you have, Nick."

"But the way they want to do it, Vanderkellen's culpability would be considerably lessened, while that of others—including mine—would be considerably enlarged. Hell, I'd likely come off as the villain of the piece."

"Wait, they did add that you should make clear you kept everything quiet because you felt sorry for Vanderkellen and didn't want to ruin his career."

"But it doesn't matter that I've apparently ruined mine, does it?"

"I understand—I do. I'm not recommending you take the offer; I'm only telling you what it entails."

"Even if I give them what they want, I'd still look mainly responsible. Jesus Christ, Hugh. Vanderkellen wouldn't need to accuse me in the interview, for I would have already hanged myself by the time he spoke his first word."

"Nick, I can call them back now and reject the offer while you're sitting here. But I strongly advise you to take at least a few hours to think about it. They just want to know your answer by noon tomorrow. Again, they plan to run the interview with Vanderkellen— or your statement and the interview—at 10 p.m. And remember—the network would also run a response from you if you reject Vanderkellen's offer—live on camera or written—but in that case it would come *after* the interview with Vanderkellen. So please, take some time—sleep on it. There are several ways to go here."

Lockhart twirled the bourbon with his finger. He knew some prudence was in order given his level of frustration and anger, but he still couldn't help chastising himself for taking his attorney's advice to think about it. Why didn't he just insist that Hugh get right on the phone with Vanderkellen's representatives and flatly reject the offer?

Jenny bolted into the house from the garage as if Livy were just then turning into the driveway. All the way back from Washington Park, she feared her friend would somehow overtake her, and then she'd be forced to explain why she broke her promise to remain home while Livy met Peter at the airport.

Running into the living room, Jenny grabbed a magazine and placed it open on the arm of her favorite cushy chair. She returned to the kitchen and poured a little coffee into a mug, grabbed a coaster, rushed into the living room once more, placed both items on the table next to her chair, and headed for the mirror near the front door. Examining her face, she started rubbing her lips with the edge of her forefinger to remove some of the color, while her other hand messed a section her hair. It was at this point she realized she was unnecessarily and absurdly trying to make it look as though she hadn't left the house.

"You are one psycho chick," she cracked as she rearranged the mussed up section of her blonde mane. She grabbed the mug and coaster and closed the magazine before returning again to the kitchen, this time filling her mug with coffee. Why not head down to the bench by Memory Lake—which would make it look even more as though she'd never left? Suddenly, she had a frightening thought. Livy would of course pull Davis's car into the garage and might well brush up against Jenny's, feeling the heat from the automobile, and conclude, rightly, that her friend had lied to her. Jenny ran to where she had dumped her keys and pressed the automatic garage door button. She grimaced as she heard the door closing, praying Livy wouldn't just then be pulling into the driveway.

After waiting a moment to be sure all was well, Jenny took her mug of coffee and opened the back door. She looked up. The sun was trying to peek through the gathered clouds, but the residue of the earlier rain would still be on the bench. She stepped back in the kitchen and retrieved a large towel from under one of the cabinets. It had been used for the purpose of bench drying many times before.

When she stepped back outside, she heard the sound of two voices before her eyes focused on Memory Lake. The voices were both young and the female one was playfully resistant.

"I said stop it, Troy. Everyone can still see us. And the bench is wet! My jeans are getting soaked."

Jenny was half way to the bench by now.

"Come on, Haley, that's what makes it so dangerous and fun." Her "No!" was punctuated by a pleasurable giggle.

"Then we'll come back here later, when it gets dark."

"But they'll probably be back by then."

"Oh, I think even earlier than that, buster."

The young male—probably sixteen or seventeen—lifted his head as if he had heard the most unexpected sound in the world. But then, he did. It was Jenny's voice.

"What are you kids doing on this bench—on my property?"

The female—probably fifteen or sixteen—leaped up from the bench and started sputtering an apology sprinkled with a hopeless attempt at an explanation. The young man leaped up right after her and, of all things, tried to shield his girlfriend from what he assumed would be a violent attack by the tall blonde early thirtyish woman sporting the menacing scowl. But Haley jumped away from him, as if he she knew for certain that the tall blonde thirtyish woman with the menacing scowl was really only interested in assaulting her boyfriend.

Jenny saw that the three top buttons of the girl's long sleeved flannel shirt were unbuttoned, but at least all fasteners were properly secured on her jeans.

Noticing the canoe pulled partially up on the shore, Jenny concluded easily enough that the couple had set sail for the seat of love—formerly called simply "the bench." It was the only bench around Memory Lake, after all, and perhaps that was why it drew the attention of the young Tristan and Isolde, who were both thinking frantically about a plausible and innocent explanation for their trespassing. Normally, Jenny would have laughed uproariously—that is, after having frightened the young couple with images of disappointed parents and merciless juvenile judges—but at this moment she felt nothing but uncharacteristic indignation.

"Just get in your canoe and don't ever come over here again without my permission. Do you understand me?"

The simultaneous "Yes, ma'am's" were followed by Haley's "We're really sorry." By the time they pushed off the shore and Troy grabbed the single oar, Jenny had calmed down to indicate to Haley that she needed to fasten those three buttons on her shirt. Haley shouted a "Thank-you" as Troy began a furious paddling toward the other side. Jenny remained standing until she saw them pull the canoe ashore across the water. She didn't care enough to wonder if either or both of them lived in one of the other houses surrounding Memory Lake.

When the pair disappeared between two of the houses across the way, Jenny finally dried and sat on the bench. What the hell made her react like that? She sipped her now lukewarm coffee and sought an answer. In a few seconds it came. Her mouth dropped into an ugly frown as she thought of the day when one of the two young lovers making out on this bench would be a resident of the house that Jenny and Davis had sold right before or right after they moved to Boston— or to Baltimore—or to Atlanta—or to Cleveland—to wherever Davis might next pitch.

Last night she had the dream again—the one she'd been having every several nights since the first week of April, when it was clear that Davis hadn't fully gotten his arm back to previous form. In the dream, she found herself in a new house in a new state. Davis was also in the dream and he was in good spirits about the move. There were palm trees swaying and the weather was warm. Jenny was lamenting the loss of snow and cold weather. She walked through the new house finding peculiar defects—damp walls, vegetation growing through the carpet, palm tree branches through the glass windows. She wanted out of that house. She begged to go back to her *real* home in Minnesota. Davis ignored her pleas. And in each of these dreams she cried until she awakened.

Although she was wide awake now and sitting on her favorite piece of furniture in the entire world, Jenny thought it best do what she did at the end of these horrible dreams. Perhaps she'd get lucky and Livy wouldn't get back for another ten minutes or so. That would give Jenny enough time to purge her unhappiness and get her face back in order so that she could be ready to hear what had happened at the Lindbergh Terminal. But then Livy's face might be as much in emotional disrepair as Jenny's was about to be.

Chapter 23

Livy knew it had to happen. She made the wrong turn. The woman's dreamy British voice on the GPS didn't make enough of a distinction about exactly when she should "make the next left." Unfortunately, Livy turned left one road before the one she was supposed to turn on. Never comfortable using a GPS system, Livy turned it off when the now indignant British lady began raising her voice, telling Livy to stop and take another bloody left. Livy relied on her basic sense of direction to get her back on the road from which she had just turned off, but that sense of direction completely failed her and she started up an off ramp before realizing her mistake. A foolish belief she could circumnavigate her way back to the correct road forced her, ultimately, to do what Peter and the rest of his sex refused ever to be caught dead doing. She stopped at a poultry plant, went bravely into the main office, nearly gagged on the odor of condemned chickens, and with a false dash of the devil-may-care asked how to get to where she needed to be.

But now—finally—she was on Jenny's road and she couldn't help laughing. It was all simply perfect. Talking to thick-skulled Peter Garner was akin to the nearly-disastrous and circus-like lefts, rights, reverses, and sudden stops she just made with Davis Montgomery's car. It was flat-out absurd but oh so good. She'd rather Jenny see her cracking up when she walked into the house than with the hopeless expression she wore when she left the airport and began her journey back to the Montgomery's.

When she entered, Jenny was on the phone, daubing what appeared to be a tear from the corner of her right eye. What had happened? Was it Davis? Did something happen to a member of Jenny's family? Or had Peter called Jenny either to accuse her of coming between him and his wife or more likely to solicit her help in getting his wife to meet him at the airport with her bag packed when he flew back from California?

But then she saw Jenny smiling—so it couldn't have been Peter.

"Wait, Nick, she just came in. It's Nick Lockhart. Here." Jenny checked the corner of her right eye with the tip of her finger, as she strolled out of the room and into the kitchen.

"Hi, Nick."

"Livy, hope I didn't get you at a bad time."

"No, no. I was just out driving around—and getting lost." She felt warm and content hearing his voice

"That can happen, and you don't have to be a new resident of the area to find yourself heading down a wrong street."

Livy liked the sound of that phrase—"a new resident." "So what can I do for you, Nick?" She feared he was going to ask her to dinner or a movie. She would have to decline if he did. As much as she would love to be with him on a normal date, she knew her present situation wouldn't allow it.

"I've called to see if I can come over and let you interview me about my military service. For your thesis, I mean."

"Oh, well yes, of course. But are you sure that wouldn't be too much trouble for you?" She was thinking of the impending interview with Paul Vanderkellen and the effect all that was having on Lockhart's spirits.

"No, no trouble for me. None at all. How about for you?"

Livy knew she needed time to tell Jenny what happened at the airport, as well as for the two of them to make and eat dinner. "Nick, if you can give me, say, until 8:00 tonight, I'll be happy to interview you. It won't be *60 Minutes*, but I'll do my best." She winced at having used the world "interview," given the one ESPN would be having with Vanderkellen.

"Perfect. I'll be there at eight." He paused. "And I hate to ask this, but can we go down to the bench by Memory Lake—just the two of us? I'm not sure I'd feel comfortable revealing everything with Jenny there." He paused. "Oh, boy. That sounds so wrong. I can't be rude to Jenny."

Livy lowered her voice. "Nick, Jenny mentioned to me that tonight she has her monthly meeting with the charity organization she and

Davis have set up in Minneapolis. I told her she needs to go and that she doesn't have to bring me. I have a feeling that she'll stop insisting I go if she knows you're coming over to sit for...my questions."

"Sorry if I sound *un*charitable in my asking to talk about my experiences just with you."

"I understand, Nick. I really do."

Livy was surprised she didn't react with more caution to Nick's request to speak with her alone. But she was certain nothing would be attempted or implied that would make her feel uncomfortable. Was it mere rationalization of her part, she wondered? At this point it didn't matter. She wanted to share more time with just him, regardless of the limits she imposed on herself. More than that, she was struck by the sound of his voice as he made his request for privacy. He was going to tell her something important, she knew. And she sensed it was going to be something she wouldn't be able to use in her proposed Master's thesis.

"Livy, you remember that old expression, "Those were our salad days"? Jenny held up a massive clump of greens freshly speared on her fork.

"I think so. It means the time of our innocence and youth, I believe."

"Maybe, but for you and me, it mainly represents the number of cheap meals we had to eat when we were roommates during our years at Chico."

Livy smiled broadly. "I remember them well. Bacon salads, pasta salads, American cheese salads, chicken salads."

"And don't forget the occasional shrimp salads with that cheap bagged shrimp that we never could get to defrost thoroughly." Jenny dramatized the memory by clamping her jaws together and managing a sneer of disgust while doing so.

"Those meals were fun, Jenny" Livy looked at the pieces of the beautifully cooked filet mignon nestled invitingly among the romaine, arugula, radicchio, and baby bok choy in one of the attractive salad bowls she had given Jenny at the latter's wedding shower. "But this salad is heavenly. And the bread is great. I can't believe you have such good bread in Minnesota."

"Yes, the state finally allowed bread baking after the 2016 election. We need another election to permit cookies and cakes, but the lobbying effort is well underway."

This time Livy's smile only made it half way, whereas Jenny's turned immediately into a grimace.

"I had to mention the 2016 election, didn't I? Just crown me Empress of the *Faux Pas*."

"It's okay, Jenny. It's over and Peter won his seat. But it's now 2017 and I'm sitting here with you and not with Peter and his new political acquaintances in Washington."

Livy wondered if Jenny was thinking, "Right, but where will you be around the time of the 2018 election?" Peter would no doubt double or triple his efforts to have her at his side when he stood for a second term in the House.

"Livy, I have to say I'm very, very, proud of you for standing up to him at the airport."

"I wish I could say I won the day, but he wouldn't allow me any sense of victory. It's funny, but on the way back from the airport I recalled the line from *Hamlet* that said, 'When sorrows come, they come not single spies, but in battalions.' My father loved that quotation. Telling Peter "no" today was like defeating a single spy. I'm afraid he's yet to unleash his battalions."

"Just kill the bastards one at a time. He'll eventually run out of soldiers."

"Vigorously and graphically put."

"Thank you. I try."

Livy took another sip of her pinot noir. "As I told you, he's going to call tomorrow and ask for my decision about flying back to Washington with him for his big dinner."

"Livy, why not issue a blanket statement—I'll write it—that says something like "No need to call me again. I'm going to say no to anything you ask me—you stubborn ass-hole."

"I can't."

"Why not?"

"I have to face him—or actually hear his voice—every time he asks me something like that. If I don't, I'll feel like I'm hiding from him.

He'll only be more insistent if he senses I'm afraid."

"Livy, can I ask if Peter noticed you weren't wearing your rings? Or did you put them back on before you met him? Wait, wait. Sorry. I know you didn't."

"You're right. I didn't. And no, he never noticed or seemed to notice that my finger was bare. But then his pride probably wouldn't allow him to admit to me that he had noticed." Livy lifted the bottle of pinot noir. "You want more wine, Jenny?"

"I better not. I need to finish my steak salad,..."

"Which is indescribably delicious, by the way."

"Thank you....and get ready to head on out to the charity meeting. Sorry to leave you for a couple of hours, because I'd much rather be here chugging grape or drinking...the margaritas...that I forgot to make earlier, but..."

"No, no. You invited me to go with you, and anyway Nick Lockhart's coming over so I can interview him for my proposed thesis."

"You better not keep it to just interviewing."

"Jenny, how many times do I have to scold you for saying things like that? You of all people should know I'm nowhere near a place in my life where I'd feel free enough to do anything like what you're suggesting."

"And if you were?"

"Ask me then."

"Ha--I knew it. Look, I'm just having some unacceptable fun with you."

Livy offered a benign smile, suggesting she wasn't at all put off by her friend's teasing. But in a moment her look again turned serious.

"Jenny, how did you and Davis do it? I entered the relationship with Peter not ever imagining how so much can change in the space of only a few months. How so much can go so horribly wrong. You'd think that once you got through your late teens and early twenties that your perceptions would be set. You never imagine that you'd still have a lot of growing to do. I don't know—it just seems to me now that it's a miracle two compatible people can actually meet, let alone remain with each other happy or at least contented."

Jenny remained silent as her friend paused for another sip of wine.

She knew Livy usually needed to pause when she was speaking from the heart.

"Jenny, I've concluded that you and Davis have been blessed. Or rather that the two of you have won some kind of cosmic lottery and your reward was each other." Livy twirled her wine glass and watched the pinot noir circle and splash inside the glass. Now she was through. "Oh, just put a piece of duct tape over my mouth and throw me in the basement."

"Remind me to do that when Davis gets home. I love you, Livy."

"And I you—really and truly."

Chapter 24

"Thanks for carrying down the wood, Nick. Jenny insisted we make use of the fire pit by the bench. She didn't think hot coffee and tea would keep us warm enough."

"I think a fire will be nice." He had already carried down the kindling and several small pieces of oak. Now he was having a little difficulty securing the seven larger pieces of wood he was cradling in his arms. Livy wished to relieve him of one or two pieces but she was doing her best not to drop the coffee and tea in two separate thermoses, along with a small tray of almond and chocolate chip cookies.

"Jenny also insisted that the fire would complement the interview. What she meant by that—well, I'm still trying to figure that one out."

Livy's laugh made Nick feel even more justified in his decision to trust her with the most important admission he would ever make to another person.

As Nick lit several pages of the morning paper, he gave little thought to the connection between the immolation of the newspaper he worked for and the fate of his career with that publication.

Livy was impressed by how adept Lockhart was in starting the fire and placing the pieces of wood to assure an effective and an attractive blaze. Although she and Peter had a fireplace in their California home, she couldn't recall a single time when he used it. His reply when asked was usually along the lines of "Then I have to clean out the fireplace, and I haven't time for that."

"Nick, I hope the coffee's how you like it. Medium sweet, right?"

"Did Jenny tell you that?" Livy nodded. Nick chuckled. "It's a phrase from one of the early Bond movies. One night Davis, Jenny, and I sat down here and discussed the Bond phenomenon, sharing our favorite "Bond-isms." He then poured the coffee into the thermos lid.

"Yes, perfectly medium sweet."

"Nick, Jenny suggested we refrain from drinking anything stronger than coffee and tea until she gets back from her meeting. She didn't want either of us to get a head start on the 'good stuff.'"

"My guess is that she'd soon catch up."

"No doubt."

They both laughed, but their laughter subsided until their smiles sank in perfect synchronization.

Livy knew she couldn't, but her present desire was to cuddle with Nick and simply enjoy the fire. "So, Nick, I guess we should start now so we can finish before Jenny's return."

"I'm ready to begin."

But Livy thought his voice belied that assurance. She reasoned that he must be going through a really tough time on the eve of the ESPN interview with that young quarterback, who for some reason held a grudge against him. But she still had difficulty believing Lockhart's job—his career—could in any way be in jeopardy. She was tempted to ask if he'd rather not subject himself to her questions tonight, but reasoned that the exchange would at least take his mind off his present worries.

"Livy, here. You sit closer to the fire." He moved down to the left side of the bench. Livy placed the tray of cookies between them and they both kept a thermos propped up against their hips—his against his right, hers against her left, thereby creating a further barrier between them. Livy deftly shifted her thermos to her other hip.

"Well, here we go." Livy pulled a digital voice recorder from the pocket of her light jacket. The weather was cool enough to require the garment, although she assumed the warmth of the fire would soon make its wearing unnecessary. "Nick, I want you to know I won't record anything you'd rather keep just between us—meaning that I won't use it when I come to write my thesis. And please know I won't mention you by name at all, if that's your desire."

He smiled. "Quoting 'an anonymous but fairly well known sports writer from Minneapolis' probably won't do much to protect my identity."

"I see your point."

"You can use my name. Don't worry about it."

For a few moments they both gazed out at Memory Lake and listened to its unique sounds, enhanced by the snapping of the wood in the fire pit. The earlier rain had refreshed the air. It was as delightful an early evening as Livy could remember. It seemed almost a shame to bruise it with a series of questions about Nick Lockhart's military experience.

"Okay, Nick. As I think I said, I'm interested in how military service affected you. That is, how it influenced *positive* decisions you made and how it stayed with you as you began and then succeeded in your career. So, if it's all right with you, we'll just start with those general questions."

Lockhart took a very deep and long breath, which Livy found somewhat peculiar, as she did the expression of strained enthusiasm and delight that came across his face. Was he about to indulge in sarcasm, ending the interview with a blanket statement that his military experience didn't do a damn thing to help him once he left the Army?

"First of all, Livy, ever since leaving the service I have always made my bed—every single morning. And I'm not like a lot of men who leave the covers untidy. I still fold military corners at the bottom of each side."

It wasn't really sarcasm, and Livy found his initial revelation amusing enough. But there was still that look on Nick's face. Even though he wore a fairly thick sweater, she could see his chest was elevated and static, as if his body were at attention. He took shallow breaths that didn't involve the chest or diaphragm—at least not visibly.

Livy sipped her tea and found it just to her liking. "I'm ashamed to admit that even I haven't always made my bed. My...never mind. No need to go down that trail." At the end of that trail stood the image of a grumbling Peter Garner re-making the bed because his wife "never tucked in securely enough" the top sheet at the bottom of his side.

Lockhart reacted to what he was sure was a suspended allusion to Livy's congressman husband. "Sorry. I'll try to be more serious from here on out."

But he found he couldn't come up with anything more than the fact that the Army taught him self-discipline, even though he shared it without conviction. Livy was intrigued by what lay behind the difficulty he was having answering her general questions. Finally, he stood and walked several steps away from the bench and toward the edge of Memory Lake.

"You know, I used to think I could hit a stone with a baseball bat all the way across the lake—from my old house directly over there right to where you're sitting now. But I never even came close."

She turned off the recorder and returned it to her jacket pocket. "That's a pretty long way to hit a stone, Nick."

"I know, but when I was a kid I never believed I wouldn't be able to do it."

"When was the last time you tried?"

Lockhart lifted his head. "The night before I joined the Army."

"Come on and sit back down and have some more coffee. Forget the specific questions. Just tell me everything from the day you were inducted until you were discharged."

Nick's shoulders slumped, but it was more from a release of the tension he manifested from the moment he first sat on the bench. He was grateful Livy invited him to give an account of his experiences without recording it or taking notes. In truth, the only honest answer he could give to the question of what he learned of a positive nature from his experience in the military was that it made him forever thankful he got out, not so much in one piece, but psychologically fit enough to make something of his life. It was only years later that he began to question just how fit he really was.

Livy had unwittingly assumed the role he required—more a therapist or psychologist than an inquisitive graduate student or eager journalist.

"Livy, before I begin, can I ask you something?"

"Of course." She feared the question would be about going out with him, even though part of her truly wanted to.

"Do you have any siblings?"

"No. I'm an only child."

"For some reason I guessed that you were. I am too."

Livy was pleased he had guessed correctly and that they shared such a status. For his part, Lockhart took comfort in yet one more reason why he believed he could open the locked door to his past and trust this woman whom he had known for only a short time. Now he was firmly convinced that in addition to love, one could find trust at first sight.

"All right, the day I was inducted, I foolishly thought they would assign me, after basic training, to Fort Benjamin Harrison in Indiana, where they sent would-be Army journalists. Any thought I had of going overseas was always accompanied by visions of sitting at my desk typing up the latest report or human interest story that would be printed in every Minnesota newspaper, if not in Chicago and New York."

"But it didn't work out that way, I take it."

"No, it didn't. They flattered me into thinking I would make an excellent MP"

"Military Police?"

"Yes, and I thought why not? One of my uncles was a cop and I thought he'd get a kick out of my being an MP."

Livy marked how Nick wished to please the older men in his family—his father and uncle. So you did your basic training—where?"

"I did both Basic and my MP and AIT at Ft. Leonard Wood in the sun and fun capital of the world—the Missouri Ozarks."

Livy grinned at Nick's joke. "I know MP, but what's AIT again?

"Stands for Advanced Infantry Training. But Ft. Woody, as I liked to call it, houses the big MP school."

"Okay, so I assume you were sent overseas at some point."

Nick nodded but his face sagged. "I was sent to an MP unit in Wiesbaden, Germany for most of my time in the Army, and..."

Livy knew from Lockhart's demeanor and unsteady voice that something very serious had happened in Wiesbaden that still deeply affected him. There was no war there, but might he have done something in his line of duty that required physical force—or worse, the discharging of his weapon—with the result that he had harmed or even killed someone? Livy needed to be strong for him if he related the specifics of what happened, because if there was any chance for her to provide comfort she wanted to be strong enough to do that effectively.

"Nick, please tell me everything. Don't be afraid." Livy saw relief and gratitude in his eyes as he stared at her.

"One night, not long before I shipped back to the States, I was on duty and received a call to check on a disturbance outside the

Spielbank Wiesbaden, which was a gambling complex in an eighteenth-century building that had table games and slot machines—as well as an upscale restaurant. When I arrived, several off-duty soldiers expressed their concern that one of the commissioned officers left the casino after drinking heavily and was headed for trouble." Once more Nick paused, seemingly afraid to continue. Livy reached over for his thermos and filled his cup. "I want you to stay warm, so here drink some more coffee." He took a swallow and looked out toward the darkened lake. His body shivered, but more from anxiety than the cold, Livy thought. "Nick, go ahead. I'm listening."

Lockhart began to relate the specifics. The men informed him that Major Gerrard, who was in the casino with three junior officers, had drunk way too much, making his conversation audible to many around him. One of the other officers related that John McEnroe as born in Wiesbaden. Gerrard launched into an overly-excessive attack on the tennis great and his controversial behavior during his prime, leading to Gerrard's threatening to punch another of the lieutenants who dared to defend McEnroe. But then Gerrard turned his attention to his sexual conquests, bragging that he had been with several of Wiesbaden's prostitutes, even though he was a married man with two small children. Trying to shift the subject, one of the other officers threw Elvis Presley into the conversation, reminding the group that Presley's former wife Priscilla lived in Wiesbaden, where her father was stationed in the Air Force.

Lockhart would never forget the next thing one of the enlisted men told him. "One of the officers said Elvis met her over in Bad Nauheim when he was in the Army in 1959—when he was twenty-four and Priscilla only fourteen."

Nick said he asked the enlisted man who informed him of what was said. The soldier answered, "No one. We could hear every word."

Nick told Livy he asked the soldier what the problem was then. The enlisted man replied, "Major Gerrard got all quiet all of a sudden and then started repeating 'fourteen'—until one of the other officers asked why he was saying that. Then Gerrard said, 'I'm going to get some fourteen year old cunt—right now.' The other officers laughed all fake-like to humor him and just stood there when Gerrard headed out. We at first figured he'd go out and pay for a prostitute, but then I got to thinking that Gerrard might really try to find a fourteen year old girl and do something bad. So we called the MPs."

Lockhart grimaced when he ended this part of the account. "Forgive me for using that word, Livy. I was just quoting what Gerrard supposedly said."

"It's okay, Nick. So did you go looking for him?"

"I did. My partner and I drove toward where prostitutes had their apartments. Prostitution wasn't legal then as it is now, but it was still a thriving business, as you can imagine. Well, my partner and I talked to some women on the street, and they said they saw an Army officer come down the *Wilhelmstraße* and then go into an apartment complex. My partner began searching the area for Gerrard, and I asked a woman if any families had teenage girls living there. She told me there were three or four families who had them but added that a girl presently babysitting in one of the apartments would know exactly how many teenage girls there were because she was popular with all of them. She told me the girl's name was. . ."

"Nick?"

"A creeping sense of fatalism came over me, Livy. I just knew something horrible was about to happen. My partner went to the one apartment the woman identified as having teenage girls, and I headed up to the one where the girl was babysitting. This apartment building was not where anyone went to meet a prostitute." Nick picked up two more pieces of wood and placed them in the fire pit. The well seasoned wood sent a new sputter of crackling sounds and confetti-like sparks hurling upward. The fire momentarily lessened the tension Livy felt in anticipation of Nick's account. "Her name was Gerlinde Schreiber. A very pretty young girl of fourteen." Nick paused as he stepped around to the other side of the fire pit and poked at the wood. The fire now separated Nick from Livy. He remained silent until Livy spoke.

"Did you find Gerrard there?'" She was immediately horrified she had asked this question—but even more frightened that the answer would be yes.

"I went to the apartment where she was babysitting and first heard an infant crying. I just put my ear to the door instead of knocking. I must have listened for a full minute before I heard Gerlinde's muffled scream above the baby's crying. Then I heard more crying, but it wasn't the infant anymore."

The wind picked up just enough to periodically blow the flames of the raised fire pit, therefore giving his face an almost demoniacal hue. The smoke drifted out over Memory Lake.

Livy felt the lake was also listening to every word Nick spoke. Her eyes were filed with tears, although none had yet dropped. "Oh, Nick."

"Before I could even bring my hand up to bang on the door, Gerrard came out, still tucking his shirt into his pants. He wasn't even startled by my being there. He just looked at my name tag and said, 'You saw nothing here, Lockhart,' as he pushed past me. I called my partner before I stepped inside the apartment, and he came in as I tried to comfort Gerlinde, who was just sobbing, but saying nothing. I asked my partner to take her to the hospital. I knew I couldn't answer the questions they would ask me there."

Lockhart dropped his head. From Livy's vantage point, it looked as though he was lowering it into the flames. She now understood the nature of the burden Nick had carried with him for twenty years. But she could also tell he wasn't done with his account.

"I later discovered that Gerlinde had babysat several times for Gerrard and his wife. He'd been told earlier in the day that she would be sitting for the new baby of one of the women staffers in his office. He was the one who recommended Gerlinde to the woman. Lockhart rubbed his open fingers over the right side of his face. "Sorry that I'm going on and on with so many details. I want to get to the end of this, I really do."

"I know; I know. Can I pour you some more coffee?" She had to get up and walk around to where he was standing on the other side of the fire pit. Nick glanced back up at the house, frozen in thought. She feared he was too emotionally exhausted to finish his horrible recollection of that night. She didn't want him to postpone the ending of what he seemingly needed so badly to share with her—with someone. She handed him a fresh cup of coffee. "Do you want to sit with me?"

"I can't." He took several steps toward the edge of Memory Lake and faced out toward the water. Livy couldn't bear his looking away from her. "Nick, please come back this way—or at least turn around and talk directly to me. I'm here for you."

Without protest, he did as she asked but again he took his position behind the fire pit, into which he placed another piece of wood. Livy understood that for whatever reason, he wanted something between them if he looked at her during the difficult reminiscence. What he chose was the fire.

"I went to see Gerrard the following afternoon. I entered his office and saluted. I stood mute. I didn't know why I couldn't say anything. He stared at me as though he would paralyze me with his gaze. To this day I can't understand why I just stood there."

Livy stood. "Nick, he outranked you. It was natural you would react the way you did. You wanted to confront him, but..." Nick took a step nearer the fire. Livy tried to do the same on the other side of the fire pit, but the heat was too intense for her to get much closer. The flames rose straight up. There was no wind she could feel. If there was any, it seemed to rise straight up from the ground, lifting the flames.

"Gerrard finally spoke to me. 'At least you had the decency to wait until I was done' was what he said. He didn't laugh or even smile. He just said that one thing. I know I could have banged on the door as soon as I heard her muffled scream. I could have shouted. But I didn't. I knew he was in there. I knew damn well."

Lockhart backed away from the flames. The breeze came up and blew the flames directly toward him. Livy's entire body trembled, even though she was near enough to the fire pit that her face felt almost burned. She stared at Nick across the flames, which started to subside. In a moment, his entire face was visible without being blocked by the fire. Livy tried to characterize the expression on his face. His mouth was open several inches; his eyebrows were arched upwards, but his eyes seemed sunken. To her, his face registered a kind of lifeless relief. Now was time for her to say something, but she couldn't find the words.

Nick expelled a labored sigh. "Two days later I reported what had happened—it took me two days—but nothing was ever done, except that Gerrard was transferred to the unit in Grafenwoehr. You see, Gerrard was a real up-and comer. At the time he was primed for promotion to Lt. Colonel. Besides that, the Army was greatly concerned about our image over there. They would do anything they could to cover up Gerrard's crime. They gave Gerlinde's parents a healthy financial settlement, letting them know that Gerrard had been sent away and that therefore discretion was advisable for everyone's benefit, especially for their daughter's reputation. I prayed there would be some kind of trial or court martial."

"You would have testified, wouldn't you have, Nick?"

"Yes. I am as sure of that as I am sure of anything."

"And you did report it."

"Yes, I did—two days after the fact. But I didn't try to stop it, Livy. Don't you see? I hesitated at the door."

"No, Nick. It wasn't quite like that. It was already happening when you arrived."

"That poor girl. I didn't even have the guts to take her to the hospital and tell them I knew had happened. I just don't think I could have survived it if her eyes met mine. But I have seen her eyes many times in the worst of my dreams. I never found out what became of her—and I hate myself for that as well."

Livy walked around to the other side of the fire pit and took him by the hand. She led him back to the bench.

"Please sit. Do you want me to go back to the house and bring you some brandy or something?"

"No, Livy. I have to make use of all my time before Jenny gets back. So, I have to know. What do you think of me now? I can't blame you if you loathe even being on this bench with me."

"I came and took your hand, didn't I?" They both looked down at their hands, which were still clenched in each other's. "Nick, I understand why you have felt the way you have for all these years. Yes, if the situation were different and if you had it all to do again, I know you would have attempted to stop it, even if it would have been too late. But you were so young then."

"That's no excuse."

"Remember that you took a big risk reporting it while you were still in uniform. You did go to see him. And you just said you would have testified willingly had they followed up on it."

"Yes, I reported it, but with no result."

"You couldn't have known that at the time you reported it. I understand you might have done more at the moment, but think of what you did do. And, Nick, you've lived with this terrible memory and paid a huge price for your failing to act—more than anyone could have expected, given the situation you were in."

This time Lockhart didn't protest. He looked at Livy with gratitude, still holding her hand.

"Nick, forgive my asking this, but could all this be a reason why you've never married?"

He stared at her for several seconds, amazed she had drawn that conclusion.

"I think what happened over there has made it impossible for me to commit to any long-standing relationship of any normal kind. I suppose I came to accept that because of what I did and failed to do I would never deserve the love and loyalty of a woman. I'm afraid that for the most part I have carefully selected the women I have been with based either on their lack of availability, or their stated disdain for marriage."

"So you've mainly seen divorced or unhappily married women?"

"I'm ashamed to admit it, but yes." At this moment, neither of them gave any thought to Livy's marital status.

Reading his expression, Livy asked, "Nick, is there something else?"

"Yes, Livy, there is. What happened that night has come back to haunt me in another way." He rubbed the edge of the wooden bench. Livy noticed the flames in the fire dying.

"I'm here to listen, Nick—to everything."

"During my career, I've been privy to personal information on professional and collegiate athletes—some of it merely unflattering and embarrassing; some of it far worse than that. From extra-marital affairs and other sexual practices to recreational drug and anabolic steroid and HGH use. In each case, I sat on my information. If you check my most aggressive pieces, you'll find that my attacks and exposure restricted themselves to organizations, and larger issues involving a number of athletes, coaches, and administrators."

"And that should all be to your credit, Nick. I'm sure you've received praise and respect for your decision."

"I have, but I hated to hear or read it."

"But why?"

"I simply refused to expose anyone for his or her individual failings because of what I failed to do in Wiesbaden that night. What right did I have to expose someone for doing something far less offensive than I did? I didn't have the moral authority to reveal anything like that. You see, that's why I couldn't expose Paul Vanderkellen. Again, I thought—what right do I have to reveal his personal sins?"

"Nick—"

"I know what you want to ask. Was it cowardly of me to remain silent because I was afraid someone would find out what I had failed to do in Germany? In large part it was."

"Nick, I was only going to say that you can talk to me anytime about any of this. I will always be here to listen."

Nick released Livy's hand and stood up, seemingly anxious to walk away from the bench. But he halted after a single step and again stared across Memory Lake to where his old house once stood. This time Livy stood and moved to his side.

"Since I started coming back here after the Montgomerys moved in, I have stared across this lake and thought often about having looked from the other side before I left for the Army. I used to look over to this spot and ponder with pleasure where I would be going in my life. Now I look to where I have been, and I can't allow myself to think with delight over all I've accomplished in my career because of what happened in Wiesbaden. I look to where I used to live and wish so desperately I had never left."

"But you did and now...well..."

"Go ahead, Livy. Say what you think."

"And now you've got to—you've finally got to forgive yourself and allow yourself to feel deserving of all the best that can come your way."

Lockhart turned to her and smiled. "You have a very persuasive way about you, you know that?"

She thought of her husband's refusal to accept the end of their marriage and wished to reject Nick's compliment, but she refrained. "I hope I can persuade you to forgive yourself, that's all. I mean, how much more self-inflicted punishment will satisfy your sense of justice? You deserve to forgive yourself. I can't help seeing you as a forgiving person."

"I have been—all my life. With everyone but myself."

Livy put her arm through his. "Well now it's time to be all-inclusive in your forgiveness."

"I can only promise you I will try."

"I'll accept that—for now. Come on, let's just sit and listen to Memory Lake until Jenny gets back. Then we'll force her to make margaritas."

Chapter 25

"It was a good meeting, Jenny."

"It was, wasn't it? But that's because you are all just so damned wonderful. I really appreciate your getting the swing sets and basketball goals up so quickly. A lot of kids are going to be excited as they can be. You and your husband are the best, Lauren."

"Well, thank you, but we couldn't have done a darn thing without you and Davis."

"Hey, we all make a great team—if you don't mind the inexcusable sports pun."

Jenny hugged her friend and headed rapidly to her car. Near the end of the meeting, she felt the tingle of her cell phone letting her know she had just gotten a text message. She took a quick look, assuming it was Livy, but her eyebrows leaped into her hairline when she saw that the text came from Davis. He never texted her, and even if he had the inclination, she wouldn't expect him to contact her while a game was still in progress. It was just a little past nine, so unless it was raining in Baltimore, he would still be in uniform. Did something terrible happen? She locked herself in her car, turned on the overhead light, and began reading his text.

Hey, I'm texting! I sent email to your phone. Read now. Jenny quickly opened her email and read his message. *Had to let you know right away. My shoulder very sore from other night. Afraid I pitched 2 innings 2 many. Pain feels different than usual. Probably messed something else up. Made up my mind tonight. If I can make it thru this yr. great. But I'm thinking this is it. Not going through this anymore. I can't return to my old form. Should not affect HOfFame if I retire after this yr. Know you've been worried about moving. Forget it. We are staying on Memory Lake! Love u. D.*

Jenny was absolutely stunned—especially after all Davis said about not retiring from the game after this year, even if it meant moving on to another team. But it was obvious from his email that he re-aggravated his shoulder and perhaps injured something new in the process. Coming out of her state of shock, Jenny gave thought to the possibility Davis would change his mind after further rehab—perhaps after surgery—and wish again to pitch until he was forty. But his reference to the Hall of Fame pushed her to accept that he likely agreed with Nick Lockhart's assessment that Davis's Hall of Fame chances would only be enhanced if he retired now rather than pitched less effectively for another two to three years.

A rush of emotion overcame her. She should have been more concerned about his shoulder, but she couldn't help it. She was thrilled his shoulder was so messed up—because of what that meant. For the rest of her life she could live with her husband in their house on Memory Lake.

She was startled by the tapping on her driver's side window. Lowering the window, she saw Lauren, whose face registered deep concern. "Jenny, are you all right? I saw you begin to cry. Did anything happen?" Jenny grinned broadly, the wetness from her tears draining into the corners of her mouth. "Only the most wonderful thing in the world, Lauren."

• • •

"I turned the phone off for awhile. But I'm back home now, Hugh." Nick's attorney shared the latest offer by Paul Vanderkellen's representatives, which allowed Lockhart a chance to have his regrets or apology expressed on air by his lawyer or anyone else he wished to represent him.

"Are you kidding me, Hugh?

"They were very serious. This way you wouldn't have to humiliate yourself by appearing on the air either visually or through audio transmission. I could do it for you."

"You're not doing anything for me."

"Okay, okay. But I promised to run the offer by you."

"Then run this back to them. I decline this and all other offers, okay?"

"Got it."

As soon as he finished the conversation, Nick wondered if it was merely his pride that so quickly dismissed this latest offer, which if accepted might keep him at the paper and allow him to go about his business with just a spot on his tie, as the sartorial metaphor might have it. He knew it was his pride, but he reasoned it was more than that and any sense of integrity that made him refuse to play Vanderkellen's game. Should he lose everything he had worked so diligently to build, Nick understood he'd still have his self-respect. Jenny and Davis would be in his corner no matter what. And Livy Garner—that incredible woman with such an understanding heart—assured him she would be as well.

.   .   .

"Livy, where's Nick?"

Jenny had just stepped into the kitchen and discovered Livy eyeing a bottle of tequila.

"He told me to tell you he was sorry but he had to go. He needed to talk to his attorney about the Vanderkellen interview tomorrow night on ESPN." Livy didn't tell her best friend that Nick was too emotionally spent to see anyone else tonight, least of all an exuberant Jenny Montgomery.

Jenny frowned. "I feared he wouldn't be in the mood for partying, with that damned jackass kid about to ruin his career. Well, did you at least get the interview you wanted?"

"I did, Jenny. Thank you for the lighted torches and the fire pit. We both found the fire conducive for serious discussion."

"Good. Fire is good for a lot of things—from illuminating to purging to lowering inhibitions." Jenny grinned impishly.

"Jenny, why the delighted expression? Did you get a whole punch-bowl load of money donated or pledged to your charity?"

"We did all right, but I'm giddy over some other news I just received."

"And that would be...?"

"I'll make some frozen margaritas first; then I'll tell you. Besides, the way you were ogling that bottle of Cuervo Gold, I wouldn't dare keep you waiting any longer."

After Jenny informed her dearest friend about Davis's email and the end of her progressive fear of having to leave Minneapolis, the women hugged, and Livy felt her spirits lift even higher. But her body was beginning to sag. It had been quite an eventful day.

"Oh, Livy, I feel like such a shit being so giddy because Davis's shoulder is in such bad shape—I really do—but I can't help being so happy."

"Jenny, I wish you had told me before that you were so worried about having to move, but I'm so, so very happy you'll be staying here until you're old and..."

"Dead. I plan on having a Viking's funeral out on Memory Lake. If you outlive me, you can have the honor of pushing the barge from the shore—after lighting the blaze, of course."

Jenny's reference to honor, fire, and the Vikings spoke to the incredible evening Livy had spent with Nick Lockhart down on the bench. She decided she would call Nick the next night as soon as Vanderkellen's interview was over.

"Jenny, what's on the docket for tomorrow?"

"Sleep in. Bagels and coffee. Lunch at one of my favorite spots—Victor's 1959 Café, which is a little south of town. You'll love this place—a bit quirky in appearance but the best Cuban food I've ever had in my life."

"You know, I don't think I've even had authentic Cuban food."

"I know. Peter only eats American. Didn't you tell me he won't even eat Canadian cheddar?"

"No, I never told you that. Besides Canadians don't even know what that is."

"Oh. Well then tomorrow night I'm making you some Lake Superior white fish. You've not lived until you've tasted that regional favorite."

"From the Caribbean to Lake Superior all in one day?"

"Hang with me, little matey, and I'll sail you to places you've only dreamed of going."

"Well, for now I think I'll hang as close to Memory Lake as possible."Jenny sighed with as much satisfaction as she could muster.

"Oh, I know what you mean, Livy. I know just what you mean."

"Jenny, I think we should watch the ESPN interview tomorrow

night."

Jenny grimaced. "I've been debating it. I want to watch so I can make a call and write a nasty email to ESPN, but I'm afraid I'll get so mad I'll work myself into a frenzy and break something in this house worth real money. Tell you what. If you watch, I'll watch. Then you can make me control myself."

"It's a deal. So...how about another margarita before we call it a night?"

"There's enough left in the pitcher for one and a third glasses each."

"What are we waiting for?"

Livy's right eye opened, but the left one refused to cooperate. The bedside clock read 7:15 a.m. Her cell phone just finished its fourth ring. She reached over and saw that it was Peter. He wanted the answer to his invitation to meet him at the airport later today and fly back to D.C. with him. Her left eye finally broke its seal, but her fingers decided to shut down completely. She let the cell phone ring out until her voicemail message began. Assuming Peter was still in California, it would be 5:15 local time. Why would he call her this early? Livy had fully intended to sleep until nine. Why hadn't she turned off her cell last night before going to bed? Did she expect her husband to call? And did she expect to answer the phone when he did? She played back the voice message.

"Livy, I assume you're up at 7:15 your time. You hardly ever sleep past seven, so I'm guessing you're in the shower. Anyway, I'm calling to tell you that I'm staying another night in California. Met some important people yesterday—every one of whom could assist me greatly when I decide to run for the Senate. We're getting together for dinner tonight, and they've arranged for me to say a few words afterward. So, I'll call you again later tonight—when I hope you'll tell me you'll fly back to Washington with me. It would be great having you at my side when the press asks about my California trip. Think about it today and try to understand how important your presence is during times like this. You can fly back to Minnesota in a few days and start your classes. Just wanted you to know that I'm still fine with that. Okay, I'll call in the morning. Have a good day with Jenn. Bye."

Not one word about missing her or wanting her with him for any other reason than politics. And yet Livy was relieved he didn't send his love or attempt any expression of romance. Yes, she was relieved by that but not by the fact that she now had a one-day stay of execution.

.　　　　.　　　　.

The next twelve hours seemed to fly by, that is once Jenny staggered down from her bedroom. Livy and Jenny had their bagels and coffee at 9:30, lunch at Victor's 1959 Café at 12:45, and the whitefish diner at 7:15. The women then headed down to the bench by Memory Lake with weak frozen margaritas in tow, where they remained until it was time to watch the ESPN show featuring the interview with Paul Vanderkellen. Livy thought Jenny's attitude while they were down on the bench was a treat to behold. She seemed to look out at Memory Lake as might a young woman discovering that her love had rejected her hated rival and finally pledged his undying devotion. Several times, she spoke to the lake and to the bench, "I'm here to stay" and "You and I are going to be together forever."

The two women remained on the bench in relative darkness, with only the houselights surrounding the lake providing illumination. Livy asked Jenny if any of the houses surrounding Memory Lake were for sale.

"The Robertson place is about to be. He's retiring right before Thanksgiving and they're moving to Ohio to be near their children and grandchildren. Are you telling me you might be interested in buying it?" From Jenny's beaming face came another source of illumination.

"It just popped into my head to ask you. I don't know. Could I afford it?"

"Probably not. Unless you get half of Peter's government check."

"Not going to happen. I'll be using my own money."

Jenny grinned impishly. "There's a lovely trailer park fifteen miles out of town."

"Okay. I can redecorate it."

"Stop. "You'll have the money you put in the bank and then your salary from the great job you'd get in Minneapolis after you finish your masters."

"I can only wish."

"Stay positive, my friend. Davis and I have connections."

"So I can get a job working concessions at Twins' games?"

"Don't laugh. You'd be perfect."

"The Robertson house is probably way too big for me anyway."

"Look, it's got four bedrooms. Sleep your springs in one; your winters in another; and so on."

"Funny."

"Okay, so when Davis and I have one of our titanic fights, I'll move in with you for several weeks until he apologizes."

"Ha, ha."

"Hmm. Maybe Davis and I can get the neighborhood covenant changed and build you a mother-in-law bungalow right down here near Memory Lake."

"Now you're talking."

"Well, come on, Livy. It's time to listen to that little Vanderkellen twerp try to ruin Nick's career. I'll make us another batch of 'ritas so we can stomach what we're about to see and hear."

•   •   •

Nick had spent the day going through several boxes of memorabilia, tossing out some of it and organizing the rest. He knew he was acting more like a man about to move than one desiring to engage in spring housecleaning. But whereas the visual reminders of his career might have otherwise depressed him, he felt in large part free of the guilt he had carried with him for the past twenty years. Yet, he wasn't sure how long the residue of his talk with Livy would sustain his brighter outlook. Perhaps it would all return to the unfortunate normal before the day was out, but for now he felt relief, gratitude, and considerable affection for the estranged wife of a United States congressman.

Taking his evening meal downtown at another of his favorite haunts—Ikes on 6th—Lockhart was approached for his autograph by an elderly man accompanied by his wife. As Nick signed, he was tempted to add to his signature, "My last requested autograph ever." He smiled as the couple left, imagining himself the disgraced but once notable sports scribe traveling from town to town signing discounted autographs at a buck a pop.

●   ●   ●

"Finally, they're getting to the interview. Only seven commercials from now." Jenny and Livy chose to sip mimosas during the broadcast rather than margaritas—but not for any reason of preference. Jenny had finally run out of margarita mix and triple sec, although she had five bottles of Prosecco chilling in the "overflow" refrigerator in the garage. Livy was pressed back in the sofa, apparently awaiting the stomach-churning attack on Nick Lockhart on live television. Jenny sat forward on the cushion next to Livy, apparently ready to pounce.

After the products were pitched and endorsed, the program returned, with a three chair set. The host was in the far left chair and Paul Vanderkellen in the center one. Smugly positioned on the right was someone Jenny didn't recognize, although she was certain it was Vanderkellen's attorney.

As Jenny informed Livy, the host was known to her from her San Francisco days. They had even met for lunch when Davis first started pitching for the Giants. As the host set up the story, Jenny shook her head. "If he simply kowtows to Vanderkellen and his legal baby sitter, I'll get his ass. I know where to strike to hurt him the most.

"What? Is he having an affair or something?"

"If I drive my knee up into the right place, he won't be up for any affair—not for a very long time."

Now churning with nervousness, Livy didn't know whether to laugh or to chide her friend for another vulgarity. The look on Jenny's face suggested she ought to do neither.

At the host's prompting, Vanderkellen related the meeting he had with Nick and what he had confessed to him. His silver-haired attorney then took the reins and made the case that the sports writer should have chosen to intercede either directly or through someone else who would have "the common sense and humanitarian instinct to help out a young man in serious trouble." Livy missed several of the attorney's words, owing to Jenny's interjection of two one-syllable words of profane clarity.

When Vanderkellen's lawyer finished, the host turned to the camera. "We have offered Nick Lockhart a chance to respond to Mr. Vanderkellen's remarks and his attorney's assessment, either by being here with us, by telephone, by video hook-up, or through a statement which we would have read—but Mr. Lockhart has declined all invitations to do so."

Vanderkellen's spoiled-little-boy face and his lawyer's affected and arrogant expression of indignation were difficult for Livy to witness. She pushed herself further back against the sofa, fighting the latest contraction of her stomach muscles. For her part, Jenny was up on her feet slandering all three men on camera. Livy feared her best friend would knee the host through the flat-screen TV.

The host finished his overly lengthy pause and continued. "Now..." Again he paused.

"Why don't you just shut the hell up, you dick-head." Jenny flung herself back on the sofa.

The host began again, as if he heard and dismissed Jenny's colorful suggestion. "Now I'd like to ask the both of you whether you've given any thought to the possibility that Mr. Lockhart kept what he learned to himself because he didn't wish to cause you, Mr. Vanderkellen, any further harm to your reputation. Couldn't you then argue that he acted out of a very strong sense of decency?"

"I love you, and I'm not going to kick you but kiss you—but not in the same place—the next time I see you, you beautiful man." Jenny's transformation was topped off by her lifting her glass of orange juice and Prosecco to the host's image on the television.

Livy's smile took some time to blossom, but it came to its full flowering the moment the camera panned back and caught Vanderkellen's look of stunned surprise and his attorney's expression of utter horror.

When neither man answered his question, the host plowed right ahead. "Although Mr. Lockhart didn't wish to appear with us tonight or to provide a comment relating to what you gentleman have accused him of..."

Livy loved that the host used the word "accused."

"...a number of others have taken the time to make their feelings known on the subject and on the issue of responsibility when it comes to the kind of difficulties you admitted having, Mr. Vanderkellen."

In succession, the host read one and two-line statements in support of Nick Lockhart as a master writer and a gentleman. "Mr. Vanderkellen, if you or your attorney wish to respond to any of these please do so." Neither man was able to articulate a sound as the tributes to Lockhart came from current and ex-professional and collegiate athletes, athletic directors, front office personnel, and several other big-name sports journalists across the country. Some of these ran as a crawl at the bottom of the screen.

"We have time for only two on-air comments. Again, Mr. Vanderkellen, if you wish to comment, I'll give you a chance after these two current athletes have their say. That way you'll have the final word before we end the program."

The first to appear live via satellite was Niki Dawsey, one of the brightest young stars of the WTA and recent winner of women's singles at the Australian and Miami Opens. Dawsey said she "spoke for many female and minority athletes," who—to a woman—had the highest respect for Lockhart's fairness and unqualified support of women's sports at all levels.

Both Livy and Jenny sat on the edge of the sofa, daubing tears while drinking healthy sips of their mimosas. Then Jenny abruptly put down her glass so she could bring both palms of her hands to her temples as the next athlete appeared on the split screen. For one of the rare times in her life, she was unable to speak. Therefore it was left to Livy to scream, "Oh, my God. It's Davis!"

Davis Montgomery spoke in glowing terms of his friend Nick Lockhart, providing three significant examples of Nick's judgment, integrity, and generosity. Jenny was a wreck by the time her husband finished. Livy ran into the kitchen to get a tissue box and got back in time to see Vanderkellen and his silver-haired attorney concede to the tide against them, evident by the attorney's reply to the host's offering the last word: "We'll just stand by what we said earlier."

There was no doubt that justice was done and Nick Lockhart would remain in Minneapolis with his reputation not simply intact but very likely much enhanced.

"Nick? Did you watch it? Please tell me you did." Livy's excitement made her voice elevate half an octave, or so it sounded to her. She called Lockhart's cell phone ten minutes after the show ended.

"I did, Livy, although I hadn't planned to." Lockhart explained that earlier in the day he had turned off his cell phone and after dinner at Ike's decided to return home, pack a bag, and head east to a friend's in Eau Claire, Wisconsin for a few days to avoid all media attempts to contact him. But when he returned to his place, he saw taped to the door a note from Hugh Martin.

"Nick, watch the interview. I received a call from a former law student of mine who works at ESPN. She said that you definitely had to watch. I think there's going to be a surprise no one is expecting. Something in YOUR favor. So WATCH!!!!"

Livy was so happy Nick was able to see all the outpourings of support. Because of their talk down at the bench and her concern for his career, she felt very close to him at this moment.

"Livy, you're the only one who knows the full reason why I have never engaged in exposing athletes like Paul Vanderkellen."

"I am honored to be that one person. Listen to me. You deserve every wonderful thing said about you on that broadcast."

"I hope so. I really hope so."

Before giving the phone to Jenny, Livy wanted to ask him if he would remain in Minneapolis and continue writing for his paper. But she didn't want to spoil the night by hearing him say either he was leaving the city or even that he hadn't yet made up his mind about what he was going to do.

"Nick, let me just insist that when the time is right—hopefully very soon—we'll get together..." She paused and knew she shouldn't ask to see him alone.

"...with Jenny and Davis and celebrate your victory."

"My victory over the forces of evil and darkness, you mean? Well, I'm not sure I'd call it a victory—but whatever I end up calling it, it will be worth celebrating. The Twins have an off day when they get back from their road trip, so perhaps we can do it then. But whenever we do it, I'd like you to be around me when I don't have the weight of the world strapped to my back."

"I would love that, Nick. I really would. Well, here's Jenny."

Nick had no sooner gotten off the phone with the effusive Jenny Montgomery than he received a call from the powers that be at his paper. For some strange reason they chose this night to inform him how much he meant to their publication and to the sports world in general. Lockhart was sorely tempted to ask why they couldn't have offered their praise and support when he really needed it, but he reasoned that getting in a good dig at the moment of his triumph was a bit petty. Besides, he had been around a long enough to know how the game was played.

He gave the idea of a career change or a change of cities a respectful hearing, but he kept imagining himself down at the bench on Memory Lake. He was anxiously looking forward to getting back to the Montgomerys so he could look across to where his old house used to stand and to see if he felt differently now that he had overcome the major crisis of his career and finally admitted what he had failed to do that night in Wiesbaden. He sensed it would take some time to clear his memory and truly escape from that dreadful place, but thanks to Livy Garner he was finally beginning to move away from it. He decided not to push matters but to make clear to her that he was willing, if she was able and desirous at some time in the future, to see where their relationship might take them. Regardless, he would gratefully accept whatever relationship they were destined to have in the meantime—provided, of course, she remained here in Minnesota. There were so many other chats he'd like to have with her on the bench by Memory Lake, from the lighthearted to the therapeutic— and perhaps, in time, the romantic. Perhaps he could even return the favor—that is, if she struggled with the decision to break permanently from her husband. For now, he dearly wanted her to be free from her marriage.

It was ten minutes after midnight—a new day had commenced. For the first time in what seemed like forever, Lockhart didn't mind being awake and alone past the witching hour. His thoughts so delighted and calmed him that he didn't want to sleep.

Chapter 26

Livy emerged quietly from the basement door and strolled into the living room. She hadn't expected Jenny to be awake, and she wasn't. The two friends didn't part for bed until 2:30 a.m. Jenny spoke to her husband right before midnight and was as happy as Livy had ever seen her. She several times repeated the fact that not only had Nick won the day but that she and Davis would be staying at this house forever.

"Livy, I just can't decide where I want Davis and me buried. In the little arbor area outside our bedroom window or under Davis's grill set-up off the back patio. I guess I should choose the arbor area. That way my rotting flesh can help fertilize the trees and grass. There are enough ashes to ashes near the grill anyway."

"Why don't you have them lay you to rest under the bench by Memory Lake?"

Livy was only teasing, but Jenny's reaction indicated that she could think of no better place.

"You're a genius, Livy. But then we've always known that."

"You've always *said* that. I've never known any such thing." Smiling from recalling that conversation, Livy glanced at the clock. 8:27 a.m. Peter had left her a text message at 1:00 a.m. Central Time that said, *"Sorry I missed you again. Will call you tomorrow morning 8:30 your time. P."*

"P" was his closing whenever he sent her a text or email message. And every time she saw it, she'd think of several vulgar words that began with the letter "P." Words Jenny had no trouble articulating, but not Livy. She'd only think them, and still feel guilty doing so.

Livy didn't have enough time to brew tea or coffee before Peter called. Dressed in a long-sleeve shirt and pajama pants, with a University of Minnesota sweat outfit over the shirt, Livy grabbed a slightly stale bagel and bottled water and headed out the back door.

She managed to take a bite of bagel and wash it down with two swallows of water before Peter called. She didn't answer until she was seated on the bench by Memory Lake. The sky was cloudless and the wind perfectly still.

"Hello."

"Livy, where were you last night when I left my text message?"

She refused to get angry at the rudeness of his opening line.

"My phone was down in my basement apartment. Jenny and I were upstairs talking."

Garner processed his wife's reply. She assumed he was deciding whether to ask if both she and Jenny were talking about him.

"Well, I'm glad you're on the phone now. Are you alone?"

"Completely." Livy startled herself by her answer. She was pleasantly surprised she didn't just say "Yes."

"Good. So—have you decided to join me when I fly back today? I can get you on the flight to Washington, but you might not be able to sit next to me. Remember what I said. You'll get back in time for school. Well, you might miss one day—two at the most—but they don't do anything important the first couple of days anyway."

"Peter, listen to me. We—"

"Many political VIP's to meet. A couple of big parties—bigger than any we've yet been to. I can see to it that you get interviewed by one of the cable news shows if you want."

"Peter, please. Just listen to me."

"But...okay, okay. I'll listen. Go ahead."

She heard the exasperation in his voice. She visualized him looking at his watch, wishing to get off the phone as quickly as possible. He was likely thinking, "Damn it, Livy. Just say yes. I've got a lot to do today before I go to the airport."

"Peter, I know you don't believe I can make up my mind about something and refuse to change it, in spite of your arguments to the contrary."

"No, Livy, don't talk like that. You just get on these tangents every once in a while, and I—"

"Peter, just listen to me and for once don't interrupt—all right?"

The softness of her voice belied the seriousness of her request, and her husband understood that ignoring or interrupting her wouldn't serve to his benefit, as it had so many times previously.

"All right, Livy. Go ahead."

"Peter, I'm not meeting you at the airport today, nor am I flying back before classes start." She stopped herself from adding secondary and explanatory comments such as "I have to get my books and get my mind prepared for the first day." She wanted to be more direct and resolute, sparing of any language that would invite him to argue with or to assure her. "Peter, you need to understand that I've not changed my mind about our marriage being over, no matter how dismissive you've been of my decision. I've told you enough times that we needed to part ways, and although these past months I could have been more insistent that I saw no way to save our marriage, I did tell you—and you cannot deny it—that I wasn't happy and that it would be best if we split—permanently."

She wanted to pause and allow what she had said so far to sink in, but she feared she wouldn't be able to regain her momentum once she halted. She took one shallow breath and continued. "I have no intention of making any of this public. I have no desire to hurt you or your career, and I'll refuse any request for a statement or interview by any member of the media. You can say what you want about it, even if it misrepresents the state of our relationship—I don't care. But please do not call or see me if you are going to try and talk me out of a divorce. I'll have to hire a lawyer, but I have no intention of asking for any large settlement. And you know there has been no one else that I have seen, let alone fallen in love with. There are some things we possess that are from my family, and I want those, of course, but anything we bought together you can have. I will make this as easy as you want to make it—believe me. I'm...No. Peter, the plain truth is that we just can't be together." She stopped herself from articulating the mitigating phrase "I'm sorry."

Livy squeezed her eyes waiting for Garner's counter-argument, which she guessed would be full of anger and recrimination. But for several seconds all she heard was his breathing. Finally, he cleared his throat with a soft "um-um."

"Livy, I understand what you are saying. I really do."

Her eyes reopened and her facial muscles relaxed. Could it be that he was just going to let it be as it had to be?

"I'll let you get started with your classes and then fly out in two or three weeks and spend a couple of days in Minneapolis. We can talk about all this then. I agree. It's best to let you settle in and settle down a bit. Then you'll better be able to see that divorcing each other is the very last thing we should do. Well, I have to go. I'll call you sometime next week to see how you are. Okay?"

"Good-bye, Peter. Good-bye."

She closed her cell phone and wondered if the finality inherent in the way she said the second "good-bye" would convince him that he wasn't going to change her mind—ever. She couldn't believe it would on its own, but he at least to accept that his short-term plans were neither appreciated nor acceptable to her.

Livy returned to the house and brewed coffee, a mug of which she brought back down to the bench. Jenny would likely sleep another hour at least. The day would be filled with further sight-seeing, good meals, and plenty of weak margaritas to make Jenny's humor even more delicious and the celebratory mood more pronounced in the wake of the good news about her remaining in her house and Nick's crisis being resolved.

As she sat on the bench, Livy laughed softly and somewhat sardonically. Of course, Peter would refuse to believe she could live without him, and he would indeed come to Minneapolis to "talk some sense" into her. She understood she would have to see him. They would have to talk about matters relating to the divorce, regardless of his initial rejection of what would eventually occur. But much of the agitation and convincing would be diverted to the lawyer she chose to represent her. She would see Peter when he came and politely accept his calls, only to take each step without any chance of regret. If he still refused to accept the divorce after they met in Minneapolis, she would, again politely, tell him that she wouldn't see or talk with him until he did accept that their marriage was over.

She went back over everything she had just said to Peter on the phone. She had spoken truthfully and without bitterness or any suggestion of her changing her mind about the divorce. But she now realized that one thing she said was a qualified truth. She had told Peter, "there has been no one else that I have seen, let alone fallen in love with." It was true that her decision to leave him had absolutely nothing to do with any other man. She hadn't seen or fallen in love with anyone else. But given her present feelings, she realized she couldn't say with such unalterable assurance that she hadn't fallen in love with someone else. Her better sense reminded her that it was way too soon to be in love with Nick Lockhart and that her current predicament had to be resolved first before she could share any affection with him. Other women might brush aside such niceties, but she couldn't. It was just the way she was made. Yet she felt very confident that when the dust had settled, Nick would be around—and she smiled at the prospect of seeing how her then free heart would respond to a man she truly cared for, regardless of how brief had been their acquaintance.

Looking to the sky, Livy saw that the sun had just slipped behind a single intruding cloud, and she felt the wind picking up, making her react to the chill in the air. But she didn't view either of these as an ominous sign that difficult times lay ahead or that she would come to regret her decision to part from Peter. Instead, she smiled at her new friend Memory Lake and ran the palm of her hand on the wooden bench that had over the past few days become so special to her. No, the clouds, wind, and Memory Lake were just telling her she could withstand any forthcoming aggravations and maintain a most pleasurable anticipation of her future. With the wind cutting across Memory Lake and blowing back her hair, Livy never felt stronger or more confident than she did at this moment.

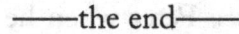

——the end——

View other Black Rose Writing titles at www.blackrosewriting.com/books and use promo code **PRINT** to receive a **20% discount** when purchasing.

BLACK✿ROSE
writing™

www.ingramcontent.com/pod-product-compliance
Lightning Source LLC
Chambersburg PA
CBHW01044510726
47904CB00008B/2491